FLAMES TO A MOTH

VICKI STEVENS

with

GARY HORWOOD

BLOODWOOD PRESS

Published by Bloodwood Press in 2020
Armstrong Creek, QLD, Australia

ISBN: 978-0-6483831-3-0 (paperback)
ISBN: 978-0-6483831-2-3 (ebook)

Little Icarus © Alina Fatima 2019

Cover design by cal5086: Fiverr
Cover images by Mohamed Nohassi/Anatoliy Gleb

A catalogue record for this work is available from the National Library of Australia

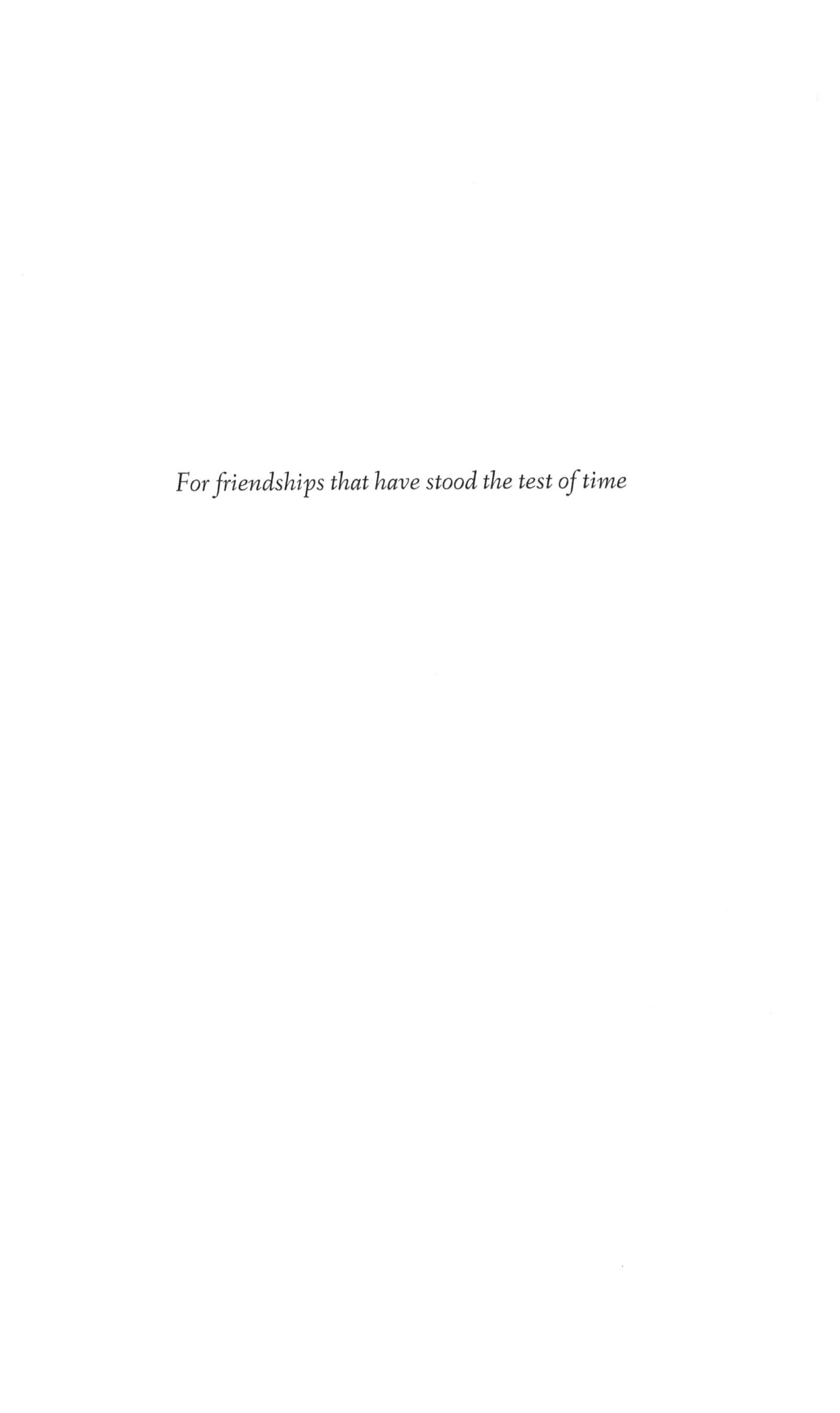

For friendships that have stood the test of time

LITTLE ICARUS

I watch a moth
fly in and out of an open fire
again and again
burning away its wax paper wings
Little Icarus
who uses the stars to navigate
has mistaken a furnace for a map
I wonder how easy it must be
to mistake scorching heat for warmth
To think that maybe
if you flew close enough
these flames might take you home

~ *Alina Fatima*

I

SPARKS AND SHADOWS

1

____

ASHLEY

2017

FRIDAY

Life is not so much like a box of chocolates, but rather a dish of lasagne stacked with repetitive layers of the good, the bad, and—in the seriously dark times—the downright ugly. In my forty-six years on this earth, I reckon I've had my fair share of experiences spawned in the shadows. Now it's time to enjoy a thick layer of happiness. *Let the good times roll.*

I entertain this thought as I place my home-cooked pasta meal into my father's oven to heat. Opening the dishwasher, I lift out my mother's favourite knife and my thumb easily finds the indentation in the wooden handle caused by decades of use. As light glints off the worn, yet still sharp blade, a pang of loss grips me, and I blink away painful memories and drop the knife on the chopping board. I look inside the fridge, surprised to see a stash of jars and bottles lining the shelves but a scarcity of fresh produce. The BO stink of a cut onion has me wrinkling my nose and searching until I find the wizened culprit hiding under a wilted spinach leaf along with a mouldy orange. They get tossed in the bin, while a heart of lettuce, a lone carrot, and two almost overripe tomatoes are extracted for a salad. Making a mental note to remind Dad that a grocery shop is in order, I hear a shout soar above the din of the television.

'Ashley! I'll have a beer with my dinner.'

'Oh, will you now,' I call back to my father in the adjoining room. 'How's your sugar level?'

'Hey? Shook a devil? That makes no sense, girly.'

I groan and walk into the lounge room. As usual, Dad is ensconced in his recliner in front of the TV—one hand gripping the remote, the other inside a Tupperware container filled with Liquorice Allsorts.

'I said, how's your sugar level? Have you done your prick test?' I point to the blood glucose testing kit resting on his side table.

'Of course I have. It's all good. No worries.' He holds out a hand. 'Where's that beer?'

I leave and return with a glass of iced water. 'Here, this'll do you.'

Dad gives me a look I've learnt to ignore. He knows I won't back down and doesn't like it one bit. Grabbing the glass, he takes a gulp. Then, with exaggerated flair, he chooses the largest piece of liquorice and pops it into his mouth.

I roll my eyes. 'Well, don't call me if you fall into a diabetic coma.'

He glares back. 'I wouldn't be able to, would I?'

His scowl becomes a grin and I shake my head. 'You silly old bugger. What am I to do with you?'

'Get me a beer?' he winks.

In the kitchen, I assemble the woeful salad and then ease the hot dish from the oven. I delight in the hiss and bubble and mouth-watering aroma of such a simple dish, but before I can slice the lasagne into portions, a clatter comes from the lounge room, followed by a cry.

God, what has he done now?

He's had a few falls recently, and the last one resulted in a wrenched shoulder and an injured hand he won't let me re-bandage. Stubborn old fool. I pop my head out of the kitchen and see my father leaning sideways over the armrest of his chair, arms flailing, moaning.

'Dad!' I shriek, rushing over.

His head turns, face flushed, eyes wild. 'The remote,' he gasps, pointing to the floor. 'I dropped it.'

I kneel amongst a scattering of liquorice, swearing under my breath as I shove a hand under the chair and drag out a fluff-covered remote control.

'Geez, Dad, you had me—'

'Give it here!' he snarls.

Hesitating at his rudeness, my ears prick to the voice coming from the television.

'Just repeating. The body of a man found this morning at Lake Mitchum has been identified as 46-year-old West End resident, Bryden Edward James.'

I snap my head around and see the face of the female newsreader replaced by an aerial view of a dam wall with a spillway on one side, and a lake hemmed in by bushland on the other. I recognise it at once. The camera operator in the news helicopter zooms in on the reedy shallows and an area on the grassy bank sectioned off by crime scene tape. Within this cordoned zone, a team in protective overalls encircles a shape covered by plastic sheeting.

My chest tightens. With eyes still glued to the scene, I push up from the floor and drop onto the armrest of the chair that had been my mother's until her passing eighteen months ago. The image on the TV now cuts to a suited man surrounded by a clutch of microphones. According to the screen text, he is Detective Sergeant Neil Collett. Though he stares without expression into the camera, I catch a twitch under his left eye before he speaks.

'Due to the nature of the deceased's death, we are treating this as a murder investigation. If anyone has information that could be of help, we urge you to contact Crime Stoppers.'

As an 1800 phone number travels across the bottom of the screen, I feel Dad watching me. One sideways glance proves this.

'Didn't you go to school with a Bryden James?' he asks.

I don't have enough spit in my mouth to swallow let alone give an answer. I nod slowly and return my attention to the broadcast, which has now cut to a report about a koala rescued from a suburban swimming pool. A thrumming in my ears drowns out the newsreader's comments, and the room spins.

I get to my feet and hand the remote to my father. 'I've got to go. You'll be all right, won't you?'

His face crumples. 'I guess so. Are you okay? You've gone all pale.'

'I just gotta go,' I say, collecting my bag from the sofa and groping inside for the car keys. 'The lasagne is ready and there's a salad.'

'What are you going to eat? Take some dinner with you.' He hoists himself up from his chair.

'No, it's fine. I'm not hungry.'

I go to give him a simple peck on the cheek, but he envelops me in a hug tighter than normal.

'Thanks for helping me out, luv,' Dad says, releasing his hold. 'You're a good girl, you know.'

The trembling of my jaw hinders my attempt at a smile.

• • •

I'm not aware of the five-minute drive home; I'm too busy concentrating on breathing.

Pulling into the carport, I turn off the engine and stare into a wall of darkness that becomes a backdrop to the visions swirling in my head: the dam, the plastic sheeting, Bryden's lifeless form beneath. My hands cramp, the pain coursing up to my shoulders. I have to contact Cam. I peel my fingers from the steering wheel and pull my phone from my bag, scrolling through the list of contacts without success. Had I deleted Cam's details? I slide out of the car and almost trip over a geranium pot plant on my way up the front steps.

I rush through the open-plan living area and down the hall to my bedroom. Though I'm quite tall, I have to stand on tiptoes to reach the camphor wood box on top of the antique wardrobe that complements my vintage cast iron bed—leftovers from the décor of my previous, much older house. The box lid creaks open, releasing the wood's rich cinnamon-like aroma, and I flinch at the sight of a pale blue envelope. My hand shakes when I drop it onto the bed. In the box, amongst sheets of writing paper, used envelopes, and odd scraps of notes, I discover the Christmas card Cam sent a few years back. Under his brief seasonal greeting, he'd scribbled his mobile phone number in the hope that I'd respond, which I hadn't. Is it still current? There is only one way to find out.

Tapping those ten digits on my phone, my finger hovers over the call symbol. Do I have the nerve to speak with him? The words that had come from our mouths the last time we'd spoken had been nowhere near civil.

2

CAMPBELL

2017

FRIDAY

As funerals go, ol' Charlie's was run-of-the-mill sad. But it had a silver lining—a chance encounter with one of his daughters.

There'd been the usual standing around, waving the hearse goodbye. Not so usual was me tripping and falling backwards into a neatly trimmed hedge. The crack of twigs and scratch of thorny branches had me protecting my eyes as I became wedged in the dense vegetation. 'Bugger,' I growled.

'Are you okay?' came a female voice from the other side of this shrub of embarrassment.

'Yeah, yeah, I'm good ... just clumsy,' I said, taking her hand and allowing her to help pull me to my feet.

The clean white hanky she offered to wipe the leaves and moist compost from my trousers and ripped suit jacket smelled of patchouli. She said I could keep it in case I tumbled into more foliage. We laughed about the timing of my fall as we walked into the church hall together and spent the rest of the wake chatting and enjoying each other's company.

That was several hours ago. Now I am back home, in my apartment.

I look out the open kitchen window and see the clouds forming a grey dance on the horizon. A quick glance below and I spot Mrs Dabiner in her house garden next door snipping flowers from her gardenia bush. The scent emitted by those creamy white blooms comes to me now on a gentle breeze and I take a deep breath to savour their heady fragrance before flicking the switch on my new artisan dual-wall kettle, a gift from a friend back from her travels to London.

'It's a KitchenAid,' she'd said all expectantly.

My response must have underwhelmed her somewhat as her smile fell when I replied, 'It looks like a shiny baby potbelly stove with a heat dial in the middle of it.' Though I have to admit its shape and bedazzling shine does add a bit of glamour to my white bench tops, white tiled walls, and hardwood timber floors.

While I wait for the water to boil, I unfold the Qantas boarding pass on which I'd scribbled her phone number after Charlie's daughter mentioned she'd like to catch up again over coffee. I have a surplus of these passes in the pockets of my jacket from regular flights to and from Canberra for conferences, and today I re-used one to my advantage. I ponder this fortuitous meeting and smile, wondering what Charlie would have thought.

He had been in charge of the government department that kick-started my career in Aged Care, and we'd bonded immediately, maybe because he'd recognised my desperate need for a challenge. Five years on, I am—as a state co-ordinator of funding within the industry—influential in making decisions that are of benefit to the elderly.

Things have changed for the better for me in recent times. The purchase of my first home—a quaint two-bedroom, first floor apartment that suits my need to escape the demands of giving out to everyone—was a true achievement. Though neatly furnished, an intricate patterned Persian rug for the lounge, and a native American dream catcher perched alone on the opposite wall are the only eye-catching features this compact 'pad' offers up to visitors.

As I gaze at the blue-inked mobile number left by Charlie's daughter, I take this as another good sign. Adding her contact details to my phone, it bleeps, and a different name appears on the screen.

Ashley.

I stare at the phone. Ashley McCabe—or whatever surname she goes by now—has messaged me. In my last memory of her, she is standing in my apartment doorway, her face flushed from ranting at me. Turning away, her long red hair flicks, sways, and bounces as she hurries down the stairs and out of my life. I've tried deleting her number but my childhood crush on her won't allow it. I hesitate, then press the text message symbol. It opens.

'Bryden is dead.'

Fear grips my stomach. My head loses its sense of space. The two people who'd most shaped my early years, and then drastically altered my adult life forever, once again crash in on my existence with those three typed words.

Damn you, Ashley. And fuck you, Bryden.

I wish the three of us had never met.

Another message, this time from an old school friend I haven't spoken with for months. *'OMG! Check this.'* It includes a link to a news update. With dread, I follow it and read that Bryden's body has been found at Lake Mitchum.

I throw the phone. It hits the wall and rebounds, skidding and spinning as it slides across the floor to rest at my feet. I kick it away.

Feeling sick and dizzy, I splash my face with cold water from the kitchen tap and douse my head in a futile attempt to cool the heat in my brain.

3

ASHLEY

FRIDAY

I chickened out. Instead of attempting an actual conversation, I sent Cam a text. That was ten minutes ago, and the room has darkened with night falling. I flick on the light and sit on the bed with the silent phone lying in my lap. Cam's lack of response makes me think he's obviously not one of those people who check their phone every few minutes like I do. I tap the screen app for the sixth time and am surprised to find the message has been read. *When did that happen?* I wait some more. Nothing.

Falling back on the mattress, I spread my arms out on the brocade bed cover and stare up at the ceiling where two black and white moths flitter around the light shade in a shadowy game of cat and mouse. A ball of pain lodges in my chest and I roll onto my stomach to force it out. Clutching one of my many pillows, I release a strangled cry into its kapok filling.

My father was a soldier and, after living in various houses in several interstate locations, my mother convinced him to put down roots when he was posted back to his home town, Brisbane, in 1981. A few weeks later, we bought our first family home in Madsen Park, north of the city, and my sister, Lauren, and I, were enrolled at Thornleigh State School at the start of second term.

On my first day at the new school, I felt anxious as I waited outside the Grade 5 classroom with the Deputy Principal. Being my sixth school so far, and shy, I worried about making friends. Ushered into a room smelling of kid sweat, old books, and chalk dust, I was handed over to a portly, kind-faced teacher, I squirmed as thirty-one pairs of ten-year-old eyes sized me up, assessing where I'd fit in the pecking order.

'This is Stephanie Taylor,' Mr Perry said, seating me next to a girl with a shock of curly blonde hair cascading from a high ponytail. 'She'll show you around the school at lunchtime.'

'It's Stevie,' the girl whispered as I loaded my newly covered books into my desk. 'Like Stevie Nicks.' Her full, pink lips formed a wide smile and her pale blue eyes seemed to sparkle with magic. I hoped we would become best friends.

It wasn't long before I felt one of my braids being tugged. Twisting around, I found two boys seated behind me engrossed in reading their social studies textbooks. I frowned and turned back. The next time my hair was pulled I caught them snickering.

'Stop it,' I hissed.

'What?' said the kid with buck teeth.

'You know what.' I slipped my plaits into the front of my shirt.

'Everything okay, Ashley?' Mr Perry asked, coming alongside my desk.

I nodded, my face aflame with the attention.

Stevie pointed to the two boys behind us. 'They pulled her hair, sir.'

Mr Perry rolled a piece of chalk between his fingers as he studied them. 'Is that correct?'

'No, sir,' they chanted in unison.

He gave a nod and walked to the front of the room, telling everyone to return to their books.

A few seconds later, I felt a sharp poke between my shoulder blades.

'Chicken,' I heard the boy directly behind me say. He then made a clucking noise.

I whirled around and my elbow knocked his textbook, sending it crashing to the floor.

'Bryden James!' Mr Perry shouted. 'Stand up!'

The boy took his time getting to his feet, and his shoulders slumped as he stood next to his desk.

'What do you think you're playing at?'

'Nothing, sir,' he replied, peering through a long mess of jet-black hair.

'I'm not sure I believe you,' Mr Perry scolded. 'Remain standing until I tell you to sit. Everyone else, eyes to the front.' The piece of chalk screeching on the blackboard as he wrote made my teeth hurt.

From the corner of my eye I caught movement and saw this kid, Bryden, dancing a jig in the aisle. Others in the class began to chuckle.

Mr Perry spun around and flicked his wrist, sending the chalk flying. It clocked Bryden on the side of the head before he could duck.

'Stand still and stand tall,' Mr Perry barked. 'Is that too much to ask, Mr James?'

Bryden snapped to attention like a soldier on parade, a smirk playing on his lips.

When Mr Perry picked up another piece of chalk and

returned to his task, I heard a scrape on the floor nearby. Another glimpse revealed that Bryden was now standing on his chair. I glanced back at our teacher, wondering what his reaction would be this time.

Mr Perry turned with a sigh, his eyes narrowing as they focused on Bryden. 'What are you doing now?' he asked.

Stony-faced, Bryden remarked, 'Standing tall, sir, just like you said.'

Kids giggled. I didn't. I sensed worse was to come.

Mr Perry wagged a finger. 'Get down this instant! Toe the line, boy, or it's up to the principal's office.'

Bryden jumped from his chair and once again stood beside his desk.

Mr Perry wiped his forehead, leaving a smear of chalk dust, and returned to the blackboard.

Another scrape followed by a creak of timber. I peered over my shoulder, surprised by the sight of two wiry legs with sockless feet stuffed into a pair of grubby joggers.

A whole classroom of eyes darted from Bryden on his desk to the centre of our teacher's back. The air felt thick with anticipation.

'Okay, class,' Mr Perry said, dropping the chalk into the groove at the bottom of the blackboard and swivelling around, 'I want you to—'

His face went from pale to crimson in a microsecond, and I expected his head to explode.

'Bryden!' he yelled. 'What in God's name are you—'

His words were cut short by Bryden belting out the chorus from Rocky Burnette's, 'Tired of Toein' the Line'.

I don't think I've ever seen a grown man move so fast.

Mr Perry tore across the room and yanked Bryden down to floor level, scattering books and overturning the chair. Shoving

Bryden to the front of the room, he leaned over his desk and wrote on a slip of paper.

Pointing to a freckled boy in the first row, he growled, 'Campbell, take this note and this show pony to the principal's office, NOW!'

As the two boys walked away, Mr Perry glared at the rest of the class, daring anyone else to muck up and suffer the same fate. No one budged or made even the smallest sound.

In the playground at lunchtime, Bryden proudly displayed the welts on his hands from getting caned, yet his red-rimmed eyes hinted that the punishment received had not been as painless as he made out.

While Bryden may have been a troublemaker, he didn't lack intelligence or concern. One day as I was struggling with a difficult maths test and on the verge of tears, I found a wad of paper wedged in my braid. Unfolding it, I discovered he'd given me the answers I needed. I never thanked him for helping me, and he never mentioned it—it was just his way. However, as time passed, his motivation for assisting others changed.

4

CAMPBELL

1980

'How high can you stack 'em?'

I turned from my hiding spot behind rows of beer bottles to see a face that was vaguely familiar: hair almost black; a long fringe brushed sideways over dark, squinting eyes. The boy looked around the same age as me, approaching nine.

'How did you find me?' I said.

'I didn't. I'm hiding too,' was his reply.

He'd caught me crouching on my knees because of the neighbourhood hide-and-seek game that was underway. As usual, most of the kids in my street were scattered between the four or five houses that bordered the suburb of Thornleigh. Sometimes you weren't too sure how many had joined in after seeing their brothers climbing a roof, lying underneath the family car, or perched on the highest branch of a mango tree. And now, as we both leaned hard up against the house with beer bottles stacked ten high in front of us, and brown glass only centimetres from our faces, the stench of stale beer heated by the sun was strong.

'So, how high?' he repeated.

'Not much higher,' I said, my eyes drawn to a cockroach running in circles inside an empty bottle, 'because the bottles roll out from the sides and Dad doesn't like them broken.'

'My old man drinks so many we pile bricks at the ends and stack 'em twenty high,' the boy whispered, leaning out and searching for our trackers.

The phrase 'my old man' shocked me. I'd never used that term to describe my father. The way he used it bordered on disrespectful, and my dad didn't seem that 'old' anyway.

This excessive drinking by our fathers became the catalyst for a future bond between us as we experienced moments of fear that alcoholism brings to a family. But on this day, we only shared this 'brewed' space for a short time for he soon slid from our secure glass enclosure and glided over a nearby fence to disappear behind the neighbour's blue Volkswagen beetle. As he did this, I noticed the faded canvas shoes on his feet, worn without socks. For barefoot-loving street urchins—as most of us kids were—the sight of what appeared to be tennis shoes was unusual. In time, this boy proved that unusual was commonplace for him.

Our next meeting was a fortnight later, when he sidled up at school lunchtime and said, 'I know you, you're the beer bottle kid. I'm Bryden James.'

'Yeah, I remember you,' I said, checking his feet and finding them still hidden within those canvas shoes.

His face drew close to mine. 'What class you in?'

I gazed into piercing eyes similar to that of a cat—oval-shaped with black pupils ringed by marbled brown.

I looked away. '4C, Mrs Simmons.'

'I'm in Ma Frinkle's, 4A,' he grinned, turning to survey the playground. 'Did ya get caught?'

'At the beer stack? Er ... yeah, my brother and Dicknose finally found me.'

'Dicknose?' Bryden laughed and turned back.

'Yeah, that's what we call Darryl, from up the road. Tall guy, plays footy with my brother.'

Our conversation continued until the bell rang, with Bryden calling over his shoulder as he hurried away, 'I'll come over this arvo and we can kick a footy.'

'Okay, I'll ask my mum!' I shouted back. But he was already talking with another kid as they headed back to class.

Self-invitation became a trademark of Bryden's. When he wanted something, he didn't wait to see if it eventuated, he just made it happen.

He arrived at my house that afternoon and we kicked a football around. My mum offered soft drinks and chocolate Wagon Wheels as a welcome treat to my new friend.

We progressed to regular catch ups and doing stuff like skipping stones in the local creek and going on adventures in the bushland around Thornleigh. He even helped me mow our yard one Saturday afternoon.

'Thanks, son,' Dad said, patting Bryden on the shoulder as he raked up the last of the grass. This made Bryden stop and smile—a sad kind of smile. The gesture also caused him to leave early to head off home.

Bryden had arrived in Thornleigh just before Christmas, when his parents bought a house in Percival Street, three streets away from mine. The first time I ventured to his place I got to see the extent of his father's bottle collection and obvious drinking problem. The entire length of the back fence was indeed stacked twenty high with discarded 'tallies'. It looked like a blockade I'd seen in an old war photo, but instead of sandbags, sunlit Pilsner glass provided the barricade.

Meeting Bryden's mum, I was surprised by how young she looked, reminding me of my eighteen-year-old cousin. Mrs James seemed welcoming enough until I started using Bryden's initials as a nickname. After hearing me call her son 'BJ', she swooped on me and dutifully told me that Bryden was Bryden, and nothing else.

'Yes, Mrs James. Sorry, Mrs James,' I replied meekly.

Months later at a rock throwing session by the creek, Brydon revealed the story behind that outburst.

'Mum was up the duff pretty young, Cam', he said while drawing with a stick in the sand. 'She was Julie Bryden before Dad came along. Grandad Bryden is some sort of fancy lawyer and he wasn't happy about her getting pregnant, so he kicked her out of home. Even though Mum was cut up about what they did to her, she named me after her family. How screwed up is that? They're all screwballs,' he added, stabbing the stick into the sandbank.

I thought on how his name could have been Bryden Bryden if his mum and dad hadn't married. But I didn't tell him that. Out of spite, he might have stabbed me too.

Bryden wasn't much into group sports at that age. He'd fill in for a team when the interest took him but was essentially a loner. He had an artistic streak that led him into school plays, and enabled him to draw cartoons of teachers that had most of us giggling—except when those long-nosed, big-lipped character sketches were intercepted by the class teacher as they slipped from hand to hand under the desks.

'Bryden James, up the front of the class,' the teacher would screech.

His easy-paced movements made him glide towards her. He'd

stand near the teacher and flick his hair over those unblinking cat eyes while she berated him.

'Silly mindless pictures ... you should know better ... up to the principal's office ... tell your mother ...'

Bryden didn't flinch, didn't move, just stared.

The teacher—more intimidated than annoyed at his defiance—finally faded off with, 'Back to your chair, young man, and I'll see you after class.'

This is the same tactic he used whenever the schoolyard bullies came within range: stand close and stare. When the pushing began, he chose not to retaliate until after the final shove. Then grabbing hold of the offender, he'd fall back, dragging them to the ground with him. Throwing punches, pulling hair, using dirt and stones for weapons, it was better described as a scrap than a fight, and often ended with Bryden screaming and thumping his chest like an angry ape as he pinned his opponent down.

I found out soon enough that Bryden was also a seeker for experience. His intelligent mind—bored by schoolwork—and his restlessness, led him to involve me in his quest for adventure. I should have known this coercion would one day get us into a whole lot of trouble.

5

—————

ASHLEY

FRIDAY

Now changed into pyjamas, I take my phone into the darkened living area and plonk down on my new sofa, whose streamlined form and tapered legs are reminiscent of the 1950s. Annoyed to find there is still no response from Cam, I search for him on Facebook. This proves futile, though I notice a few old school friends have posted 'R.I.P. Bryden James'. Unable to bring myself to read the additional comments, I get up and go into the kitchen. Returning with a vodka and orange in a highball glass, I rest back on the sofa, shut my burning eyes, and revisit the past.

———

1982

Maybe it's because I had no brothers that I was drawn to boys. Or maybe it resulted from a craving for male company due to my father's regular absence. Whatever the reason, I wasn't a tomboy, but I wasn't one of those girls who got all giggly and silly around them either. Stevie did become a close girl friend, yet when our entire class at Thornleigh stayed together when graduating to Grade 6 in 1982, I gravitated towards two boys in particular.

Bryden's frequent disobedience was often excused because of his humour and intelligence. However, most people blinded by his strange appeal did not witness his more sensitive side. This was sighted in fleeting fragments by only the intuitive or the observant. Like the time when Bryden got into a fight at school with an older kid.

It was a full-on punch-up and it attracted a spurring crowd. While Bryden laid into a boy for saying nasty things about his mother, I scanned the playground hoping to spot a teacher coming to break it up. That's when I noticed Campbell Druery. The short kid from our class who hung around with Bryden, stood to the side —hands in pockets, frowning. When our eyes met, and we shared looks of concern, a strange bond formed between us. While my body fizzed all over like I'd stuck my finger into an electrical socket, I saw Campbell's shoulders twitch as if someone had walked over his grave. Then he ran away, returning soon after with a teacher who stopped the messy brawl and dispersed the disappointed onlookers.

Other than getting into lunchtime fights, Bryden had a habit of testing others to see their reaction. One week, our Grade 6 teacher, Miss Harris, sat Bryden next to me—well-mannered, quiet, too frightened to rock the boat—to curb his need for attention. She must have done this out of sheer desperation for she certainly wasn't thinking clearly.

Sitting with me in the far back corner, Bryden took the opportunity to keenly reveal some hidden talents—one being the fact he liked to draw caricatures, the other, his knowledge of anatomy. Putting the two together, he got a thrill out of shocking me with his drawings of people I knew doing things I'd only recently found out about.

'Hey, Cinders, have a look at this,' Bryden said, nudging me in the ribs.

Unsure if I appreciated the new nickname he'd given me, I took the note he passed me under the desk. Naively, I unfolded it and gasped at yet another rude drawing. In this one, a smiling and naked Miss Harris slapped the bare backside of a boy bent over in front of her. Sticking out from between the boy's legs was something huge and revolting. The speech bubble above Miss Harris read, 'I see you're enjoying this, Campbell Druery.'

I peered over at Cam seated a couple of desks to the right, and he must have caught the movement because he cocked his head and stared back. My face went hot, and I screwed up the piece of paper. Cam frowned and eyed Bryden who was making a show of silently laughing behind his hand. Grabbing his eraser, Cam threw it over the heads of the two kids between us. But his aim was off and instead of hitting Bryden, it struck me in the face. I squealed.

Miss Harris glanced up from helping Sandra Gillingham with her work and scowled. 'What's going on back there?' She probably saw me rubbing the spot where the eraser had bounced off my cheek for she added, 'Ashley, was it you who made that noise?'

Every head in the room turned, and every eye focused on me. I nodded.

'On your feet,' Miss Harris ordered, walking up the aisle towards the back row.

Bryden chuckled as I stood, so I gave his shin a sideways kick.

'What happened, Ashley?' Miss Harris asked, redirecting her gaze to Bryden.

'It wasn't me, Miss,' he said.

'Then why is your cheek red, Ashley?'

Too afraid to look her in the eye, I glared at her nose, watching her nostrils flare. I was also aware of Cam waiting for me to dob him in. My heart pounded. As I gripped the edge of the desk to steady my shaking, the wad of paper fell from my hand.

Miss Harris looked at the floor. 'What's that?'

My face burned. There was no way I would show her that disgusting picture. She might even think I was the one who drew it. I swiftly dropped and picked it up.

'Nothing, Miss,' I said, stuffing Bryden's drawing into my mouth. Two chews and I swallowed it whole.

I'm not sure who was more startled by my action—Miss Harris, Bryden, or me. This wasn't something I'd normally do. I was the good girl. Yet, Miss Harris sent me to stand outside the classroom until lunch break.

When the bell rang and the class filed out, I waited for Bryden to pass and punched him in the arm.

He just laughed. 'Cinders, that was way cool. I owe you big time.'

'No you don't!' I snapped, pushing him away. 'Leave me alone, you sicko.'

Eager to replace the taste of paper in my mouth, I went to the bag racks outside the classroom and searched inside my school bag for the corned beef and tomato sauce sandwich my mum had provided for lunch.

Cam came alongside. 'Thanks for not ratting on me,' he whispered. 'I thought I was a goner. What was on that bit of paper, anyway?'

I considered the freckled face before me and the way the pale eyelashes fluttered like caught insects and decided against expanding on the truth. 'A drawing,' was all I said.

Fair eyebrows arched. 'Of what? It must've been good.'

'No.' I shook my head, my ponytail swishing across my back. 'It was bad. Way bad.'

Cam's eyes lit up. 'Did Bryden draw something?'

I peered over at Bryden sitting on the bag racks further down, chatting to a pack of stupid girls, and nodded.

He chuckled. 'What was it? You can tell me.'

'No, I can't,' I said, brushing him aside, and heading for the stairs that led down to the playground.

Cam stepped in front, blocking my way. 'Come on, Ash, spit it out. Did he do one of Miss Harris? Was she in the nuddy?'

'I'm not telling you.'

'It's okay. I can draw it again,' said Bryden from behind.

I swung around and mouthed a 'no', but he just grinned and pushed past. Slinging his arm over Cam's shoulder, he led him away.

I wasn't surprised when I heard there'd been a scuffle near the tennis courts and both boys failed to return to class that afternoon. Still, it didn't take them long to sort things out and, having somehow proven my worth, they began to include me in their weekend activities.

6

CAMPBELL

FRIDAY

If ever there was an ache, a slow bleed in my soul, it has been because of my longing to be noticed by Ashley. Over the years, we have shared our pain, and occasionally she let me hold her when the world became too big and dark for her sensitive grip. But she rarely reciprocated my depth of feeling for her. In the past, I have been a loyal puppy, eagerly awaiting any scrap of recognition thrown my way. Yet, there have been times I've hated this weakness and loss of dignity in believing that one day she would see 'me'.

Ashley, Ash, Cinders ... bitch—no, maybe that's too harsh—slid into my life in Grade 5.

1981-82

I barely observed Ash's arrival that day in June. However, Bryden—in my class since the beginning of the year—was fully aware of her presence and soon got a kick out of stirring her because she seemed so very proper. Pulling her long, red hair, or sneaking up behind and whispering in her ear to give her a fright was fun for him. This annoyed Ash, who only welcomed attention when being complimented on her schoolwork.

And then in Grade 6, she was simply there: joining in with Bryden and me to chat at lunch, jostle in line at the tuckshop, and sit at our kitchen tables after school sharing in our respective mother's offerings of sustenance. Ash's athletic build and extra height—at least ten centimetres taller than me—made it easy for her to keep up with our boyish exploits and I became fond of her because she was the only girl, other than relatives, I knew well. In time, this innocent appreciation of the opposite sex would alter, and I would seek further expressions of affection.

The only close physical contact we had—apart from rescuing each other from adventures gone wrong—was during the regular dance classes in preparation for the annual school fancy dress ball. Partnered for dances such as The Pride of Erin, Ash's long fingers never matched my squat hands and often slipped because my palms were moist—the nervousness more to do with trying to get my feet moving in the right direction. Her tentative smile would meet mine as we attempted the waltz section, then the tripping began. Embarrassed, I found myself peeling away, allowing Bryden to step in and take the lead, and together they'd move off with a grace and timing that even surprised the teachers. Entranced by Bryden's competence, I searched for ways to transform myself from a sandy-haired, freckle-faced nobody into someone more noticeable, like him.

Boredom stalked Bryden one humid Saturday as we sat on the back steps of Ashley's home slurping on Redskins before the heat stole the ice cream off the sticks.

'Hey, Cinders,' Bryden shouted from the carport under the high-set house, 'what are all these hessian bags used for?'

Leaning to peer through the wooden slats, Ash's ice cream dripped onto her thigh and trickled down one slender, tanned leg.

'Dad takes them when he goes crabbing with his Army mates,' she called, using the hem of her T-shirt to mop up the sticky splotches.

Moments later, Bryden emerged carrying five hessian bags.

'Put 'em back,' Ash cried. 'Dad'll hit the roof if he finds out we've touched his stuff.'

'Aw, come on, Ash. I've got a plan. It'll be fun,' was his dismissive reply.

Before long, we were dragging a reluctant Ashley down a few streets to some bushland nestled between new housing estates. Two more street wanderers, Barnesy and 'Windy' Winslow, joined us after hearing Bryden say we would become firemen.

Ash was still protesting as we gathered in a circle, each gripping a woven bag and sweating from the heat mist rising from the tall grass.

'Look, it's simple,' claimed our leader. 'We'll light a small fire and then bash it out with the bags.'

'Bryden, it's too hot to be doing this,' Ashley whined, 'and we'll burn Dad's bags.'

'Not if we hit the flames hard enough. It will go out quickly,' countered our thrill-seeking fire expert.

Windy Winslow offered up a can emblazoned with the word Ampol. 'Will this help?'

'Where'd you get that?' Ash cried, her eyes wide with alarm.

'Swiped it along the way,' he smirked, twisting the cap free and releasing petrol fumes into the air.

My stomach twisted when Bryden produced a box of matches from a pocket of his shorts. It knotted further when Barnesy grabbed the can from Windy and poured a small circle of petrol, thirty centimetres in diameter.

Bryden had a match out of the box and lit before anyone could protest. Cartwheeling from his fingers, it set the ground alight with a gentle 'whoosh' and had us pounding the orange flames with the bags. In no time, the fire was out with the grass only singed. Cheers followed from our youthful brigade.

Ashley's flushed face, glistening with perspiration, had only just regained composure when Bryden ushered us further out to create a bigger circumference.

'No!' she cried, but soon the ground was alight again.

The pounding that took place had this second, larger circle of fire under control within a minute. Jubilant about our prompt actions, we also felt like oven-roasted potatoes from the bristling heat.

'One more,' Windy said.

And with that, a blaze erupted from a wider ring of petrol. But this time it overpowered our efforts to stamp it out, and the crackling, biting monster racing through the long grass had us all turning in panic and dashing away. Under a rising cloud of blue-grey smoke, Windy and Barnesy peeled off in opposite directions while Bryden and I raced back with Ash to her place.

We heard distant sirens as we checked ourselves for injuries. Other than scratches on our legs from long, sharp blades of grass whipping us as we retreated, no one was hurt. Still, Ashley was in tears, and the smouldering bags lying on the front lawn had her running upstairs and into the house. I turned to quiz our leader as to what we should do next, but Bryden was already rushing out the gate.

I ran after him and we both arrived back at the wild blaze to discover the scene now included two fire trucks and a crowd of gawkers. The acrid smell of smoke tinged with petrol fumes and burnt wood had us gripping our noses. We watched from a safe distance as firemen equipped with large hoses clamped onto the trucks by shiny couplings tackled the flaming beast.

When the fire was conquered, and the throng had dispersed, a brigade captain approached us and asked if we'd seen who had started it.

Bryden's face beamed as he eyed the sweat-dripping man who appeared larger than life in his thick-coated uniform and helmet. 'Yes, sir,' he said with confidence. 'I saw some boys run off into those bushes. I reckon they were the ones who started it.'

The fireman studied us through narrowed eyes, his drooping moustache quivering as he chewed his lip and nodded. Then, removing his helmet and tucking it under his arm, he moved away to motion his crew back onto their red chariot.

We watched as the trucks departed. Gazing over the vista of burnt earth, smoking knolls, and black skeleton trees we were amazed that our little game had cleared acres of vegetation in a matter of minutes.

Bryden elbowed me and grinned. 'It's funny that we started the day with Ash and finished it with another kind.'

Finding no amusement in what we had done, I ran back to Ashley's place and arrived just as the family car pulled into the driveway and her father stepped out.

'Hi, Mr McCabe,' I said, my voice coming out as a nervous squeak.

Ash appeared on the verandah in a change of clothes. Hurrying down the stairs she stood next to me, her hair wet, face mottled from crying.

Mr McCabe's gaze dropped to the singed pile of hessian on his lawn. 'What the hell is this?'

I looked at Ash and caught her eyes darting back and forth

between me and her dad. My thoughts quickly turned to Bryden's ability to stand firm and lie.

'Th... there were three boys,' I stammered, '... and ...and we saw them light a fire in the bush and ...well ... we ... Ash, had this great idea that we could put it out by ... er ... using your hessian bags. She was ... well ... Bryden and me ... we did our best.'

Ash nodded in agreement and gave me a sideways glance. Here was a lie that must have gnawed at her sense of honesty—a lie her parents would never query because of their trust in her. It was not the last time she would look at me with both gratitude and disgust.

7

ASHLEY

1982

Cam and Bryden's visits became regular, especially during school holidays when we'd take off on our bikes around the neighbourhood in search of adventure.

Drawn to Bryden's popularity, other kids joined in and we morphed into a rowdy mob of mischief-makers rather than a trio on a quest for fun. I jokingly referred to Bryden as The Pied Piper of Thornleigh, though I secretly resented being thrust aside like an outgrown childhood toy in his pursuit of a wider group of hangers-on.

One Sunday, Bryden dropped into my place more excited than usual. Sitting cross-legged on the verandah, reading a book on Howard Carter's discovery of Tutankhamen's tomb, and envisaging my life as an archaeologist, I heard my name shouted. I glanced up to see Bryden leap from his bike and race up the stairs, unconcerned that his Malvern Star had wobbled into a hibiscus shrub.

Red faced and wide-eyed, he cried, 'Holy toledo. You've got to come right now.'

'Why? I'm busy.' I waved the book at him.

He grabbed it and dropped it on the tiles. 'We've found a way into the food store on Fargo Street. There's some wire mesh broken around an air vent. You've gotta help us get in.'

'Why me? I've never broken into a shop before. Do it yourself.'

'We can't.'

'Why can't you? I'm sure you've done it heaps of times.'

He shook his head, his dark hair falling over his eyes. 'The hole's too small. We can't squeeze in.'

'What about Cam? Is he there? He's not big.'

'He's short, but he's not skinny like you.'

I cringed. Tall, with stick figure limbs and a stomach that wasn't just flat but concave, I had bony ribs that stuck out and a chest that didn't. It made me mad that I ate as much as anyone else my age, yet I never put on weight. There were plenty of books and magazine articles written on how to lose weight, but nowhere had I come across information on how to put it on. I even clung to the hope of waking up one day and finding I'd magically sprouted boobs overnight which Stevie said had happened to her. My mother kept telling me to be patient and appreciate not having to worry about leering boys. Yet, part of me wanted to be gawked at—in a good way.

'Okay,' I sighed, getting to my feet, 'as long as it doesn't take long, and we don't get caught.'

'Thanks, Ash,' Bryden grinned, slapping me on the back. 'You're a champion, a real mate.'

I rolled my eyes and went to find my bike.

Being Sunday, the store was closed. Though the rear of the small building was obscured from prying eyes by a high timber fence, we discovered Cam and another kid, Barnesy, hiding amongst piles of empty crates and cardboard boxes.

'Geez, you took your time,' Barnesy scowled.

Bryden smacked him over the head. 'Well we're here now, so you can stop playing hide-and-seek.'

'Hi, Ash,' Cam smiled. 'Thanks for helping us out.'

'I haven't done anything yet,' I said, turning to Bryden. 'Where's the hole?'

He pointed to the bottom corner of the besser block wall where the removal of an iron grate and the peeling away of wire mesh had revealed a square opening. 'See if you can stuff yourself in there.'

'Then what?'

'Open the back door and let us in, dummy.'

It seemed a simple enough task. I put my arms in and followed through with my head, and then my shoulders. It was dark within and eerie shadows lurked. I wished I'd brought a torch. It smelled stuffy yet pleasant, a mixture of breakfast cereals and spices. When I tried to ease the rest of myself in, my backside became wedged.

'I'm stuck,' I yelled, my cry echoing in the darkness.

Someone—I have a pretty good idea who—grabbed my bum and gave it a squeeze. Cackling followed. I kicked out and was shoved further in until I slipped through and tumbled onto the floor.

The light now coming in through the unblocked opening afforded a better view. I was in a storeroom stacked high with boxes. Tins, bags, and packets of all kinds of foods and household needs lined the wall shelves. One whole shelf contained boxes of lollies. It was as exciting as discovering the antechamber to King Tut's tomb.

It went dark again as Bryden's head poked through the hole. 'Hey, open the door will ya?'

I stood and pulled on the handle of the storeroom door. Fortunately, it was unlocked, otherwise, I may have still been there when the owner opened up first thing Monday morning. The doorway led into the shop and I found the exit door, flicked the snib, and turned the knob. The boys raced in with cries of '*Whoa*', '*Cool*', and '*Get a load of this*', while I nervously hung back.

Though unlit, large panes of glass at the front allowed enough light into the shop for us to scoot up and down the four aisles without knocking into things. Bryden halted in the confectionery aisle, grabbed a bag of potato chips, ripped it open, and stuffed his mouth full. Barnesy opened a container of sherbet cones, and Cam picked up two blocks of chocolate. Gingerly, I lifted a packet of bubblegum from a shelf and slid it into a pocket of my shorts. I'd stolen nothing before, so for me this was as scary as robbing a bank.

Bryden chugged down a can of warm cola and then disappeared around the edge of the aisle. I followed and found him vaulting over the shop counter to the cash register.

'Bryden!' I shouted, 'No stealing cash. We're just here for a bit of fun, aren't we?'

He smiled and did a little dance, singing 'Tired of Toein' the Line'—his regular catch cry since the incident on the desk in Grade 5. Stretching up to the overhead shelving where the cigarettes were stored, he extracted a packet of Marlboro Red and a box of matches.

'Smoko,' he said, ripping open the packaging and removing a cigarette. Placing it between his lips, he struck a match and lit the end.

The other boys joined me, and we watched in awe as Bryden casually drew back long and hard, proving this was not his first time.

He lit a second cigarette and handed it to Barnesy, who took a puff and passed it on to Cam. Cam studied Bryden, then held it with his thumb and index finger and placed it in his mouth in the same fashion. He breathed in and his eyes watered, and he began to choke.

Bryden laughed and called him a baby. 'Now it's your turn, Cinders. Let's see what you can do.'

My parents smoked. Dad puffed away like a cowboy from the Wild West while Mum smoked gracefully like an olden day movie star. I emulated her by holding the cigarette between my fingers and taking a small drag. With a flick of my wrist, I lifted my chin and blew smoke into the air thinking I looked cool.

'Cheat. You didn't inhale,' Bryden said. 'Do it again.'

I scowled at him and dragged longer, breathed in deeper, felt a burning itch at the back of my throat ... and almost died. I gasped, coughed, and puked semi-digested Fruit Loops from breakfast over the floor tiles.

Bryden jumped out of the line of fire. 'Geez, what a loser.'

Barnesy roared with laughter while Cam just stood there covering his mouth with his hand.

'Let's get outta here,' Bryden ordered, pocketing the cigarette packet. 'I'm bored.'

I wiped my chin. 'What about the mess? We should clean it up.'

'Nah, leave it. Let 'em wonder what the hell happened here.'

Exiting through the back door was much easier than squishing through a small gap in the wall. Cam was the last to leave, flicking the snib lock and pulling the door shut after him. Bryden and Barnesy bent the mesh over the hole and replaced the grate as best they could.

While they were doing this, Cam sidled up to me. I took two steps away, but he zoomed right in.

'What's with you?' I asked, chewing bubblegum to replace the taste of cigarette and spew.

He forced a packet of fluorescent-coloured hair bands into my hand. 'Thought you could use them for your hair,' he said, a blush filling in the spaces between his freckles.

I was speechless. Cam had been freaking me out of late: watching me weirdly, lining up right behind me when we were waiting to enter the classroom. Stevie reckoned he had a crush on me, but I'd just laughed it off. Now I didn't feel much like laughing.

'What's that?' Bryden asked, walking over.

'Nothing,' I mumbled and slipped the packet into my shorts pocket rather than handing it back and being spotted by Bryden. He'd have made a big thing of it. The way he now glared at both of us as we fidgeted and scuffed our feet in the dirt, was unsettling enough as it was. I quickly got on my bike and rode home.

Years later, I found the same unopened packet of hair bands in a drawer, and the irritation in Bryden's eyes that day came flooding back. If I'd known it was the beginning of events so much worse, I would have ceased hanging out with those two boys right then. But that's the benefit of hindsight: seeing clearly where things first went wrong.

Another scheme Cam and Bryden roped me into had us nearly burning down the neighbourhood. Frightened by what took place that day, I ignored all boys for a month. It could have gone on longer if not for an invitation to join a group at the Druery's place for a sausage sizzle and to watch the first episode of a new TV series called *Family Ties*. My sister told me the show starred a cool, new actor, Michal J Fox, and was doing real well in America. So I thought, 'Why not?' I'd get a free sausage sandwich.

As usual, I was the only girl to show up. Just as we finished eating, a thunderstorm hit, and we had fun running around in the rain after a stinking hot day. When we'd had enough, and Mrs Druery wouldn't allow us inside with wet clothes, the boys stripped off their shirts. This wasn't an option for me, so Mrs Druery kindly handed me a towel and led me to Cam's bedroom. Opening a cupboard drawer, she removed a couple of T-shirts and laid them on the bed.

'Not very girly, I know, but they should fit,' she said, smiling. Brushing damp locks away from my face, she added in a more sombre tone, 'I almost had a daughter once. I would've loved to have been able to fuss over her, but it wasn't to be.' Then she left me to change, her strange comment drifting after her.

I surveyed Cam's bedroom. His two younger brothers shared a different room, so this was his alone. A typical boy's zone, it included a smattering of sports equipment, a desk covered in comic books, and a bookshelf lined with action figures and Matchbox cars. Instead of pictures of pop stars sticky-taped to the walls, as in my bedroom, here were movie posters: *Raiders of the Lost Ark, Mad Max, Star Wars*.

Cam's blue-painted bed under the window bore heaps of stickers on the headboard. I moved closer to read them when a scratching in the paintwork caught my attention. Carved within an outline of a love heart was *'AMcC 4 CD'*.

I pulled away, my stomach somersaulting. Stevie was right. How was I to return to the group knowing Cam's secret?

Feeling sick, I quickly chose a blue shirt printed with a black outline of a cassette player. It was clean, but still had a sour boy smell about it. Nervously venturing into the lounge room, I found everyone seated in a clump in front of the TV, chips and lollies at the ready. All eyes lifted to me.

'Isn't that your T-shirt, Cam?' asked a grinning Windy Winslow.

'Ooh, I think she likes you,' stirred someone else.

'No way,' I growled, taking a seat on the carpet far away from a blushing Cam.

My arm was nudged. 'You sure about that?'

I glared at Bryden sitting on my right. 'Of course. I'm just wearing his stupid T-shirt 'cos mine's soaked. Is that a crime?'

His lips curved into a smile. 'Nope, guess not.'

The TV show was good, but I missed parts because Bryden was sitting so close. His scent—sour, salty—and his arm brushing against mine as he passed bowls of munchies had a confusing effect on me.

The next evening while dumping a bag of rubbish in the bin at the rear of my house, I heard someone cough in the dark. Fear ran icy fingers down my spine at the idea of a prowler lurking in our yard, and I jumped when a figure appeared in the ray of light streaming from our kitchen window.

'Holey moley, Bryden! What are you doing here?'

He gave a shrug and sat on the rear steps, cradling his left arm.

'What happened? Are you hurt?'

'It's nothing.'

I squinted into the shadows. 'Where's your bike? Did you have a stack?'

He shook his head. 'My dad can be a real shit sometimes, that's all.'

I glanced at his arm and was tempted to ask if his dad had hit him, but I chickened out. 'Why are you here, then?'

He peered up at the kitchen window. 'I like coming here ... listening to a regular family doing regular things.'

'Listening?'

'Yeah, from outside. I look through windows, watch people glued to the TV together, eating dinner, having silly family squabbles then making up.'

The image of him spying on my family gave me the creeps. I made a mental note to close my bedroom curtains at night.

'My family's not normal, Ash.'

'In what way?'

He paused for a beat. 'You know.'

I think I knew what he meant. Rumours flying around hinted his parents fought a lot and that Bryden sometimes got caught in the middle. Maybe that was what went on tonight.

'You're lucky, Ash, having the family you've got.'

I considered my parents, how they annoyed the hell out of me at times, and of my sister and how irritating she could be. Still, we loved each other. My parents weren't shy when it came to sharing their feelings.

I heard a sniff and caught Bryden rubbing his eyes.

'Don't tell anyone,' he urged.

'I won't,' I said, unsure if he meant the crying or being a peeping Tom. Either way, his secret was safe with me.

He gave me an awkward sideways hug and then ran off into the night, while I stayed where I was, wondering if the strange thrill of his touch had something to do with puberty. If that was the case, then I wasn't the least bit ready for it.

8

CAMPBELL

1982

There were only two times our parents met face-to-face. One was at a primary school fete.

Bryden and I were nudging each other and engaging in boy banter when Ash marched past as a member of the school band. She was the tallest of that ear-splitting recorder and drum-banging troop, and her short skirt made her legs look even longer, which Bryden and I had noticed, hence the elbowing.

The band circled the parade ground, marching with high-legged steps before coming to a ragged standstill, ending their performance. Bryden and I joined the crowd in whooping and clapping enthusiastically. We ambled over to poke fun at her when Mr and Mrs McCabe edged through the throng and greeted their daughter with a hug.

'Well done, sweetheart,' her father congratulated.

Another voice had me spinning around.

'Campbell Druery!' my mother shouted, pushing through the

crowd. 'Where in the dickens have you been? Your father has been looking for you for ages.'

Dad appeared behind her, scowling, and holding a misshapen hamburger. A slice of beetroot slipped from the soggy bread roll and dropped to the ground.

'Sorry, Mum,' I apologised. 'We were watching Ash and the band.'

Mr McCabe extended his hand to my dad. 'John McCabe, and my wife, Nancy. Campbell knows our daughter, Ashley.'

Dad wiped his beetroot-stained hand on his trousers before offering it to Ash's father. 'Hi John. We're Phil and Dot Druery. Yes, Cam and Ash spend quite a bit of time together.'

This sent a blush to Ash's cheeks and a rush of heat to my own, provoking a jab in the ribs from Bryden. His smirk vanished when a large hand clamped onto his shoulder.

'Bryden, time to go, mate.'

His dad wasn't the school fete type of guy, and his expression registered his impatience.

Bryden shrugged out of his grasp. 'I'll be home later. Where's Mum?'

Mr James tilted his head to the right. Standing a couple of metres away, Bryden's mum—looking as young as ever and only slightly taller than Ash—motioned Bryden over.

Before Ash's father could utter more than, 'Hi, I'm ...' Mr James had walked off, leaving Mr McCabe with his arm still outstretched.

Bryden's mum took three paces forward and clasped her slender fingers around the strong hand of this military man. 'Julie James. How do you do,' she offered. 'That friendly chap was my husband, Peter,' she added, with a roll of her eyes.

While our parents engaged in small talk, Bryden and I sidled up to Ash and pretended to admire her uniform.

'Nice hat you've got there, Ash,' said Bryden, pointing to the maroon wedge cap pinned into her hair. 'Didn't know the Air Force was having a garage sale. I could've got myself one.'

'Nick off, Bryden,' she countered, pushing him away, 'you're such an idiot.'

'Takes one to know one,' he quipped back, giving her long plait a tug, and causing her to squeal.

Bryden jolted when his neck was grasped.

John McCabe's grip hinted at a strength that could be unleashed if necessary. 'Come on now, boy. Enough with the tomfoolery. You should know better than to tease girls.'

Ash's eye roll showed she disagreed with her father's view of girls being unable to withstand a little bit of ribbing.

The next tension-filled time our parents got together was at the Thornleigh police station when we were offering an explanation for a crime being committed.

9

———

ASHLEY

1983

'Puberty: The process of physical changes through which a child's body matures into an adult body capable of sexual reproduction.'

This is pretty much what was taught one day in Grade 7, when boys and girls had been separated into two groups and given the low-down on what to expect during adolescence.

It began with confusing symbolism—pollinating bees, metamorphosing insects, and the life cycle of a frog—and ended with graphic and clinical information on things that would grow, sprout, curve, deepen, and gush. Giggles and elbowing were greeted by stern warnings from teachers who preferred to be anywhere other than in a puberty awareness class packed with sniggering students.

What they didn't tell us—and we soon discovered for ourselves—was that puberty also turned kids into strange creatures. Girls would have sudden outbursts of crying, blushing, and sulking, while boys would squawk, become moody, and get into more fights. 1983 was, therefore, an odd time.

Though fascinated by the changes finally happening to my body, I hated what was going on in my head. Emotions heightened in all aspects. I became upset about the smallest of things—much to my parents' dismay—and began to like boys in a way I'd never expected. Confused by my feelings, I ditched weekend adventures with Bryden and Cam for times hanging out with a group of girls who, like me, were infatuated with movie stars and pop stars and used pillows for kissing practice. Then, to my horror, I developed a crush on Bryden, whose reputation as a joker and rule breaker had grown to legendary status.

'Why him?' I asked myself. *Why did I search him out in the playground? Why did my heart race when he looked my way, or my stomach flip when he neared?* It was stupid. I felt stupid. But I couldn't shake the fact that brooding, angst-ridden males on the edge drew my attention. I blamed my sister, Lauren, who had urged me to read classics like *Wuthering Heights* and *Catcher in the Rye* and watch James Dean in *East of Eden* when the movie aired on TV.

Then came our primary school break-up party, held on a Friday night at Stevie's place. Ignored most of the year by Bryden, I was surprised when he offered me a can of soft drink when I arrived and dashed over to make the odd remark between entertaining kids with his silly antics. I wondered what had sparked his interest in me. Maybe it was my short, frilled skirt, or my hair falling free around my shoulders, or that I wore a little makeup. Whatever it was, his attention made me edgy.

Later in the evening word got around that a game of Spin the Bottle was about to start. Though curious about who would be taking part, there was no way I would join in. Not having properly kissed anything human, I wasn't keen to have my first attempt witnessed by a group of gawking kids. Hanging out at the food table, I happily watched kids zombie dance to 'Thriller' until Stevie grabbed my arm.

'C'mon, we need another girl,' she urged, dragging me outside.

Christmas lights strung around the Hills Hoist clothesline lit up the backyard where eight kids sat in a circle on the freshly mown lawn. Stevie pushed me down next to Russell Higgins and took her place alongside Windy Winslow. Across from me sat Alice Cummings wedged between Cam—disinterested, plucking at blades of grass—and Bryden, his narrow eyes glinting red, yellow, and then green as the Christmas lights flickered through their range of colours. He smiled at me, and I dropped my attention to the glass soft drink bottle lying on the grass in the centre of the circle—the holy grail of the Grade 7 set.

Resigned to my fate, I sent up a prayer. '*If I have to spin the bottle, please make it stop at Bryden.*' To my relief, the bottle ignored me.

Stevie, on the other hand, got to kiss both Russell and Bryden, and heartily showed her appreciation. The boys responded with the same exuberance, proving truth to the rumour that some kids had been chalking up experience behind the school sports shed during lunch breaks. Stevie's actions didn't surprise me as she'd already confided in me her exploits with boys. Yet, seeing her and Bryden pash, niggled me.

I checked my watch. Fifteen minutes until my mother's arrival to take me home. I started to get up to make an early escape when Stevie tapped me on the arm and said it was my turn to spin. All eyes focused on me compelled me to stay.

Hesitantly taking the bottle by the neck, I glanced around the circle. On my right was Russell, who'd latched onto Stevie like a starving suckerfish. Nick O'Connor, the kid with the worst breath at school, was on my left. Next came Windy—sweat beads forming above his fleshy upper lip—then Bryden and Cam. There was only one person I wanted to kiss. Uttering another silent prayer, I gave the bottle a good spin.

It whirled, and wobbled, and slowed, edging its way past Windy and Jill Morrissey. Then, just as the bottle stopped at Bryden, he gave it a nudge with his foot, and it halted in front of Cam. Bryden grinned, Cam turned bright pink, and I felt betrayed. The urge to run away was strong, but everyone goaded us on.

I glared at Bryden and got to my knees. Cam did the same. As we leaned over the bottle, Cam hesitated, blinking, and chewing the corner of his mouth. I wanted to get it over and done with, so I grabbed him by the shoulders and wrenched him close.

I always thought my first kiss would be like in the movies— gentle and so very romantic, but it wasn't. It was forced and cringeworthy, full of teeth, wet lips, and noses that got in the way. Pulling out of the kiss, I noticed a strand of saliva linking me to Cam before it snapped apart.

Bryden cackled and punched Cam in the arm. 'What was that, mate? It sure didn't look like kissing to me. What were you doing, munchin' on a Big Mac?'

Everyone laughed, and Cam jumped up and scurried away.

I gave Bryden a dirty look. In deriding Cam, he had also mocked me. 'Stop it!' I snarled. 'Stop being so cruel!'

Bryden pulled a face. 'Geez, loosen up, Ash. What's wrong with you? Is your training bra too tight or something?'

I slapped him across the face—another first—and stormed off.

Fuming with humiliation, I waited at the front gate for my mother to arrive. Tears poured hot and stinging, and I rubbed them away with the heels of my hands, not caring if I smudged my carefully applied eyeshadow.

A noise came from behind and I twisted around.

If I wasn't so caught out, I might have sunk my teeth into the lips that pressed against mine. Instead, I let Bryden kiss me.

I didn't see him again until after the holidays. A lot can happen in six weeks. I went camping at Coolum Beach with my family and spent time with the girls from school—going to the movies, having sleepovers and stuff. By the time we started high school in the new year, Bryden was just a bad memory.

10

―――――――

CAMPBELL

FRIDAY

Sitting in the lounge room, with crumbs from leftover pizza I barely recall eating scattered in my lap and over my black leather couch, I struggle with memories that have pursued and haunted me. Over the years, I've found that the only thing that keeps these dark thoughts at bay comes from what I can shake out of little brown pill bottles.

Attempted escapes—running breathless, head snapping back to see who was chasing, my mind so frenzied that the stumbling, falling was not felt—became frequent in Bryden's company, starting with the frantic fleeing from the grass fire.

―――――――

1983

That running away painfully reappeared one night at the Grade 7 break-up party. Bryden's sick attempt to out my private feelings for Ash in a childish game of Spin the Bottle, and the ridicule that followed our awkward kiss, had me hiding at the side of the Taylor house. In that quiet, shadowy space, I saw Ash race into the front yard, equally upset. Then seeing Bryden chase after her and give his own version of passionate kissing was a breaking point for my sensitive twelve-year-old heart. I back-pedalled and jumped the neighbouring fence. Climbing a wooden gate, I sprinted down the hill and dashed through parkland in an attempt to outrun the pain of embarrassment.

It wasn't long before the darkness proved disorientating and I tripped, tumbling onto the bitumen, and grazing my chin and hands. Though winded from the heavy fall, I picked myself up and continued running, gulping air through sobs, and hating Bryden with a murderous depth.

My mouth dry, my lungs aching, I slowed to a stagger and found the perfect place to rest. A large cylindrical drainage pipe big enough to stand upright in, was the sanctuary I needed. Halfway home, and with time still on my side before my expected arrival, I decided to stay awhile.

As best as any boy my age could, I tried to understand why Bryden made life so difficult for Ash and me. These thoughts intertwined with ways I could get back at him. Yet, the idea of buying bombs to blow him up, or building large, covered pits for him to fall into, seemed too fantastic even for my active *Raiders of the Lost Ark* and *Mad Max* imagination. After twenty minutes, I noticed a small red glow approaching through the darkness— someone sucking on a cigarette.

'Well, well, well,' came a familiar voice. 'Having a conference with your friends, are you?'

'Piss off, Bryden,' I said, backing further into the pipe.

'What's up, Cambo?' he said, stepping inside the cement cylinder. 'You're not all funny about kissing Ash, are ya? I thought you'd be happy that you got to smooch your girlfriend.'

Though Bryden was physically stronger and taller than me, I lunged, hoping to knock him down with a rugby tackle. But he turned his hips as I rushed in and I hit the wall of the pipe instead —more indignation.

'Cut it out, Cam. I'll flog ya if you want,' came his unsympathetic response.

'You shithead!' I yelled, tears refilling my eyes. I continued to protest, yet it was only when I stammered, 'My m ... mum even thinks you're c ... cruel sometimes ... and my d ... dad was going to invite you on holidays with us,' that Bryden's mood changed.

He flicked his cigarette away and blew the last of the smoke from his mouth. 'Hey ... I was only trying to help. I thought—'

'Don't! I saw you kiss her,' I said, wiping snot on the sleeve of my shirt.

'Cam, you're my best buddy. I'm sorry. I was ... well, you know, just stirring Ash.'

He put his arm around my shoulders and we both slid down the curved wall onto our backsides.

'Hey, you're like my brother ... and your mum and dad ... well, they ... well your mum makes great ham and salad sandwiches,' he said, with a slow grin.

I wiped my nose again and smiled. 'Yep, she does,' I sniffled.

'Mate, I won't hurt you again. I promise.'

This naively calmed me. 'Promise?'

'Promise!' Bryden ruffled my hair, and we sat in the dark for a while, making silly noises that echoed around us like ghosts.

Walking home together, Bryden attempted to make me laugh by relating what Stevie had been getting up to at the party. It helped ease the sting of my grazed hands as I tucked them under my sweaty armpits, and numb other body aches that were surfacing.

.   .   .

Bryden holidayed with us over the Christmas vacation period and came to see that, even though our family lived modestly, we enjoyed each other's company and revelled in our mum's generosity. Her meals, filled with kid-satisfying tastes, urged Bryden to say things such as, 'Your mum puts together real salads, Cam, not like the strange things my mum makes from canned stuff.'

He even liked the simple building projects my dad involved us in, using stumps and branches and whatever was at hand.

'They're the best outdoor cubbies and gunyahs anywhere in the world,' Bryden exclaimed.

His parents' drinking and arguing had reached gossip stage throughout the neighbourhood, and I wondered how he was handling all the crap going on at home.

'I'm gonna leave one day, Cambo,' he told me, while we were in the middle of playing the board game, Operation. 'I'm saving money just in case.'

'In case of what?' I asked, my interest more in trying to remove Cavity Sam's Adam's apple with a pair of tweezers and not setting off the buzzer.

'I dunno ... in case it gets too much. Any cash I find lying around, I'm putting in an old sock and hiding it behind a loose bit of skirting board under my bed. Got about fifteen bucks, I reckon.'

'That's not gonna get you far.' I chewed my lip and went for the plastic heart.

'Well ... if I can get to the Gold Coast, I'll be right. I'll become a beach bum. I could surf out to an island and live like freakin' Robinson Crusoe. You could join me and be my mate, Friday, and run around fetching me coconuts and fish and stuff.'

My hand jerked and the buzzer went off. Cavity Sam's red nose flashed like Rudolph's at Christmas. 'The hell I will!'

Our short ten days stay near the beachfront seemed to calm

Bryden and allow our friendship to strengthen. Though, on returning to his troubled home life, his difficult behaviour resurfaced, and he soon broke that promise he'd made to me in the drainage pipe.

The first incident involved a game of darts—not throwing them at a dartboard but aiming them at trees and pieces of strewn timber to see how far we could toss them. We were in Bryden's backyard, hurling darts at a wooden post with a metal basketball ring attached.

Bryden turned to me. 'Do you like to dance?'

The first dart he threw landed near my left foot, and my instinctive reaction was to lift it out of harm's way. The next, by my right, had me jumping high to avoid the brass point that then pierced the ground. I called out for him to stop, but he only complied when his throw found its target, lodging in the flesh of my calf. I whimpered as I tugged it from my leg and hobbled off, hearing Bryden scoff, 'It was only a joke, Cam. Anyway you're soft.'

Another day my dad allowed us to go with him to a firing range and watch him shoot a handgun, a semi-automatic pistol a war vet friend had given him. The first time we heard it going off scared the crap out of us kids. But it was still pretty cool and had Bryden and me chatting about joining the army when we left school and becoming tough-as-shit heroes like Rambo.

One weekend, Dad hauled me over the coals for playing with the gun. When I told him I didn't know what he was talking about, he said the box he kept it in had been opened. The gun was inside, but he knew it had been handled. Though I denied touching it, he gave me a good walloping and a long list of jobs to do around home. I bailed Bryden up at the shops after school the next day and he just laughed. He owned up that it was him and told me to quit whinging or else I'd never make it as a proper soldier. Then he handed me a Rising Sun military badge he'd found and told me to believe in myself.

This was how it was for me with Bryden. I could be laughing, saddened, and then angry with him in quick succession, only to have him win me back to favour with his use of logic and silver-tongued praise.

11

ASHLEY

FRIDAY

The darkness scurries away with a flick of the lamp switch. The wall clock says 11:00 p.m. though it seems much later. I turn on the TV, yet nothing holds my attention, so I go in search of food. After staring into the fridge and the pantry, I select a bottle of cider, a bag of potato chips, and a jar of olives. Most people pick something sweet, like chocolate, for comfort food but I choose savoury every time.

Walking through the living room, I stop by the recessed bookcase to locate an aged photo album amongst the stash of books. I ease it out and sit on the sofa, staring at the padded cover. *Do I have the strength to cope with more memories?* I let it rest in my lap as I drink, eat chips, and flick through shows on a comedy channel. When the bottle is empty, I crack open the album. Like the picking of a fresh scab and knowing pain will follow, I skim the three class photos from my Thornleigh School years.

How young we look. Innocent children brimming with potential. Me—tall, thin, and positioned in the centre because of my height. Cam—always standing at attention, a little too serious for a kid of that age. And Bryden—pulling stupid faces, messy hair, shirt untucked or unbuttoned. Anyone could see he was a handful. *But could anyone have guessed how his life would pan out? How it would end?*

I quickly turn a page. Here I am posing on the verandah in my new uniform on the first day of high school in 1984. My hair is caught up in a high ponytail, and my skirt falls at the required level just above my knees. I have on new shoes and a new backpack loaded up with freshly covered books and stacks of folders. I remember being excited that day yet nervous. The transition from primary to secondary was enormous—a giant leap into adolescence. One year we were at the top of the ladder—kings and queens of the school—and the next we were back to climbing the first rung as small fry.

Chelton Hills High was fed into from several primary schools, with Thornleigh being one of four in the district. Since Stevie was in a different form class, we gradually drifted apart, and I hung around with a bunch of new girls. Boys our age were now idiots with pimples and squeaky voices, and sniggered way too much. Their immaturity encouraged us to set our sights on boys from the upper grades instead. For most of us, this was done from a safe distance.

Flipping another album page, a photo escapes and slips to the floor. I pick it up and cringe. In this one I'm wearing a bikini, hair in a single plait, skin kissed by the sun. I was in Grade 10, and this was taken during the Easter long weekend when my family travelled to Lake Mitchum, forty-five minutes from home. I remember this time with a prickling of my skin.

1986

Mid-morning and the cloudless sky was a vivid blue. I jogged from the water's edge to my towel on the grassy bank and heard my name called. Well, actually, a name that got my attention.

'Hey, Cinders!'

I spun around. Sprinting towards me and wearing only a pair of pink and grey board shorts, it was easy to see how much Bryden had grown. His shoulders were wide, and his limbs had definition. Though we'd hardly spoken at high school, I was aware that his snowballing image as a show-off and a rebel drew other kids to him like fans to a pop star. If there'd been a vote, he'd have won Most Popular Junior Boy three years in a row.

'What are you doing here?' he asked, flicking damp hair away from his face.

'Picnicking with my family,' I said, catching his feline eyes checking me out in my wet and clinging swimwear. My slowly developing figure had never attracted such a lingering gaze and it felt weird, yet nice. 'What about you?'

'I'm here with a mate. His uncle has a boat and I've been having a go at skiing. You might have seen me. I stayed upright for a solid minute.'

I shook my head. 'Nope, didn't see you. I've been canoeing with my dad.'

He nodded, his eyes darting as if checking for my father's whereabouts. 'When do you go back?'

I shrugged. 'Dunno. Before dark, I guess.'

'Cool.' His wide smile did stupid things to my heart, yet I flinched when he laid a hand on my shoulder. 'We used to have fun, didn't we?'

His touch made me nervous. 'A long time ago,' I said, bending to pick up my towel and rubber thongs.

'Want to meet up later? You know the walking track that takes you to the dam wall? I could meet you at the start in a couple of hours.'

I blinked against the sunlight. 'Maybe.'

He smiled again. 'I'll be waiting.'

After lunch, my parents were drinking wine and chatting with another couple, and Lauren had her nose in a book. Saying I was going for a walk, I sneakily smeared some of my sister's lip gloss on before leaving.

Bryden was at the track's entrance. So was a senior I recognized from school, a stocky footballer.

'I told you she'd come,' Bryden said over his shoulder. 'Ash, this is my mate, Mark.'

Mark's grin revealed two canines so sharp they might have been chiselled that way. 'I've seen you before. Didn't you used to hang around with Stevie Taylor?'

'Yeah.' I nodded, puzzled by what that had to do with anything.

Mark chuckled and winked at Bryden. 'Alrighty then.'

I frowned. 'Alrighty what?'

'Nothing,' said Bryden. 'Let's walk to the wall.'

I wasn't happy with Mark tagging along. He reeked of body odour and I didn't appreciate the way he kept eyeing my denim shorts that had shrunk in their first wash and barely covered my bum. 'Hooker shorts' my sister called them, and I now regretted wearing them.

Lake Mitchum isn't a natural lake, but a huge reservoir in a catchment area fed by several major watercourses. The dam's concrete wall with gated spillway is around forty metres high and has a fenced walkway along the top. As we walked this, stopping now and then to take in the view or gawk at the plunging descents on both sides, I got a little dizzy and had to stand back from the edge. The height didn't seem to worry the boys, and at one point Bryden hoisted himself over the railing facing the lake. With hands gripping the wrought iron, he teetered on the narrow ledge.

I told him to stop being an idiot. He laughed, called me a 'party pooper', and leaned out.

I screamed and reached for his arm. 'You're bloody crazy! Come back now!'

'I'm not going to fall,' he said, releasing a hand and swaying further out. 'Ah ... ah ... maybe I am!'

'Bryden!' I screeched.

Mark clapped his hands. 'Lovin' your performance, Bry!'

Bryden leaned in. 'I'll get back over, Ash, if you let me give you something.'

What did he have in mind? I didn't care. All I wanted was him to be on the right side of that rail.

'Okay, just get back here, now!'

'You promise?'

'Yes, yes, I promise!'

He climbed over and dropped onto the walkway. 'C'mon, let's go back.'

I followed the boys, feeling twitchy when hearing my name mentioned within a conversation I couldn't make out.

As we reached the track, Mark elbowed Bryden. 'When are you giving it to her, Bry? What about over there?' He pointed into the bush, towards a massive gum tree.

Bryden drummed his fingers against his chin. 'Yeah, that'd be a top spot.'

I checked up ahead. Being a frequented path, someone was bound to appear around the bend of trees in the next little while. Whatever the boys had planned mustn't be going to take long.

Bryden clutched my hand. 'Come on, Ash.'

Leading me through low-lying scrub to the far side of the tree, he pushed me back against the scratchy bark, pinning me there by my shoulders.

My heart thrummed in my ears. 'What is it?' I asked, sliding my tongue over my lips in readiness for the kiss I now expected.

He leaned in and grinned, and I smelled cigarette on his breath, 'I want to give you a root.'

My jaw dropped. 'You what?'

'You heard me. I'm gonna give you a root, right here.'

I stared at Bryden, then at Mark nodding behind him like a bobble-headed dog. 'That's ridiculous. You're lying.'

He pressed harder, the dry papery bark crackling in protest. 'You promised. Can't go back on a promise.'

Fear skyrocketed. I kicked out, but he dodged my foot before it connected with his shin. Gripping his arms to force them away, I found his hold too powerful, so I dug my nails into flesh.

He grunted and forced a knee into my thigh. 'Hey! Don't be like that. Don't you want a great root?'

I spat in his face.

He pulled a hand away to wipe his cheek, but before I grabbed the opportunity to punch him in the head, he wrapped his fingers around my throat and squeezed. 'I'm gonna do it whether you like it or not, so quit struggling or I'll have to let Marky boy take over.'

Behind Bryden, Mark made a show of rubbing his groin and wagging his tongue.

My body froze, yet my mind raced. *How to get away? Scratch his eyes out? Knee him in the balls?* But then his mongrel friend would grab me, and I didn't like my chances against that Neanderthal. I could scream. Someone had to be nearby.

I opened my mouth, but the noise that edged out of my constricted throat was more a rasp than a cry for help.

Bryden shook his head, 'Uh-uh,' and shoved his other hand inside his board shorts and fumbled around.

Clamping my eyes shut, I heard a crow caw from somewhere high above and willed it to go get help. A tickle on my nose drew my eyes open.

'Here ya go,' Bryden said, holding something in front of my face. 'Take it. It's all yours.'

It looked like part of a plant—the part that grows under the earth. He stuffed the root down my top and laughed until he snorted.

I slumped to the ground, tears burning.

'Geez. Don't bawl, Ash,' Bryden moaned, 'it was only a joke.'

'A fuckin' good one, too,' added Mark. 'You got her a beauty, Bry.'

Bryden's hand was on my head, stroking my hair. 'See, we can still have fun, can't we, Ash?'

I slapped his hand away. 'I hate you,' I snarled, getting to my feet. Stumbling through bracken, I reached the dirt track and ran all the way back to the picnic area.

At school on the Tuesday, I found a rumour had spread like a summer bushfire. Everyone believed that Bryden and I had 'done the deed' over the break, and it shocked me to discover how difficult it was to convince my friends this wasn't the case.

The sniggers, the whispers, and the cutting remarks were so hurtful that I stayed home the following day pretending I had a headache. Back at school on the Thursday, I confronted Bryden, only to be told I should just suck it up and thank him for improving my chances with boys.

Just when I thought things had died down, Mark bailed me up behind the school library and asked if I wanted a quick screw. My look of horror had him cackling and shoving a shiny, silver screw—probably pocketed from his manual arts class—into my hand. That incident transformed into another dirty lie, and I ended up having a sleazy reputation by doing absolutely nothing.

Once again, Bryden had taken a joke too far. My school life became a living hell until the rumours were superseded by a newer piece of adolescent gossip.

12

———————

CAMPBELL

The beginning of high school saw the relative innocence of childhood replaced with the gritty needs of adolescence. Assimilated with kids from other primary schools, Ash, Bryden and I drifted apart as companions, though I was still aware of their presence.

Bryden's life became more hectic when his father left the family on the twenty-third of December 1984. I remember the date because two days later he was sitting at our dinner table eating Christmas lunch.

The sound of a knock at 8:00 a.m. had my mum opening the front door and consoling a grieving little boy. Bryden's tears startled me. I assumed he'd hardened up for he now engaged in more reckless behaviour with scant regard for his or others' welfare. Yet, seeing him cradled in my mother's arms, crumpled and sobbing, had me feeling sorry for him. He joined in our family festivities that day, and Mum visited Mrs James in the afternoon, taking her a basket of leftovers. We said nothing to each other about that incident and only once, as adults, did Bryden ever mention it.

As for Ash, I had seen her at school and around the neighbourhood over the years but had made a point of avoiding her. Then one day in 1986, in Grade 10, I bumped into her outside the school library as I was chasing a mate who'd stolen my school tie, the only one I owned. Not having been undone since Grade 8, the knot was so small and tight that I could only slide it down a short way to allow my head through before wrenching the knot back up to sit in a crooked angle below the collar of my shirt.

'Ash!' I cried, skidding to a stop.

'Cam,' she replied, staring wide-eyed at me.

For the first time, I looked straight into her eyes. Having shot up faster that year than ever before, we were now the same height.

'Hey,' she continued, 'what's happening?'

'Just mucking ... about,' I panted. 'Someone's ... nicked off ... with my tie.'

'Don't see much of you. How's your family?'

I raised my hand and popped up my index finger to indicate I needed another breath. 'Good,' was all I could manage, as my heart pounded not just from exertion, but fear—not a fear of Ash, but the anxiety that comes from being hurt.

With recent stories circulating, I harboured contempt for the way she seemed happy to have her purity trampled underfoot like a discarded pickle sandwich. My stomach churned whenever I heard tales of what she'd been getting up to with, not only Bryden, but other random guys. Now, standing breathless in front of her, a burst of emotion tempted me to lash out. Instead, I turned away to hide my pooling eyes and took off running, shouting over my shoulder, 'I've gotta go. I need my tie!'

13

ASHLEY

FRIDAY

I stuff the photo into the album, shutting it before another leaps from its sticky enclosure. There are other pictures in there that also hide secrets. Such as one taken by Lauren on the morning of the tenth of May 1987, my sixteenth birthday. I can see it without looking at it. I am sitting cross-legged on my bed in a pale blue, long-sleeved nightie, with a pile of unopened presents in my lap. My parents sit either side of me, each kissing a cheek. Though smiling for the camera, there are shadows under my eyes, and I'm clutching my right arm close to my chest. Nobody there but me knew the great secret being kept.

My eyes drop to my right forearm, the one hidden in the photo. Halfway between my wrist and elbow is a tattoo I got for my thirtieth birthday—a stylised vine with two colourful butterflies. Unseen, but still felt if I brush my hand over it, is a patch of hardened flesh. A scar. A burn. At first it was pink and raw, over time becoming a pale blemish until concealed by ink. Now and again, I finger it and recall the night of the Thornleigh School fire.

1987

My parents were attending a Battalion dinner, and Lauren had gone into the city to watch a movie with friends. Rather than stay home on my own, I visited Kate Vincent from my Grade 11 form class who had red hair like me though worn in a short bob. The previous day, word had spread around school that a party was to take place a few blocks away. Knowing that Stevie and some other girls would definitely be going, Kate suggested we also check it out.

She informed her mother after dinner that we were popping over to Stevie's place to go over an English assignment. Not batting an eyelid proved Mrs Vincent knew nothing about Stevie, who would rather die than spend her Saturday evening doing homework. Putting on makeup and spraying on loads of perfume, we dashed out while Kate's mother was glued to the TV watching *Hey, Hey, It's Saturday.*

'One hour,' I cautioned Kate. 'That should do us.'

Our journey only took five minutes. We weren't aware who lived here, but it was easy to see no responsible adult was on the premises as kids—mostly from Chelton Hills High—littered the front yard and crowded the verandah. Kate peeled off her jacket, revealing a pink see-through blouse with a black bra beneath. I had nothing of that nature, so I just untucked my T-shirt from my jeans and tied it in a knot, exposing my midriff. Stretching the neckline, I also bared a shoulder. I'm not sure if we wanted to draw attention to ourselves or blend in with the crowd but, whatever the reason, they allowed us into the party.

Inside, the music blared, and the alcohol flowed. We elbowed our way through the throng to a punchbowl brimming with khaki-coloured liquid, where a glassy-eyed boy handed us each a full paper cup. I lifted it to my nose and recoiled; kerosene wouldn't have smelled as bad. Kate and I stood awkwardly in the living room, sipping the tongue-numbing punch that burned its way down my throat, and pretending to be cool about everything. Popular events included a sculling contest, a who-can-tell-the-filthiest-joke competition and—by the number of couples disappearing and returning with different partners—a dare that involved shagging as many people as you could in a single night. I noticed Stevie was an avid participant in this particular game.

I went in search of food, or at least a packet of chips, and found her in the kitchen hanging off an older boy.

'Bryden's here,' she giggled, before being led down the hallway towards a bedroom.

Of course he was. Way too much fun here to stay away. I peered down the hall, imagining him behind a closed door getting it on with some sleaze of a girl. Not giving a stuff, I returned to the lounge.

Holding my cup out for a second serve of punch, I scanned the room. Kate was in a serious conversation with a boy from our science class, so I left her to it and found my way down the rear stairs to the backyard where a drunken game of volleyball was in play.

I edged past a mob of rowdy kids sprawled on the lawn and aimed for a child's swing set. The plastic seat flexed as I sat, took hold of the ropes, and pushed off. Leaning back to view the star-filled sky, my tipsy mind didn't care that my hair dragged in the dirt; I was floating in space—untethered, free. I could have swung there for hours.

'Hey, Ash,' a voice called from above.

Planting my feet, I came to a staggered stop and spied a makeshift timber structure amongst the leafy branches of a huge jacaranda. Over the edge of the treehouse hung two denim-covered legs and a pair of red joggers. I walked over and jolted when a face appeared.

'Come on up,' Bryden urged.

I would have declined his invitation if the boards nailed to the tree trunk hadn't made it such an easy climb.

'What are you doing up here?' I asked, reaching the top rung, and wrapping my arm around a branch for balance.

'Perving I s'pose, and drinking.' He patted a spot on the platform. 'Sit.'

I hesitated and studied him. Bryden didn't seem all bluster tonight, just a loner hiding from the ruckus like me. I plonked down beside him.

He held out a can of beer. 'Want some? Have the rest of this.'

I downed a few mouthfuls before resting the can between my knees. It seemed weird sitting next to Bryden after ignoring one another since the 'root' business. He'd turned sixteen in February and his physical presence filled more space than I remembered.

'Just because I'm up here doesn't mean I like you,' I said. 'I'm just bored.'

'Fair enough.' He shrugged, pulling the ring tab off a fresh beer can. 'What are you doing at a party like this?'

'Well, I thought I'd check it out to see what all the fuss was about.'

'And?'

I shook my head. 'Not really my thing.'

'A bit full on?'

'Something like that.' I gulped down the remainder of the beer. The bitter taste wasn't to my liking, but it added to the buzz from the punch. 'I hear your parents got divorced.'

'Yeah. It's been much better since Dad buggered off.'

I frowned. 'You don't miss him?'

'I don't miss the fighting ... the way he shoved Mum around and beat the crap out of me. I showed him a thing or two before he left, though,' he added, pummelling the air with his fists.

'So, how's your mum?'

'On top of the world. She's found another guy ... at least I reckon she has. She's out a fair bit.'

'What do you think about that?'

'I don't give a rat's. If Mum's happy, I guess I'm okay with it. Anyway, let's quit talking about her.' He rested back on his elbows. 'It's nice up here. Look at those stars. Aren't they awesome?'

I arched my neck. Through a gap in the green canopy, I spied the Milky Way smearing a glittering path across the night sky. All five points of the Southern Cross winked at me.

'*The heavens declare the glory of God,*' Bryden said, in a commanding voice. '*The skies proclaim the work of his hands.*'

I faced him. 'Where'd that come from?'

'Psalm 19.'

My eyes widened. 'You read the Bible?'

He sat up. 'Now and then. A guy was handing them out at school, and seeing they were free, I took one. There's some rad stuff in there. You should read it.'

Maybe Bryden was reforming. *Bad boy turns good.* It could happen.

I returned his smile, yet it disappeared when he slung an arm over my shoulder. On the verge of giving him an earful, I was even more surprised when he leaned in and kissed me. Not tame like the kiss at the gate after the Spin the Bottle disaster, it was full on and sent tingles right down to my fingertips. The next thing we were both lying flat on the boards, and whatever his tongue did, mine reciprocated.

'You're keen,' he said, peeling his mouth away.

Was I? Now I understood why alcohol should be avoided, it

messed with your sensibilities. I didn't stop his hand when it glided over my bare stomach, or when it fiddled with the knot in my shirt. But when it tugged the knot free and reached under the fabric, I covered it with mine.

'What are you doing?'

'Thought I'd try for second base,' he grinned.

'Second?' My heart bucked. I inhaled deeply and slowly released my breath. 'I think I've had enough,' I said, with a lack of conviction.

He removed his hand and used it to brush hair from my face. 'Hey ... isn't it your birthday tomorrow?'

I was blown away that he remembered such a thing. 'Yeah, it is.'

He laughed. 'Sweet sixteen and never been ...'

No need for him to finish the sentence. I knew what he was implying.

He trailed his fingers down my neck, his arm skimming over my chest. It felt nice. Too nice. His face swam before my eyes, and to my fuzzy brain Bryden looked fantastical, not of this world. Caught in the orbit of his beauty, I didn't object when he dropped his hand to my breast and gave it a squeeze, as if checking the ripeness of a piece of fruit. I squirmed and hoped he wasn't thinking of plums. Peaches would be better.

Then he lifted my shirt and I gasped when his fingers slid inside my bra. New feelings were birthed, and I melted from within. My ears pricked to the song blaring from a boom-box below and INXS singing words that matched the moment. Yes, definitely 'new sensations'. A moan slipped from my mouth. I was on a downhill slide. *Good girl turns bad.*

'I knew you'd enjoy it,' Bryden said, his hand guiding mine to a spot between his legs. 'I do too, can't you tell?'

I snatched my hand from the hard bulge of denim and sat up.

Bryden sprung up. 'Hey, what's going on? We've only started.'

'I'm going back to the party,' I said, tucking my shirt into my jeans.

'Going back? To what? You'll have more fun up here.'

He was probably right, but no, I couldn't stay. I wasn't slutty. A proper boyfriend was what I wanted, not just a grope and a poke.

'I'm not a quick shag. I'm not Stevie.'

'Shit, Ash. I wasn't going to screw you.'

I glared at him. 'Are you sure about that?'

He scowled. 'Hey, don't act all innocent. You were the one moaning and groaning up here. I was only doing you a favour.' He shook his head. 'Well, if that's it, I'm gonna get another drink.'

I watched with mixed emotions as he climbed from the treehouse. Several seconds later, I did the same and followed him towards the house.

An excited Mark confronted us as we rounded a couple of boys wrestling on the grass.

'Bry, I've been looking everywhere for you.' His eyebrows leapt when he noticed me. 'Hey, what have you two been up to?'

Bryden gave me a brief glance. 'Nothing worth talking about.'

Mark grabbed him by the shoulders. 'My brother's here in his Valiant. It's really rad! I begged him to take us for a spin.'

Feeling like a dead loss, I started to move off when I heard Bryden ask, 'Is it okay if Ash comes along?'

'Oh, sure,' Mark grinned, 'the more the merrier.'

Maybe it was because I wished to prove I wasn't such a wet blanket that I joined them as they walked around the side of the house.

I caught Kate engrossed in a pash-fest on the verandah steps with the science geek and told her I'd get a lift home. She waved me away, and I was bundled onto the rear seat of the souped-up car between Bryden and Mark. A small bottle of whisky was passed around before the Valiant pulled from the kerb and sped down the street with a screech of tyres and the pungent smell of burning rubber.

14

———————

CAMPBELL

FRIDAY

I crack open a Corona and flick on my wall mounted TV. *Back to the Future* plays across the 55-inch screen. I laugh. *How often have I watched this over the years?* The current scene triggers another memory.

'Here we go,' I say, taking a swig from the bottle and closing my eyes.

———

1987

My friendship with Bryden grew distant as he became more aggravated and looked for people to blame for his circumstances. But this changed one night in Grade 11 when an orange Chrysler Valiant roared past me as I skateboarded home from a mate's place.

The car pulled up with a screech of tyres and a fog of burnt rubber.

'Hey, Marty McFly, you handsome d-u-u-de,' called the

drunken voice of Bryden as he leaned out of the back passenger window and motioned me over with a bottle of Jack Daniels.

I dragged a foot on the bitumen to slow down and came alongside.

'Nice hoverboard,' he said, with a grin.

The skateboard was second-hand, bought at a garage sale. Pretty dinged up, it still rode well enough for me. I tucked it under my arm and peered into the car, surprised to see Ashley wedged between Bryden and another guy.

'Hi Cam,' she purred with a waggle of her fingers.

'Hey buddy, come join us. We're off to the creek for a little par-tay,' Bryden drawled. 'Jump in.'

I stared at what was before me—five people in various states of stupor, laughing and hoo-ha-ing from inside a souped-up sedan. The paintwork looked new, the suspension illegally lowered, and the clutch of lights mounted on the front bumper could have lit up an entire football field. Noxious fumes spewed from the throbbing exhaust pipe as the car idled, waiting for the next rev of the engine.

'C'arn mate,' came the driver's urgent request. 'We can't wait all fuckin' night.'

My instincts screamed, 'Don't!' yet I found myself pushing my way onto the back seat. A mixture of sweat, perfume, and carbon monoxide filled that confined space as I squeezed between Bryden and Ash, crushing her into the guy on the end.

We had only travelled a short distance when Bryden shouted, 'Stop! That's our old school!'

We all shot forward and then back hard against the upholstery as the driver stomped on the brakes.

Bryden opened his door. 'Quick, everyone out. I'll give you a grand tour.'

He tumbled onto the bitumen, followed by me and Ash. Before anyone else exited, the tyres spun—kicking up gravel—and the Valiant thundered away, leaving the three of us open-mouthed and stranded on the roadside.

'Shitheads!' Bryden barked, watching the taillights become a pair of bright dots in the distance.

He then turned and eyed the school buildings lit by random lighting. 'Old Thornleigh ... remember Miss Harris, Cam?' Jogging across the footpath, he vaulted the chain wire fence.

Ash and I did the same, though my foot got caught and I landed on my face, my skateboard shooting off down a concrete path by itself.

Bryden motioned us to follow as he passed A Block, where the Grade 1 classes were in our day, and through to the lunch area under B Block.

We sat together on the wooden-planked seating that now seemed so narrow, and reminisced about the games we played under here and the lunches our mums had supplied—or hadn't, in Bryden's case—which we tried to swap for something tastier, or a handful of marbles if we were lucky.

In the semi-darkness we could just make out each other's face and the glint of teeth as we laughed, the bad blood between us disappearing a little more with each story told. Then we heard a *click, click, swish* as Bryden flicked on a silver cigarette lighter, the miniature flame in front of his face revealing an eerie smirk. My skin prickled. Mischief gleamed in those narrow eyes.

I glanced at Ash and our eyes locked. She was chewing her lip. She didn't have to say it for me to know she was having the same concern.

Bryden snapped off the light and stood. 'I'm hungry.'

Moving in the shadows, he bumped into a metal bin, knocking the lid flying. It clanged then skidded as it hit the cement. Discarded rubbish toppled out as Bryden lifted the bin and placed it on a corner bench seat up against the building's timber framework. Plunging his hand into the waste, we heard another *click* and a pale glow illuminated Bryden's face. A flame leapt up and sparks flew as the fire took hold.

'You idiot!' I yelled, scrambling forward.

He thrust out an arm, blocking me from disturbing his growing creation. Pulling the bottle of Jack from his jeans pocket, he tipped a splash into the bin. Flames flourished.

Bryden spoke in a dramatic voice. 'Let us be thankful and please God by worshiping Him with holy fear and awe. For our God is a consuming fire.'

'Stop it, you moron!' Ash shrieked.

He scowled and poured more whiskey into the bin before smashing the bottle against the wall's uprights. He arched back as orange tongues shot up and danced, licking the doused timber, and quickly spreading.

I coughed and rubbed my eyes as smoke billowed.

Ash rushed forward with the metal lid to kill the fire but stumbled and fell against the bin. An explosion of sparks. A scream. I grabbed her around the waist and dragged her away.

She curled into me, sobbing, and clutching her arm, and I held her close smelling the acrid odour of singed hair. I searched for Bryden but couldn't locate him within the veil of smoke.

'Let's get out of here,' I urged, feeling the heat from the burgeoning fire.

I pulled Ash out into the open and we followed a cement path that led us to a gate. This opened onto parkland, and as we ran across the mown field towards a dense line of trees, the crackling and popping sounds behind us proved the fire was taking hold. Clambering through scrub, we reached the creek, and even from here we could smell smoke and see the sky above the school turning orange.

While Ash slumped to the ground choking back sobs, I

climbed the gnarly branches of an ancient Moreton Bay fig. From this vantage point, I saw the middle section of the building well ablaze with flames now inside the first-floor classrooms. The howl of sirens and flashing of blue and red lights added to the scene. I trembled. Not only was our old primary school going up in smoke but also our lives.

Movement nearby. A figure running from the park into the bush.

'Bryden!' I called. 'Over here.'

A noise of thrashing through foliage. When he appeared below, I dropped.

Bryden shoved the skateboard into my hands. 'You're lucky I came across this, dickhead.' Then he doubled over, wheezing, no bravado in sight.

I took the opportunity to call him out on his stupidity.

'What do we do, now?' I asked, shaking out my right hand as Bryden picked himself up from the dirt, holding his face where I'd punched him.

Though I loathed him, I knew we would have to rely on his cunning to get us out of this mess.

15
____

ASHLEY

1987

The last time I saw Cam and Bryden on the night of the school fire, was when I raced away to follow the creek towards the bridge. Ordered home to pretend I had nothing to do with the events of the evening, I glanced back to see them heading in the opposite direction, further into the bush. My own need for safety overtook any concern I had for them. The horror of what was taking place at the school, and the pain from my burnt arm, urged me to distance myself from the boys and the situation.

Scrambling half a kilometre in the dark through scratchy lantana, with the sound of sirens in my ears, I felt like a fugitive in one of those old black and white TV shows. I reached the old, less used, bridge spanning the creek, and climbed the embankment. As I stepped onto the worn timber boards, my jaw dropped. The view resembled a scene from a disaster movie, and it seemed to have drawn the whole neighbourhood out to witness the catastrophe.

Amber clouds rolled like waves in the night sky over Thornleigh. The school was still ablaze but looked to be contained by the crew of two fire trucks to just B Block, now a charred skeleton within the inferno. It was hard to believe that one idiot with a cigarette lighter had caused such destruction.

Lightheaded, I held onto the railing for support and took in deep breaths of smoky air. I had to get home before my parents returned. I couldn't let them see me like this; couldn't have them ask questions. I walked across the bridge and followed the streets towards home.

There were people everywhere, but only once was I drawn into a conversation.

'It's shocking isn't it, luv?' said an old man wearing a coat that barely hid the pyjamas he wore beneath.

'Yes, t-terrible.' My voice was shaky.

'Have you seen it up close?'

I nodded and hid my arm under my T-shirt.

'I wonder how it started. Wouldn't put it past some bored lowlifes out to stir up trouble.'

'Well they sure did that, the mongrels,' added another man, in a tracksuit. 'Probably kids off their heads on drugs. No regard for property.'

'Somebody could have been hurt,' said the elderly bloke. 'Bet they didn't think about that when they struck the match. Hope they get locked up for years.'

'Yeah, and have their parents cough up for all the damage,' demanded tracksuit guy.

I distanced myself, my feet plodding the bitumen as if encased in blocks of cement rather than strappy leather. *Please, God, let us not have been seen.* Though Bryden had been the orchestrator, Cam and I had been involved and would most likely be charged along with him.

Thankfully, no one was home, and I was able to enter the house undisturbed. Showering to rid myself of mud and the stench of smoke, I winced when the warm water hit my injured arm. I turned the cold tap on full and thrust my arm under, watching with horror as skin peeled away in cobwebby strands. I found a tube of antiseptic cream in the vanity and dabbed it carefully over the seared flesh before wrapping my arm with a gauze bandage. I wasn't too sure if this was what you were supposed to do for burns, but I gathered it had to be better than doing nothing. Stuffing my clothing into a plastic bag, I hid it in my wardrobe.

By the time my parents arrived home, I was in bed, dressed in a long-sleeved nightie and pretending to be asleep. Still, my mother poked her head in to see that I was okay and to mention the fire. I told her I knew about it because I watched it from the street with Kate before coming home.

I was glad when Mum left me to go back to sleep, though disturbing memories kept me awake until sunrise. One that kept returning was of me falling against the burning bin. I could have sworn someone had pushed me.

In the morning I was greeted with birthday wishes and presents. Afterwards, I went to the bathroom to check on the condition of my burn when I heard a knock on the door. It opened before I had time to hide my injury.

'What's wrong with your arm?' Mum cried.

I pulled down the sleeve.

She reached over and slid it back up. 'Why is your arm bandaged?'

I couldn't speak. I struggled to come up with a lie.

'Take that gauze off,' she commanded.

I did as I was told.

'Oh my Lord! Is that a burn? How did you get that, Ashley?'

'Umm ... Kate and I were ... baking biscuits and ... and I burnt it putting the tray in the—'

'That is not a cooking burn. John!' she yelled into the hallway. 'Get here now!'

I recoiled when Dad appeared in the doorway.

'What's going on?' His jaw dropped. 'What the hell is that?'

He didn't need to force the truth from me. His steely glare and the sight of the pulsing vein on his forehead had me spilling the beans about the fire in no time.

'That Bryden James is one shit of a kid!' he snapped. 'He's gonna pay for this. We're going to the police, and you're going to tell them everything. That is an order!'

'Then we'll go to the hospital,' added Mum, rewrapping my arm.

Getting into the car, I felt like the biggest snitch ever. Soon the cops would be organising a manhunt and I had no way of warning Bryden or Cam. I hoped to hell they were safely hidden or still on the run. Maybe they'd caught a train interstate. I prayed for some kind of miracle.

At the police station, I was stunned when I saw Mr and Mrs Druery sitting in the foyer. Across from them sat Bryden's mother. I felt sick. That could only mean one thing.

16

CAMPBELL

Bryden had an instinct for knowing how far a bluff could be taken. He also knew that the sound of barking dogs was a clue to stop running. Not for me though, I kept stumbling and forcing my way through the bushes edging the creek.

Bryden was comfortably sitting in the back of the police car by the time I was delivered by a gasping cop for the same ride. A second cop had control of two sleek German Shepherds, still excited after the chase as they were bundled into the dog squad van. I think I caused those dogs to exercise for an extra two hundred metres before their handler pulled them up.

With thick smoke from the smouldering school drifting around the car, I was seated beside Bryden and our worried eyes met. *Had Ash made her way home after we'd sent her in the opposite direction to us?*

The early hours of the morning after the fire were filled with phone calls to parents, lots of tears, meetings behind closed doors— with Bryden and me separated to tell our version of events—and finally, sitting across the table from a man in a black coat and red polo neck shirt, his dark hair glinting with silver and receding at the temples.

'Campbell, my name is Francis Bryden. I'm Bryden's grandfather and a lawyer,' came his serious tone. His eyes—slits beneath heavy lids—commanded attention, just like his grandson's.

It turned out, synchronicity was on our side that night as Francis Bryden, in town visiting his under-coping daughter, had answered the phone call beckoning a family member to the police station.

'You boys appear to have erred in your decision making this evening.'

You betcha, I silently agreed.

'It would also seem that you've had a disagreement over the escalation of the night's events.'

This was no doubt a reference to the fight Bryden and I had at the creek when I exploded about his stupidity—the only occasion that I would ever be able to land a punch that left a mark on him. I peered sideways. Bryden's upper left cheek was still red and swollen, and the bruised flesh around his eye was darkening. I was surprised to see a fresh track in the soot on his face made by the trickling of a tear. His grandfather must have noticed it too, for he took a folded white hanky embroidered with a black 'FB' in one corner from his coat pocket and, without comment, handed it to Bryden.

'Young man,' Mr Bryden now looked at me, 'this is the last time I expect you'll see inside a place like this. I will be taking this matter up with the Chief of Police and hope to manage the appropriate procedures. Now, apologise to your parents and you can go home.'

In a matter of weeks, Bryden was suddenly out of our lives.

The outcome of the Juvenile Court proceedings was an eight-month stint at a youth detention centre. Urged by his legal patriarch, Bryden joined the Australian Defence Force as soon as he turned seventeen and went to Kapooka, in New South Wales, for army recruit training.

As for Ash and me, we were the benefactors of Bryden's honesty—which his grandfather's skill extracted from him—and were cleared of any charges. We resumed our schooling activities and fought off the rumours that abounded. Ash seemed to draw closer to me, and I sensed an appreciation that, for me, raised hopes in a romance blossoming.

We finished Grade 12, and I partnered Ash to the end-of-year formal and parties. Though I now received a kiss on the cheek and a well-held hug when we greeted and parted, Ash did not encourage anything further. Yet, it was enough to give me that giddy feeling as I walked home smelling her perfume on my clothes.

University beckoned for Ash. While she studied for a Bachelor of Business, my disappointing grades led me to take a less academic path and I found employment with the local bank.

17

ASHLEY

SATURDAY

A nightmare. Screaming children morphing into adults with flames for hair has me waking in my bed, tangled in sheeting. I eventually get back to sleep, only to be disturbed again by a buzzing sound.

I grab my phone from the bedside table, but my bleary eyes refuse to focus, and I have no clue who is calling. My pulse steps up a notch. I clear my throat and answer.

'Good morning, sweetie,' Dad says. 'How are you?'

I sit up and rub sleep from my eyes. 'What time is it?'

'Just gone seven-thirty. Sorry it's early, but I've been worried about you.' His voice is heavy with concern.

'I'm okay,' I lie, raking my fingers through mattered hair. 'Everything's fine.'

'Are you sure? You seemed to take rather a hit from that news report last night. Bryden James ... wasn't he the one that started the school fire back when you were kids?'

The last thing I need is to talk about Bryden. I draw my knees up to my chest. 'Yes, Dad ... he's the one.'

'A bad seed. I reckon it had something to do with drugs.'

'What, the fire?'

'No, his death. You know, a drug-related killing. Gangland stuff. You read about it all the time. Payback or whatever.' He coughs into the phone. 'Did you have much to do with him after school?'

I massage my temples where my head is tightening. 'No, not much. Look Dad, I appreciate your concern, but I need a shower and a coffee.'

'Sorry, luv, as long as you're all right. You gave me quite a fright the way you raced off.'

'Like I said, I'm fine. It was just the shock ... seeing it on TV and all.'

'Sure, I understand. Quite a shock.' A pause. The sound of a chair squeaking—the stool at the breakfast bar. 'His mom died tragically too, didn't she?'

My jaw clenches. 'Yep, she did.'

'Now this. Some families have such bad luck, don't they?'

'I guess so. Sorry, Dad, I really need to go.'

'Okay, well take it easy. It's Saturday. Head out to one of those cafes you like so much. Eat a slice of mud cake. It always cheers me up.'

I don't bother reprimanding him on his sugar intake. I kick off the bed cover. 'Yeah. Maybe I'll do just that.'

'Lauren and Brett are coming to visit me later.'

'That's nice. I'm in the bathroom now.'

'Oh, righto. Love you.' Then he hangs up.

I slump back onto the mattress and pull a pillow over my head. *Shit!* Can't I even start the day without thinking about bloody Bryden?

1990

University was great. I was enjoying my second year of studies as well as socialising. Parties were plentiful and so were the opportunities to meet guys. I went on a few dates, though nothing serious, probably because I still guarded my virginity with the tenacity of a bear shielding her cubs.

One Monday travelling home from Uni, I glanced up from reading Michael Crichton's *Jurassic Park* as the train pulled into a station a few stops before mine. Watching passengers spill onto the platform, I noticed a young man moving against the flow and boarding the train. He was a head above most people, tanned, and good looking in a broody way. *Shit.* I almost dropped the book. *What was Bryden doing back in Brisbane?* Then I remembered the shocking news my mother had shared a few weeks back about Julie James' tragic death and the rumour that she'd taken her own life.

I peered over the top of the book as he took a seat further up the carriage, facing forward like mine. When the train drew out of the station, he turned to look out of the window, and as familiar scenery passed by, I wondered if memories of sharing these sights with his mother stirred his sadness.

Arriving at Thornleigh and fearing a tense meet up, I remained seated as Bryden alighted and walked the platform with a swagger I knew so well. Yet there was evidence of a more disciplined life in the way he held his shoulders back and his head high—or was this a posture in defiance of fate? I stepped from the train just before the doors closed and headed for the carpark, sitting inside my car for a full ten minutes before driving home.

Later that night, Mum answered the telephone and called me out of my room. Thinking it might have been Cam phoning me back after I'd abruptly ended an earlier conversation, the 'Hi, Ash,' that sounded in my ear forced me to lean against the hallway wall to stop my knees from buckling.

I cupped my hand around the receiver. 'Bryden,' I said, lowering my voice. 'This is a surprise.'

'How are you?'

My tongue felt like a dry sponge in my mouth. 'Okay. You?'

'Well, considering I'm up here sorting out the house cos my mother died, I'm doing great.'

'Oh ... yeah ... I'm sorry about your mum.'

'Oh well, *c'est la vie.*'

His comment lacked emotion, yet he had to be cut up inside. There was no way he'd have dealt with his pain in such a short time.

'So, you're up here. How long are you staying?'

'Dunno. Depends how long it takes to get things sorted. Francis wants to sell the house ASAP.'

'You've taken time out from the Army?'

'Yeah, compassionate leave.'

I fiddled with the phone cord, struggling with where to take this awkward conversation. 'Have you seen Cam?'

'At the bank. He seems to be doing alright there.' A long pause. 'Hey, want to get together?'

My scalp tingled, so did my hands. Was it a chill of apprehension? I flexed my fingers. 'The three of us?'

'Yeah. Or I could find a treehouse for two, if you like?'

I squirmed as I recalled a star-filled night, the taste of beer, INXS ... and Bryden feeling me up. I gave a weak laugh. 'No treehouse. So, when and where?'

'Tomorrow night. My old house. Seven o'clock?'

'Okay. I'll bring pizza.'

'Awesome. See you then.'

'Don't forget to invite Cam,' I said, right before the line went dead.

I returned the receiver to the cradle and peeked around the corner to the lounge room where my parents were watching TV. Thank God, Dad hadn't been listening in.

'What the bloody hell are you doing, girl?' he would have growled. 'He's bad news, everyone knows that. Haven't you learned your lesson?'

Maybe Bryden had changed. I had to give him the benefit of the doubt.

18
____

CAMPBELL

FRIDAY

A throbbing headache pulls me out of a sleep that four Coronas and a Xanax had eased me into. Rolling off the couch, I slide onto my hands and knees on the floor rug and pause in this yoga position until I realise the pounding in my head needs a more upright stance.

I stand and shuffle through the dining room when a whirring sound has me looking under the chrome and glass table and spotting my phone vibrating on the polished floorboards. My throwing must have bumped it onto silent mode. I wait until it stops shimmying before I pick it up. Three missed calls have registered: two from my mother—no need to guess what she wants to talk about—and one from Ashley. The thought of answering either woman's calls quickly upsets my stomach and I flip the phone from hand to hand. *What to do? What to do?*

I flick on the bathroom light and squint against the fluorescent brightness. Filling a glass from the basin tap, I down a couple of aspirin and wince at my reflection in the mirror. It's no surprise that I look like shit because I feel like shit.

In the kitchen, I scoop ground coffee into a glass coffee plunger and boil water. The steam billowing from the kettle spout in hot clouds reminds me I'd fallen asleep while recalling the school fire. The replica train luggage rack mounted on the wall that I use to hold my few recipe books provokes me to think of Bryden's mother.

1990

Harbouring a desperate mind is a tragic thing. The humiliation of her son being sent to a detention centre and then joining the army, several failed relationships, and struggling with her guarded drug habit took its toll on Julie James. She finally succumbed to the hopelessness and confusion and ended her life in a most pitiful way. One night, clutching Bryden's childhood teddy bear, she lay down on a suburban railway track and let the next express train do its work. This set off a chain of events that changed the lives of all of us.

Bryden returned to Thornleigh a few weeks later with his grandfather to sell his mother's house. I found this out when Bryden surprised me by visiting the bank where I was a Customer Counter Assistant. After two years in their employ, I had not impressed enough to move on to higher duties.

'Druery, you spend too much time talking to the young titters,' was the accountant's summary at my annual review.

Bryden's taste of the military had given him a stronger, athletic physique with his shorter, precision cut hair pronouncing his jawline and perfectly setting off those feline eyes.

He stretched out his hand and grinned. 'Cam, you old dog.'

His strong grip made me wince. 'Bryden, good to see you, buddy. What brings you home? Missing us?'

Bryden's gaze intensified. 'No, just doing some business here. Francis has some property to settle and . . . well . . . you and I have to catch up. Are you free later?'

Before I could answer, he placed a wooden container about the size of a shoebox onto the counter and slid the lid out sideways, like an ancient school pencil case.

'Cam, I need to put this in a safe deposit box. Can you organise that for me?'

'Sure,' I replied, feeling chuffed at the opportunity to engage my newfound banking skills.

I ushered Bryden into a side office used for private access to belongings kept in the bank's custody and returned with the signing documents and the registry book. The box now sat prominently on the desk.

'Any goodies in there?' I enquired.

He shrugged, drumming the box with his fingers. 'Nah, just some of my mum's things I want to keep.'

The penny dropped. 'Oh, shit, mate. Of course. Sorry to hear about your mum.'

'Yeah,' he nodded, staring at his hands.

When nothing else was said, I pointed to the documents. 'Sign here . . . here . . . and here, and I'll get that popped away in the safe.'

'Still living at home?' he asked, pushing back the chair, and standing.

I gave a quick nod of acknowledgement, noticing his smirk before he departed with the promise to get together before he left town.

Entering the bank vault and the strongroom, I felt the heavy weight of whatever was in the box and heard a metallic sliding as I slipped it into its secure enclosure.

The phone call I received that evening from Ashley was not regarding the expected coffee meet up.

'Cam! Bryden is back in town. I just saw him on the train.'

Resentment built at hearing the excitement in her voice. 'Er ... yeah. He's here with his grandfather. Something to do with a property settlement.'

The required information obtained, she cut the conversation short. 'Great. We'll have to catch up soon. Bye.'

Catching up was frequent and painful these days, as I became a sounding board to Ash's ramblings about University intertwined with sketches of her 'terrific' and 'fascinating' liaisons.

'Cam, you're so grounded,' was her grateful and sometimes tearful response to my considered advice.

I had given up the idea of being her romantic lead some time ago. Her pattern of seeking partners who demeaned her somewhat was difficult to understand, and I took a big step back.

'Is this making you happy?' was a repeated yet disregarded line of mine.

And now, after being absent for almost three years, Bryden had returned looking more like a panther than ever.

19
____

ASHLEY

The next day dragged. I was edgy at uni and unable to concentrate. My friends annoyed me for no reason, and I bit off a few too many heads.

'What's got into you?' said Rhys, a guy from my group. 'That time of the month, is it?'

I cold-shouldered him and the others for the rest of the afternoon, which I think they appreciated.

Keen to get ready, I sped home from the train station and spent more time than usual choosing an outfit and doing my hair and make-up.

Dropping by a local pizza parlour—which funnily enough was situated in the same shop as the grocery store we broke into as kids —I picked up my order and made it to Percival Street in Thornleigh by 7:05.

Bryden met me at the front door. His black tank top showed off the results of intense physical training as a tanned and muscular arm held the door open for me.

He gave a sharp whistle. 'Lookin' good, Ash.'

I smiled. My choice of a sheath dress with long sleeves to hide my scar, and short hem to show off legs I was now proud of, had done its job.

The musty-smelling lounge room was sparsely furnished with a beanbag and an overturned plastic crate on which rested a packet of paper serviettes, a bottle of Bundaberg rum and another of Coke. Only two glasses alongside them made me frown.

'Cam?' I enquired.

'Had other plans.'

I sank into the beanbag and opened the pizza boxes, while Bryden sat cross-legged on the floor and turned up the music playing on a stereo cassette player.

'Who's that?'

'Depeche Mode.' He held up the cassette case. 'Their new album, *Violator*. You've heard of them, right?'

'Of course. Not really my taste, though.'

He sorted through a pile of cassettes and slid one over. I picked it up and recognised Madonna's *Like a Prayer* album. 'That's more my style.'

We ate and chatted, our conversation easing as we shared amusing stories about Bryden's experience in the military and my life at university. We even had a few laughs about the old school days—steering away from any mention of the fire or other hurtful incidents instigated by Bryden. It almost felt like I was on a date with a regular, normal guy.

I tentatively brought up his mother's death and expected him to flippantly brush it aside as he'd done during our phone conversation or tell me it was none of my bloody business. Instead, he spoke with red-rimmed eyes of the manner in which she'd died. Dying at only thirty-five was sad. Throwing herself in front of a train was absolutely nightmare stuff. Ruled a suicide, he believed differently, suspecting she had been coerced. He was determined to discover the truth, and I asked how he planned to do that. He just shrugged and said he'd find a way.

I stood to clear away our rubbish.

'Leave it,' he said, grabbing my hand. 'I can take it out later.'

He pulled me onto his lap and loosened the band holding my messy bun in place. My hair tumbled around my shoulders.

Clutching a handful, he raised it to his nose and sniffed. 'I've always loved the smell of your hair.'

I squinted. 'Really? I thought you only ever cared about your own.' I skimmed my hand over his cropped locks, feeling the spikes of hair tickle my skin.

Trailing his fingers down my right arm, he drew back the sleeve and the pucker of flesh glistened in the light. 'Sorry about this. I don't know what got into me that night. I guess it will always remind you of me,' he added with a grin.

He was right on the money with that, yet the thoughts it gave me were never pleasant ones.

I watched his eyes travel over me and linger on certain areas. 'You've got curves, Ash. In all the right places.'

My heart fluttered. I gave his bicep a playful squeeze. 'You've changed too. You must be fit.'

'Yeah, pretty much. My stamina's increased, that's for sure. Want to check it out?'

I laughed. 'What are you gonna do, race around the yard? Do hundreds of push ups?'

He winked. 'I had something else in mind.'

The next thing his hand was around the back of my neck, drawing my face close to his. Our noses touched, our breath mingled, our lips met. This kiss was tender and personal, unlike the urgent pash in the treehouse so long ago.

When his hand slid up my leg, I flinched. Bryden's eyes were filled with hunger, hunger for me. That was flattering, empowering even.

He lifted me onto the beanbag and knelt, gliding his hands up my calves, over my knees. Gripping the hem of my dress, he slowly peeled it up to expose my thighs, my satin underpants, my stomach, and my recently bought push-up bra. I felt like a snake being helped to shed its skin. *Was there a new me underneath?*

'Geez, you certainly have filled out,' Bryden said, kissing the flesh spilling out of the satin cups.

I giggled and slipped my hands under his shirt, exploring taut muscles, running my fingernails over goose-bumps. When Bryden freed my breasts from their confines and teased them with his tongue, my nerves sizzled. Yet when he snuck a hand between my legs, I shivered. *What was I doing?* I had my boundaries and Bryden was pushing me to the edge. I needed to catch my breath and give this more thought.

'Wait,' I cried, pulling his hand away.

His head snapped up. 'What do you mean, wait?'

'I'm not sure I'm ready.'

He pushed up on his elbows. 'You are so bloody ready it's not funny.'

'No. I mean ...' I squeezed my thighs together. 'I mean I haven't ever ...' I glanced away, newly embarrassed by this confession.

He rolled sideways and the Styrofoam beans in the bag shifted, elevating me. 'Holy shit, Ash. Don't tell me you're still a virgin?'

I raised my chin. 'Yep. I am,' I said, my pride returning.

'Well, you sure had me fooled. It's okay. I know what to do. You're not the first one I've gotten over the line.'

A scene played in my head—Bryden in football gear diving between the goal posts with a girl tucked under each arm, a cheer squad with familiar faces wearing 'Bryden Did Me' T-shirts, a referee signalling a successful 'try'.

I shuddered. 'It's not happening.'

He groaned and tugged his hair. 'Have another Bundy and Coke, it might loosen you up.'

Not wanting to hurt him, I chose my words carefully. 'This is important to me, Bryden. I want my first time to be with someone I love, someone I respect. I care about you, but ...'

He shot me a menacing look and sat up, causing me to sink back down again. 'Bloody hell! You can't get me worked up and not follow through.'

'Just watch me!' I fought against the beanbag's changing surface to sit up. Bryden's hand on my chest pushing me back down added to the difficulty. 'Let me up, you bastard!' I yelled, squirming, kicking.

A fearful darkness replaced the light in his eyes. He gritted his teeth and pressed his forearm against my throat.

Fighting for air, I clawed him, scratching bloody lines down his arms, across a cheek. But he was too strong, and with the beanbag cushioning around me and barring any chance of escape, he wrenched my underpants off and chucked them across the room.

'Please ... don't,' I wheezed when Bryden eased his hold to wriggle out of his shorts.

'Too late,' he said, spreading my legs apart with his knees.

I cried out when he forced his way inside me.

As he vigorously fed his need, my focus moved from the pulsating vein on his forehead to the ceiling light encased in a domed shade made of frosted glass. It looked like a hovering spaceship, and I felt like a specimen being horribly probed. The sound of Styrofoam crushing rhythmically beneath me as I was ground into the bean bag was overtaken by the song coming from the cassette player. Ironically, fate had chosen The B-52's 'Love Shack' to be the soundtrack to my assault.

Finally sated, Bryden slid out of me and rolled onto the floor.

While he lay there panting like a marathon runner after finishing a race, I fought back tears and winced from the deep stinging of rasped flesh.

'Don't worry, it won't hurt so much next time,' he said, reaching over and patting my shoulder.

Next time? I shuddered and tugged my dress back down. Tussling with the bean bag to sit up, I gasped as a disgusting warmth oozed out of me.

Bryden handed me a clutch of serviettes. 'Here, clean yourself up. I'm going for a piss.'

I stuffed the paper between my legs and watched as he got up and walked from the room, his tight, bare bum showing the scratches my nails had inflicted, not from passion, but from trying to pull him out of me.

Struggling to my feet, I grabbed my belongings—including my torn undies—and rushed out the front door. But not before dropping the moist wad of paper streaked with blood onto the sticky bean bag, along with the cassette case for the *Violater* album.

I drove home sobbing in snotty gasps and feeling shame attach itself to me like a weighted backpack. Flitting between blaming myself for leading Bryden on and despising him for not heeding my demand to stop, I also grieved the theft of something precious. Still, I had no intention of reporting the assault to anyone, for in my mind—and what girls were led to believe at that time—I was equally at fault.

SATURDAY

I throw off the pillow, now damp with tears, and get out of bed. Dwelling on how Bryden's life had meshed with mine, it was inevitable this scene would raise its ugly head. I stand in front of the wardrobe mirror and wipe my eyes, tuck sweaty hair behind my ears. Lifting my pyjama top, I press a hand against my abdomen where a new life had once formed.

Bryden had known. I'd told him when he came back to finalise the sale of the house to some poor schmuck who'd paid top dollar for it, sight unseen. I hadn't wanted to, but I needed to let him know that his action had consequences. As expected, he went ballistic. Said I was just like his mother and warned that if I didn't get rid of it, it would end up just as fucked up as him. A wad of cash was stuffed into my hand and he'd walked away.

I stare at my reflection and once again wonder what kind of mother I would've made. As caring as my mum? Or more like Cam's—strong, resilient, making the best out of difficult circumstances. Yes, I would like to have had Dot Druery's fortitude and non-judgmental attitude.

20

CAMPBELL

1990

Our usual meeting place was a local small eatery that served up Greek sweets and Ash's favourite Turkish coffee. I eagerly responded to her urgent request to meet up and joined her at our regular table in a cosy corner.

My excitement vanished the instant I saw Ash's puffy eyes and the handkerchief wiping her nose.

'I'm pregnant,' was all she could get out before burying her head in her hands.

As much as I was stunned, it was strangely expected. Her need to share her intimacies had me dreading such a day as this. I said nothing, just placed my hand over hers and waited.

'It's Bryden's.'

Fuck! Can't this bloke ever come into our lives and not screw things up? 'B-Bryden?' I stammered. 'But, but how ... when ... I mean ...'

She looked up, fresh tears pooling. 'When he first came back. Cam, I'm so stupid. I'm not ready for this.'

I patted her hand, my thoughts whirling like all those times before. There was a burning in my head. My heart pumped hard. *Run ... run!*

I had no solution other than to drive Ash to her house, leaving her to walk up those stairs into her family home and keep her secret hidden.

The following days were filled with moral questions regarding choices—ending a life to save another. At nineteen, we were still too young to grapple with the enormity of the situation. Here was I, standing as an outsider pretending to offer support about things I had no knowledge of, and there was Ash, weighed down by regret and the pressure of a decision only she could make.

At the coffee house during one of our desperate ponderings, Ash stopped crying and looked up with determination in her eyes. This was not the face of a young, frightened girl. The manic churning in her mind had forged something within—a strength she could now draw on, a belief she could manage.

'I'm keeping it,' she said.

21

ASHLEY

The pains woke me around dawn on the morning of the twenty-first of June 1990. We'd eaten Chinese takeaway for dinner and, as it hadn't sat well in my stomach, I presumed whatever had been off was working its way through my body.

I slipped out of bed and went to the toilet, sitting for ages without relief. Downing painkillers, I slept a few hours before the cramping returned with greater force. Hunched over and shuffling back to the loo, I noted that the deathly quiet in the house was due to everyone having left for work. With afternoon tutorials that day, no one had bothered to wake me. This time as I sat, I noticed I was bleeding.

I was scared. I'd made the difficult choice to go ahead with the pregnancy which was now in its eleventh week. Having not yet told my parents of my predicament and barely showing, I thought I could delay the shock and heartache a little longer. Now I regretted that decision. Eager for my mother's help and advice, I realised it was too late. *How could I phone her at work and ask her to come home to give aid when she hadn't even known I was pregnant?* Stupid, stupid girl.

The cramping continued, and I began to pass blood clots.

'God,' I prayed, 'please don't let me lose the baby.'

In desperation, I phoned the bank where Cam worked. Other than Bryden—who assumed I'd had a termination—he was the only one who knew my secret. Cam had been dumbfounded when I'd told him, but incredibly supportive. I was sure he would drop everything to take me to the hospital.

'Cammy's not here,' an annoyingly upbeat female informed me. 'He's in the city taking part in a training seminar.'

Shaking, I slid down the wall to the floor, and was forced to do the only thing left. I called Cam's home number.

Mrs Druery was a nurse before she'd married, and that's why I phoned her. When I blurted out what was happening, she rushed over and stayed with me until the heavy bleeding had lessened. She told me she was fairly certain I had miscarried.

'It mustn't have formed properly,' she said and assured me it was nobody's fault. 'It's just nature's way. You'll be a right as rain soon enough.' She sounded as if she was speaking from personal experience. 'I almost had a daughter,' she had told me once. I now realised what she'd meant by that.

The only question she asked was, 'Is it Campbell's?'

When I assured her it wasn't, she let out a breath and gave me a hug.

I told her that the father was a loser, had wanted nothing to do with the baby, and had moved back to Sydney. She probably guessed who he was. It didn't matter now. The baby was gone.

Before she left, I implored her to not tell my mother. She wasn't pleased but, seeing my distress, agreed on one condition, that I promise to visit a clinic as soon as possible to make sure everything was all right.

She and I never again mentioned this incident, but on the odd occasion we bumped into one another, she always asked after my health and wellbeing. Thanks to Dot Druery my family has never known that I was almost a mother.

22

———————

CAMPBELL

Ash confided in me about losing the baby.

'Promise you won't tell him.' Ash's voice became high-pitched as she leaned in, tears streaming, hands gripping the loose folds of my shirt. 'Promise me, Cam!'

I grasped her wrists and drew her hands away from my chest, wiping and smoothing out the crinkled cotton. I meant it when I replied, 'I promise, Ash. Bryden will never learn you didn't go through with the termination.'

I studied the fatigue in her stooped shoulders and the anguish in her eyes and knew there was nothing else I could say. Her child —the life she had so recently committed to—and the depth at which she prepared herself to be a young mother ... now gone.

She dropped out of Uni soon after and fled overseas to distance herself from the consuming sadness.

While loosening my serious worldview, I experimented with drugs and binge drinking until I became hooked on both. Occasionally hungover at work, I fudged my way through by volunteering for back office filing which most of the staff avoided.

. . .

Bryden returned unannounced several months later. His hair had grown, and he bore a close-shaven beard. A purple high collared shirt under a dark three-quarter-length coat, along with baggy black pants stuffed into military boots showcased his eccentric side. His enthusiasm was less kindly greeted by me this time. Yet, Bryden could cleverly read body language and to him I was an open book. He matched my mood and calmly asked if I could join him for lunch.

We met at a pub around the corner from work.

'Cam, I've moved back for good.' He paused, lifting his glass of rum to his lips. 'I'm starting Arts College next week.'

'Okay,' I said, still confused by his casualness.

'Yep, had a gut full of all that *yes sir, no sir* saluting shit. Got some money together and setting my sights on getting involved in the entertainment industry.'

I simply sat and stared, not the least bit surprised he hadn't lasted the distance. I wondered what his grandfather thought of his career change, and if Francis had played a part in wrangling Bryden's exit after less than three years in the military.

Bryden cleared his throat. 'How's Ash?'

I shrugged. 'Does it matter?'

'C'mon, Cam, let's cut to the chase. I know you know.' His eyes drilled into mine. 'Ashley's too pitiful not to have shared with you.'

My pulse quickened. 'Share what?'

'Geez, Cam, don't force me to call you stupid. You know about Ash getting pregnant and having an abortion.' He rested back in his chair. 'Bugger me if it didn't make me mad, her being so irresponsible.'

'Irresponsible?'

'Yeah. She dropped around. It was all going smoothly. We had a few laughs, even talked about you. And then things got heated. Cam, you know better than anyone what Ash is up for.' He gave a smirk and continued. 'And there she was all ... you know ... ready and begging for it.'

Uncomfortable with hearing this, I squirmed in my seat. 'Bryden ... you don't need—'

He cut me off. 'Nah, I do. You're probably the best mate I've had, even though I've done some crazy shit to you. I don't want you thinking I did the dirty on Ash. I stopped and said flat out I didn't have any protection. Quick as a flash, she said it was okay, she had it covered. I presumed she was on the pill or something. It's not my fault if a girl is willing to risk everything for a quick root.'

I gulped my beer, unable to offer more to this conversation.

'Ash is a disappointment. I always thought she was different to the other girls. She ...' Bryden seemed to struggle for his next words. 'She used to be ... decent. Yep, she was decent and had a great family and ... I dunno. Turns out she's just like all those other slags.'

'She's gone overseas,' I mumbled.

His eyes widened. 'Oh ... really?' He blew out a puff of air, as if relieved. 'I suppose that's good then, for her to get away ... good for everyone concerned. Including you, Campbell.'

'Me?'

'Yeah, you weak-arsed pussy.' He laughed and ruffled my hair without explaining this remark.

He appeared to be happy that Ash was not around to remind him of what had happened. His re-entry into his old town was now free of any walking ghosts.

As he left, I considered his explanation regarding Ash. *Was it true that she had been so reckless?* I had at times felt she took risks by playing the field or *'joure sur le terrain'* as she would say, giggling. But her drastically throwing caution to the wind while with Bryden had me puzzled. I really didn't know her at all.

My own disappointment allowed this presumption to rest comfortably in my mind, and in Ash's absence, I re-engaged my friendship with Bryden.

II

FIRE AND RAIN

23

———

ASHLEY

SATURDAY

It is well known that a particular scent can bring forth a forgotten memory. So can a song from the past, a movie, or an article of outdated clothing. The taste of certain drinks also has such an effect.

I'm sitting at a wrought iron table in the morning sunshine on my back deck. The scented Earl Grey tea I'm sipping evokes a recollection of a winter long ago: white cloaked alps; heavy snow; aching muscles; and Nat, a ski lift operator with the ability to kiss the cold away. I pop three paracetamol and ponder other beverages that hold reminiscences associated with men.

The zing of Stones Green Ginger Wine reminds me of summer, a sandy island beach and Evan, a dreadlocked surfer with broad shoulders and a deep tan. Wiley, the owner of a Harley Softail, a full beard, and a tattoo of Darth Vader on his chest always comes to mind when I drink a smoky scotch on the rocks. While Strongbow Apple Cider's crisp sweet tang brings with it the sound of 'Achy Breaky Heart' blaring through the speakers of a blue Falcon panel van as Mick the country boy showed me how to boot scoot by moonlight.

Interestingly, most of these memories were forged during a year filled with carefree fun.

1992

Not coping with my life's turn of events, I shocked my parents by suddenly dropping out of university. To escape the reminders of a life derailed, I searched for excitement further afield. A few months travelling turned into six, then twelve, as Stevie, Alice Cummings, and I backpacked through New Zealand and then hitchhiked around Australia. Funding our adventures by working temp jobs at cafes and take-away food joints, and the odd bit of fruit picking, we lived simply, but partied hard. Since the theft of my 'prize', I had dropped my barriers and eased into a more reckless existence, though one that saw me in control.

On the last leg of our journey, we stayed at a beachside caravan park on the Gold Coast. Visiting The Playroom at Tallebudgera, I met Zane, a rock musician with a voice that turned my insides to mush. He had a long blonde ponytail, an ear piercing, and wore denim and leather better than anyone I'd ever seen. I became his biggest fan that night and followed his band, pub-hopping, fist-pumping, and screaming with the best of them. Before the week was out, I'd captured his attention and we hooked up. Soon after, he had a roaring argument with the other band members and he left, determined to make a career as a solo artist.

We ended up in Brisbane where I got a job at a nightclub, Dusky's, waiting on tables. Zane scored regular gigs in pubs and clubs in the city and Fortitude Valley, and a double shot macchiato —his evening stimulant—takes me back to that wild, heady time.

Impressed by Zane's crazy ideas about changing the world through well-written lyrics, I thought I was in love. However, our relationship concluded five months later when I discovered Zane in bed with two local hookers—one male.

'It's just for inspiration,' he argued.

I walked out with him yelling, 'You're too narrow-minded!' as I dragged my bags down the stairs and through the front door.

Returning to my parents' house for a spell, I found a small, inexpensive apartment at New Farm not too far from my workplace, where life took a sharp and more horrid turn.

24

CAMPBELL

SATURDAY

I wake again. This time I'm curled up on my bed with my back and neck aching from lying in a foetal position. I hear my knees crack as I stretch my limbs and glance around the room. Sunlight threading through the window blinds tells me it's morning and, for a minute, I can't recall what day it is. Then I remember—everything. Thank God, it's Saturday. I couldn't face work: all those tasks, financial conundrums, people clamouring for my attention and demanding answers. Certainly can't call my position as State Co-ordinator for Aged Care boring. Not like my job in the bank, even if it had its interesting moments.

1992

Banking was mundane and repetitive. The release from the build-up of that life-sucking occupation came at the annual staff Christmas party where employees from a variety of departments converged on the mezzanine floor of the city head office to engage in goodwill. The first hour comprised listening to the General Manager spouting his yearly message of gratitude for our efforts towards skyrocketing bank profits. Then, as the lights dimmed, ties were removed from white collared shirts, and high-heeled shoes were kicked off for dancing to the upbeat music pounding through the in-house ceiling speakers.

My involvement in these parties was generally limited to joking with like-minded nerds and goofballs who couldn't get their fill of the small party pies and spring rolls being circulated by the hired wait staff. This all washed down with free alcohol provided by management. In fact, it was members of this senior executive group who were carried out at the end of the night and deposited into taxis as a result of their lack of restraint in partaking of the excesses they had made available for everyone.

At the 1991 Christmas party, I was at the crowded bar relieving the waiter of the two beer stubbies I'd requested, when I felt a hand squeeze my left butt cheek. I thought it was Kenny, Teller 5 from the Savings Bank section, who as a joke always squeezed or prodded a staff member's backside when they bent to put away cash tins in the main safe. So it surprised me when I turned to tell him to piss off and was confronted with a heavily lipsticked and powdered face.

'Josie,' I exclaimed, recognising the girl from the International Transfers Department. She had a round, yet voluptuous, figure, and always wore comfortable, supportive shoes—which I only noticed because of her fat ankles. As an act of kindness, I usually commented on her perfume and hairstyle.

'Hi, Campbell.' She batted her eyelashes at me, their length proving she'd been heavy-handed with the mascara. 'Are you buying me a drink?'

I was taken aback. 'No ... but I can order you one if you like, they're free.'

She stepped closer, her cheap candy-smelling perfume cloying, her stupendous breasts pressing hard against my chest. Raising both my arms to create some space around us, my gaze was drawn to the unbuttoned top of her blouse and cavernous cleavage.

'How are you?' I asked, looking for a way of escape through the throng of staffers.

Her answer came in a squeeze of my crotch.

'Cam.' Her voice lowered to a huskier tone. 'I had a dream about you.'

'Oh, yes?' was my squeaky response.

She removed her hand from my genitals and held it out, horizontal, palm up. 'You and I,' she purred, glassy-eyed, placing her other hand on top, '... like this. How about it?' she demanded, more than enquired.

The several beers I'd consumed eased me into thinking, 'Why not?' There'd been no other proposition.

These bank parties were rife with people darting down corridors and slipping into vacant offices. So nobody blinked when Josie led me along one such darkened hallway to the manager's office. Rather than open the door, she swung me up against the wall alongside and started kissing my neck.

Still holding a stubby in each hand, I had difficulty in joining in as she bit my nipples through my shirt and fumbled with my belt. She had my pants around my ankles when I grabbed her by the shoulders and forced her to look at me.

'Josie, stop ... not here. The dunny is just over there. Some pisshead will come past and we'll get sprung.'

Breathing heavy with an asthmatic wheeze, her eyes darted in desperation and she reached sideways, rattling the door handle until the lock released. We fell through the doorway and landed on the floor, the beers flinging from my hands and rolling over the floorboards.

The street lighting filtering in through the blinds gave just enough brightness for me to see Josie get to her knees and rip open her blouse—one button pinging across the room—revealing the cups of her white lace bra straining to contain the copious amounts of flesh within. Bending down, her moist lips found mine and I tasted cocktail onions as her tongue burrowed into my mouth.

Minutes later, Josie stumbled to her feet and moved to Mr Withers' large timber desk. Swiping all the items from its surface, and oblivious to the metal in-trays crashing against the wall, she grinned and removed all her clothing.

I jumped up and wriggled out of my jocks while Josie fell back on the desk and spread out over the leather tabletop. Mounting a corner of the desk, I heard the timber creak as I strategically tried to get into position. Josie wasn't so careful, grabbing hold of my arms, she wrenched me down on top of her.

The timber continued to complain as we writhed and rocked and shook until, with a loud crack, one wooden leg broke under our weight and the desk listed like a sinking ship. As we both slid to the floor in a tangle of naked flesh, the office light came on. Twisting around, we found Arthur, the security guard, standing in the doorway shaking his grizzled head.

'Geez, Druery. You'll be duck-shit when old Withers cops a gander at this mess.'

Josie swiftly covered her bare bits with dog-eared manila folders, while I rubbed my forehead where a lump was forming and realised my banking career was now in jeopardy. On a quick scan of the room, I discovered my underpants had symbolically landed in the wastepaper basket.

. . .

Bryden's knee slapping had him spilling his drink as he listened to my story about Josie in Mr Withers' office. I could tell by his laugh—loud and deep in his throat—that he thought the incident was a worthy exploit. Bryden then relayed his own recent 'mounting'.

'Cam ... mate ... this chick last week ... seriously ... she squealed like a pig.' He shook his head, running fingers through greasy hair. 'She was all doe-eyed and pissed to the max. It was all *yes, yes, yes,* and then a high-pitched squeal as I brought it home. She was a dirty slut. I even mentioned this to her boyfriend later on, and he agreed!'

Here we were, two boys sharing their conquests and exaggerating our stories to make them more interesting. Yet, Bryden's narrative shamed mine somewhat by its weird coolness.

'That makes thirty-eight since July last year,' Bryden boasted. 'The bar manager and I have a bet to see how many roots we can get in a financial year. But he's fallen behind. He's only fucked twenty-six.'

I sat there in disbelief. Josie had been a very infrequent encounter for me. And if we were keeping score, my tally was three ... in total!

My first time was an unfortunate coupling in the front of my car fighting the floor gear stick as my date and I fumbled in the cramped space of the Hillman Hunter. Debbie walked away from that romantic interlude with a long bruise on her inner thigh from the poorly positioned lever. The second time was more comfortable—on a blanket, behind sand dunes, at a late-night beach party. Yet my technique must have lacked finesse for the girl ran off soon after without giving me her name or her phone number.

'You're bullshitting me, Bryden,' I responded.

He showed surprise at my disbelief. 'Mate, look up there, over at the bar. See the chalkboard that looks like a darts scoreboard near the Bundy polar bear sign?'

I strained to peer through the crowd and the smoke. 'Okay ... yeah.'

'What does it say on the board?' he asked, nodding.

I focused and read the scrawl written in pink chalk. '26J and 38B'.

Bryden studied me with raised eyebrows as I made some calculations. It was February 1992. From July last year to now, there had been 33 weeks.

'Hooley dooley!' I blurted out. 'That means you're rooting a girl every week.'

I shouldn't have been surprised. Bryden's life—a mix of infrequent studying, performing in local theatre productions, and managing back of house for touring bands—afforded plenty of opportunities to meet girls.

He tapped his chin and pondered. 'Nah, not every week. There's a couple of twosomes in there ... and an impromptu orgy with the cast of a play we did in March, *The Sexual Manifesto*. Shit play, but there were some hotties there worth banging.' He counted on his fingers. 'Yep, four that night.'

I often accepted Bryden's invitation to tag along when he was checking out a new nightclub, though I struggled with the noise and sweaty masses brushing against me in the confined space. When the stifling atmosphere brought on a dizzy spell, I would exit into the fresh air and head home in a taxi. Bryden never complained about my sudden departures, as he was busy being the go-to man for visiting bands like The Sunnyboys. This celebrity status was no doubt a honey catcher for notching up conquests for his scoreboard.

The excitement of meeting rock stars and getting free tickets to events wore thin over time, and one disturbing evening after a concert contributed to my decision to distance myself from Bryden's boozy, drug-induced, and smoke-hazed social life.

Sliding a chair out from my table, Bryden slapped down two bottles of Strongbow cider and did his usual thing of holding up two fingers and pointing to the bar, referring to the updated score chalked on the board. I noticed he was already starched when his eyes glazed over, and he started talking about his life in the army.

'I was kicked out in the end. Got into this scrap with a corporal. The prick was lucky I didn't fuck him over completely.'

There had been many occasions when I'd had little to say in response to his rambling and this was another. I hid my shock and just nodded.

'That dirty bastard pushed me too far when he mentioned my mum. Lucky for him the knife blade missed his jugular.'

Bryden unpacked his story, revealing how, on returning from compassionate leave after his mother's death, he'd overheard a superior slagging off about her means of suicide.

'One messed up bitch,' the man said. 'Explains why Bryden James is such a twisted sack of shit.'

Bryden tracked the man down and waited for him in the shower block. Launching his wet, angry body against the soaped-up physique of Corporal Bell, they both fell hard on the tiled floor. Bryden's fists pounded with rage at his head-locked target until Bell's gagging brought others running to intervene. They drew back when they sighted the small knife Bryden pressed into the soft flesh below Bell's ear. With a flick of his wrist, he opened up a deep wound and the shower floor turned crimson. Corporal Bell recovered, but Bryden was discharged with the aid of his legally astute grandfather.

'Contract not renewed due to mental duress,' was the note that closed his file.

Bryden smiled at me. Placing a hand inside the pocket of his paisley print waist coat, he produced a small Victorinox penknife.

'This little fucker comes in handy. I had it modified.' He pressed a tiny silver button which activated a blade to flick out from its hiding place—a compact switchblade.

The smoky room made my lungs wheeze, and the sight of that knife made my stomach grip.

25

———————

ASHLEY

1992

The nightclub scene in Brisbane was booming with trendy places opening up all over town. Venues such as the Groove Kitchen catered for the grungy, alternative, and arty kids, while places like The Tube ran car park dance parties and weekly SLAMS—sex, love, and music Saturdays. There were also techno-driven events hosted by DJ's, and high-voltage gigs with live bands. My job at Dusky's progressed to regular office work, taking bookings, and implementing marketing skills I'd learnt at Uni, and on weekends I often helped with front of house or hung out at the bar. Life was exciting for a twenty-one-year-old living out of home and in the city surrounds, though one particular night had me reconsidering my career choice.

The Earwigs—a popular band known for playing a mix of 1960s garage, glam and power pop—were warming up and the patrons were rowdy in their enthusiasm. A boisterous group of women on a mystery bus ride labelled a 'booze crooze' stumbled through the entrance proving this was not their initial stop on the club hop. Half of them headed to the bar, and the remainder made their way to the dance floor. One—of a more mature age than you'd expect to see in such a venue—desperately needed the loo. Guiding her through the sweaty, squirming throng, I discovered a line-up outside the women's toilet.

Around the door appeared a woman with makeup and hairstyle so outlandish she could have been an extra in *The Rocky Horror Picture Show*.

'Hope no one's in a hurry,' she informed us.

I elbowed my way to the front of the queue, pushed the door ajar, and squeezed through to find another mob of waiting women. Amongst them a sequinned and feathered drag queen from a club down the road fixed false eyelashes onto a girl sitting on the bench surrounded by a clutter of tubes and palettes. The air smelled toxic as two other girls in front of the wall mirror sprayed their teased hair with cans of glitter.

'What the hell's going on here?' I shouted above the commotion.

'Wait your turn, lovey,' waved the drag queen. 'First in, first served.'

I batted away a drift of blue feathers. 'You can't do this. Firstly, you're taking up space, and secondly, this is not a beauty parlour. People need to use the loo.'

'Yeah,' cried a girl clutching between her legs. 'I've been waiting for ages.'

I studied the three closed doors. 'What's wrong with the toilets?'

'Occupied,' said the drag queen now brandishing a curling iron.

I pounded on the first door. 'Hey, hurry up!'

'I've got the shits,' groaned a woman on the other side.

From behind the second, both a female and a male voice told me to 'piss off'.

The third door flew open and a young woman crawled out grasping a bong made from a plastic Mr Juicy bottle. She offered it up to a girl studying an Avon catalogue. 'Here ya go,' she said, eyes rolling back in her head.

I stepped over her. 'I'm calling security!'

Walking out into the blast of noise, I pushed through the writhing throng to inform a bouncer that his assistance was needed ASAP.

Moments later I was seated at the bar swilling a silky smooth Black Russian when I heard a laugh that almost caused me to drop my glass. I swivelled my stool.

With hair now reaching his shoulders and stubble shadowing the lower section of his face, I suspected Bryden had ditched military life. It had been two years since we'd last spoken, and the sight of him holding his audience's attention like a magician about to perform a new trick brought a rush of bile to my throat. His narrow eyes flashing robotically in the club's strobe lighting seemed to have mesmerised the open-mouthed girls, while his regaling about getting caught in a hot tub with a rock star's model girlfriend brought chuckles from the guys.

'You prick,' I growled under my breath. Quickly downing the rest of my drink, I rushed away before being spotted.

Collecting my bag from the office, I was locking the door when I heard footsteps. A strong hand gripped my shoulder and I spun around, shoving the key into his stomach.

'Faark!' grunted Rob, a bouncer, lurching back and clasping his belly.

'Oh, it's you,' I said, dropping my arm. 'Sorry.'

He checked his hands, his uninjured stomach, the key still in my grasp. 'Bloody Hell! Who did you think I was?'

'Somebody else. Don't worry.'

'Don't worry? Shit a brick, I thought I'd been knifed.'

'Well, you shouldn't sneak up on someone in the dark and grab them unexpectedly. What do you want, anyway?'

'Wanted to let you know it's all sorted in the ladies' loo. I cleared out the trash.'

'Great,' I said, edging past his bulky frame. 'I'm off. Have a good rest of the night.'

'I will now that I haven't been gutted like a fish,' he called as I hurried away.

I safely exited without bumping into Bryden, though I was still shaking when I arrived home.

Most of a bottle of vodka later, I fell into bed only to be disturbed from slipping off to sleep by the sound of my phone. I answered, more to stop the shrill ringing than to speak with anyone.

It was Cam. He wished to catch up. Amid the fuzzy cloud settling over me, I felt a need to be with someone I could trust. Before blacking out, I agreed to meet up sometime soon.

26

CAMPBELL

1992

I struggled to rise after a late Saturday night watching Deni Hines and the Rockmelons at a club with Bryden when my mum popped her head into my bedroom.

'Ashley's back home with her parents,' she whispered loudly.

I shot up from the mattress, my gelled hair matted in such a way that my mother let out a laugh.

'My goodness. You look as though you've put your finger in an electrical socket.'

'Yeah, yeah, Mum,' I groaned, trying to pat crunchy spikes down. 'When did she get back?'

'I was speaking with Mrs McCabe on Friday.' She paused and frowned. 'Ashley's changed, Campbell. She needs ... oh, I don't know. Just make sure you keep an eye out for her, okay?'

Mum withdrew with no further comment, leaving me confused and unsettled.

I had only received two postcards from Ash since she hastily left eighteen months earlier. One from Auckland with a scrawled *'the world is a book and those who do not travel read only one page'* on it. The other from South Australia's vineyard region with a short note: *'Hi Cam, drink more piss.'*

My heart fluttered in my chest whenever I heard from her, and now I was hurt that she'd not come to visit on her return.

By the time I'd worked up enough courage to make contact, my mother informed me that Ash had moved out again and was living at New Farm. It was another three weeks before I phoned her by using the number my mum had gotten for me.

It was a Friday night, and I'd plied myself with alcohol to ease my nerves. I dialled Ash's number, and she answered after only two rings—a little too quickly for my liking.

'Hello?'

'Hi, Ash.'

'Who is this?'

'It's me.'

'Me who?'

This was not going well. Why hadn't she recognised my voice? Words tumbled out. 'It's ... it's me ... Cam. You know, Cam.'

'Sorry ...'

'Campbell Druery.' I was now annoyed.

'Oh, Cam! How are you, darling?'

My heart jolted. She had never referred to me in that way. It embarrassed me when I later realised that *'Hello darling'* was her new stock standard greeting to anyone she talked with.

'Hello ... are you there?' she followed up after a few seconds of silence.

'Yeah ... sorry, Ash. I just rang to say hi.'

'Wow, it's been a while.'

Silence again.

What should have been a simple chat between old friends was heavy with unspoken truths, new interests, and knowledge that we were no longer kids. The call ended with a promise to catch up, but it left me standing, with the receiver still in my hand, feeling sick and stupid in equal measure.

One afternoon a few days later, there came a knock at the front door. Opening it, I found Ash on our doorstep. Lit by the sun, the tips of her red hair—now a shaggy mass of curls—glowed bright orange. With bare shoulders, skin tanned a honey brown, a smattering of freckles dotting her nose and cheeks, she was perfect.

'Campbell Druery?' she queried playfully.

My mother appeared behind me. 'Ashley! So glad you've dropped over, dear. Kettle's on, come on in.'

Ash brushed past me and smiled in a way that disassembled my mind. She was simply too overpowering for any shield I held against her.

'So,' my mum said, 'I hear you've been gallivanting around the countryside, and overseas. That must have been a wonderful experience.'

'It was amazing,' she gushed.

I sat across the kitchen table from Ash, with my arms folded, as she gave a quick run-down of her adventures—leaving out the juicy bits, I assumed.

'In a nutshell, New Zealand was beautiful, and our lucky country is huge and diverse with so much more to see. Met heaps of interesting and friendly people. You should give it a go, Cam. Get out and explore the world.'

I shrugged. 'Yeah ... sometime. Too much to do here at present.'

Mum coughed and raised an eyebrow at me. A smirk played on her lips.

'Oh yeah? Like what?' Ash asked.

'Work. Earning a living.'

'Sounds boring to me,' she sighed, giving my foot a kick under the table.

My feet scraped the lino as I pulled them away. 'Having security is important. Preparing for the future makes better sense than running off and living like a—'

'Cam!' Mum broke in. 'Give me a hand with clearing the table.' Already on her feet and stacking the cups and saucers from our afternoon tea, she looked none too pleased with my reaction.

'Can I use your loo?' Ash asked, pushing up from her chair.

'Sure.' Mum smiled. 'You remember where it is.'

In Ash's absence, my mother gave me a dressing down for being so rude.

'What's with the cold shoulder? Stop sulking and ease up. Choosing a more sedate life doesn't give you an excuse to rain on her parade.'

She was right, but there was more to it than that. Though I hadn't quite unravelled what it was.

Ash seemed to be taking an awful long time relieving herself. I headed to my bedroom and came to a sudden stop in the doorway.

'Hey, what are you doing?' I barked.

Ash was inside, standing next to a shelf near my full-length wall mirror. She had a finger in a jar of hair gel.

I rushed in and snatched it from her.

'A nice collection of toiletries you've got here, Cam,' she sneered. 'Who are you trying to impress? Don't tell me you've got a girlfriend.'

'None of your business,' I said, replacing the lid on the jar and returning it to the shelf alongside an assortment of hair products and aftershave bottles.

'Oh,' she grinned, 'my mistake. A boyfriend then?'

I glared, gritting my teeth. She was getting under my skin.

Ash frowned. 'Sorry, that was a cheap shot. But I've never seen such a collection of beauty products in one guy's room before.'

'And I guess you've been in plenty to know,' I snapped back.

'Touché, darling,' she said, moving in front of the mirror and fluffing her hair. 'What do you think of my crimped locks? It takes forever to do, but it's all the rage and the guys love it.' She smoothed out the wrinkles of her strapless dress and lifted the hem high, revealing the length of her legs. 'Do you like my tan? There's a roof terrace on my unit block where you can go sit and relax. It has a great view of the city. I go up there to sunbake. Sometimes I wear my bikini ... sometimes I don't,' she added, eying me from her reflection.

If she was looking for a reaction, I wasn't giving it.

I looked away, raking fingers through my gel-spiked hair. 'You've changed, Ash.'

'So have you. You used to be nice. I thought you wanted to see me again, but all I've gotten from you is a wall of ice.'

She stepped closer and peered up at me. This was a first. I hadn't realised how tall I'd grown.

'Don't you like me anymore?' she asked.

I stared back, catching a whiff of her floral scent, and being reminded of the time we rode our bikes as kids through some old lady's rose garden and being hosed with water for our disregard. I still liked her—too much, that was the problem.

She sighed at my lack of reply, and crossed the room to my bed, running her hand over the black iron headboard.

'Sad to see you've replaced your little wooden bed. No love hearts scratched into the paintwork of this one.'

My stomach knotted. 'How did you know about that?'

'This isn't the first time I've been in your bedroom, you know.'

When might she have seen this small evidence of my crush?

The heart was only there for a short time before I'd covered it with a Rambo sticker.

She gazed around the room, her eyes taking in the framed prints of sports cars and James Bond movie posters that now hung on my walls. Pointing to a shelf, she smiled.

'Cool stereo. Got any music worth listening to?'

I nodded but didn't bother doing anything about it. I wanted her gone. Having her in my room made me nervous.

The bed springs creaked as she flopped onto the mattress. Giving an unsettling smile, she bounced up and down and the squeaks turned into shrieks.

'Hmm ... that could be embarrassing,' she giggled. 'You ever been caught going for it with someone?'

My face went hot.

She clapped her hands to her face. 'You have! Oh God, Cam, tell me. Who found you? Your Mum? Your Dad? Not your brothers.'

I dropped on the bed beside her. 'No ... it was at work ... on a desk ... during a Christmas party.'

She punched me in the arm. 'You sly dog. So, you have been laid.'

'Sure I have. Plenty of times,' I exaggerated.

She elbowed me. 'Well good for you. I'm not surprised. You've turned into a bit of a spunk .... in a boy-next-door kind of way that is, which is what the girls go for. All those guys strutting around shaking their tail feathers like horny roosters aren't really keepers. I mean, just take Bry ...' Her face fell, and she jumped up.

So, mentioning Bryden was still a sore point for her. I didn't blame her.

She moved over to a framed poster of a Harley Davidson and slid a hand over the print. 'I went out with a biker a couple of times.'

I got up and joined her. 'Was he in a gang?'

'God, no. Just a guy who rode a bike. He had a tattoo of Darth Vader.' She placed a hand on my chest. 'Right here.'

Her touch made my heart race, and I wondered if she felt it pounding beneath her fingers.

'What would you get tattooed here, Cam?'

I took a while to answer. 'I dunno. An eagle, or a lion. Maybe a spider ... a redback.'

Ash grimaced. 'That doesn't sound like you.'

A cough came from the doorway. Mum stood there smiling and holding a casserole dish. I swiped Ash's hand away.

'I'm dropping this off to Mrs Anderson,' Mum said. 'She hasn't been well. Then I've got to pick Tim up from his friend's place and your father from the tavern. Have no idea where Scott is. Will you two be okay? You're welcome to stay for fish and chips, Ashley.'

'Thanks, but I reckon I'll head home soon,' she said.

'Well, nice seeing you again. You're always welcome.' Then Mum was gone.

Ash sauntered over to my desk and played with a glass paperweight encasing a marijuana leaf. A Christmas gift from Bryden.

'I have one, you know.'

'One what?'

'A tattoo. Got it in Sydney. I may have been a little drunk at the time.'

I eyed her with curiosity. 'Where is it?'

She smiled. 'If you guess where, I'll show it to you.'

I stepped closer, my eyes examining her. 'Not on your legs ... or your arms.' I spun her around. 'Or your shoulders. Maybe on your back, lower down?'

She shook her head. 'Nope.'

'On your stomach?'

'Nah.'

'Your hip? No, I've got it. A bum cheek.'

She laughed. 'No.'

While I tapped my chin in thought, she sat on my desktop and rested back on her elbows, her breasts straining against the fabric of her dress.

I swallowed hard. 'How about on a boob?'

She shook her head again. 'Still wrong. I'll give you a hint. It's only small, and not easily seen. And it's in a very, VERY, sensitive place.'

My pulse quickened. *Play it cool.* I lifted her right leg, removed the sandal, and checked the sole of her foot. Nothing. I did the same to the other foot.

'Bugger,' I groaned. 'I thought I had it for sure.'

She rolled her eyes. 'You're really shit at this guessing game, Cam. C'mon, you're not that stupid.'

I chewed the inside of my mouth and felt my face warm as I thought of the only other place it could be. Stepping back, I held up both hands. 'Nah. I give up.'

'No you don't.' She stretched out her legs and caught her heels around my waist, drawing me in. 'Give me your hand, and I'll guide you to it.'

I hesitated, feeling a vein at my temple throb, and offered a hand. She moved it downwards in line with her stomach, then over her thigh, then the space between her legs. My hand was a Geiger counter, my heart beating faster each time it stopped and hovered.

I glanced up, catching a glint in her eyes. Ash was enjoying this game as much as me.

She suddenly lifted my hand to her mouth and brushed the tips of my fingers over her lips. A moan bubbled from my throat as her tongue flicked out and licked them. She smiled and slid my hand around to the back of her neck.

'There,' she whispered.

I frowned, disappointed. 'There?'

She dropped her head and pulled her hair to the side. 'Can you see it?'

I bent for a closer look, sighting a small red heart just below the hairline.

She giggled. 'If I'm kissed there at the right moment, I go off like a rocket.'

When she lifted her head, my hand stayed on her neck, on the spot that was a key to her arousal. I wished to God I could turn it with my mouth and witness her explosion.

Our eyes met, and the energy between us was palpable. I held my breath, my pulse pounding in my ears. If she hadn't broken the tension by unclasping her legs from around my waist and dropping to the floor, who knows what might have taken place. Actually, I have a good idea what could have happened. A big mistake, that's what. I chose to believe she passed up a moment of passion because she hadn't wanted to mess with our friendship. Sex only complicated matters, and our relationship was tenuous enough as it was.

My heart rate returned to normal as I watched Ash retrieve her sandals and fasten them back on in readiness to leave. Then, like the gentleman my mum expected me to be, I walked her to the front door.

Before taking the steps down to the path, she grabbed my arm. 'Hey, it's your twenty-first soon.'

'Yeah, in a couple of weeks.'

'We should go out. Have a party. Do something freakin' awesome. I was away for mine, so we could have loads of fun.'

'Bryden's already planning something.'

'Bryden?' Her eyes became slits. 'You still see him?'

'Occasionally.'

Her hand dropped from my arm. 'I can't believe you still hang out with that bastard. From what I saw, it looks as if he's heading even further down that highway to hell.'

'You've seen him?' my voice rasped.

'At the club ... where I work. He came in one night with a band of groupies, or whatever, fawning all over him. I wanted to puke.'

'Did you talk to him?'

'Of course not. Why would I do that?'

'He's into some seriously crazy shit. I wouldn't go near him if I was you, Ash.'

'Don't worry,' she assured, 'there's nothing in this world that would make me go within a kilometre of that stinking turd.'

27

ASHLEY

1992

Clouds edged the evening sky, and, by my calculations, it was only a couple of days short of being a full moon. Standing on the rooftop terrace of my apartment building it felt like all I had to do was balance on my toes and I'd be able to touch the pockmarked lunar face hanging from the heavens like a bright disco ball.

To my left, the city sparkled with jewels—diamonds, rubies, and emeralds—their beauty reflected in the waters of the serpentine Brisbane River. Flashing and flickering, the lights beckoned me down. Even the iconic Story Bridge seemed to be smiling. It was Saturday night, party time. A few glasses of red wine had eased my tension from a crap week at work and I was raring to visit a place where I could relax, have fun, and not be on duty. *But where?* I peered over the brick railing at the front of the building and caught sight of a gaudily decorated and well-lit bus slowly approaching from the far end of the street. The strobe light mounted on its roof indicated it was on a club hop—just what I needed.

I raced down the stairs to my apartment, stepped into high heels, and grabbed a Glomesh shoulder bag to accessorise my black harem pants and gold sequin top. I was outside and on the footpath in time to flag down the bus.

The first two clubs were pretty tame and nowhere near as grungily cool as Dusky's, but at least they had DJs and specials on cocktails. The third one, the Smooth Cat—a hangout for the rich and famous—looked more promising.

I located the bar in the smoky, noise-filled interior and elbowed through the masses to buy my seventh drink for the night. Turning back with a Piña Colada, I accidentally side-swiped someone familiar.

'Cam! What are you doing here?' I shouted above the clamour.

Bleary-eyed and teetering, he pointed to a large coloured badge pinned to his shirt. *21 And Loving It*, it proclaimed.

'Oh my God,' I squealed. 'It's your birthday!'

Wrapping an arm around his neck to kiss him on the mouth, I stumbled and planted one on his chin instead.

He peeled me off. 'How come you're here?'

'A booze crooze,' I yelled, slurping my cocktail and being careful not to stab my eye with the little paper umbrella. 'I should buy you a drink.'

He leaned close as if to hear me better and I noticed his pupils were dilated. There was also a splotch of white powder under one nostril and a smear of lipstick on his cheek.

'Cammie,' I said, clutching his shirt. 'What have you been up to?'

'You should bloody go,' he demanded.

I pulled a face. 'Go, where?'

'Out of here. I'm warning you. Get out.'

'That's not very nice,' I pouted. 'We could at least have a dance together.' I tried to bump his hip with mine but missed and knocked into a man standing behind him.

The man looked up from eying the splash of my drink on his jacket.

'Shit!' I cried, poking him in the chest. 'You look a lot like Slade Delaney.'

He gave a toothy grin. 'That's because I AM Slade Delaney.'

I stared open-mouthed at the legendary music critic and record producer, so recognisable in his pin-striped trilby hat. 'Holy crap.' I swung around. 'Cam ... it's friggin' Slade Delaney.'

'I know,' he growled, gripping my arm. 'You gotta go Ash, now.'

I tugged my arm back. 'I don't think I like you anymore, birthday boy. You're a real—'

A hand slid around my waist. I twisted around and I couldn't have been more horrified if it had been a pasty-faced Dracula standing next to me.

'Well, if it isn't Ashley McCabe,' Bryden said, beaming. 'You here to join in the celebrations for ol' Cam?'

He looked similar to when I'd seen him at Dusky's—unshaven, long hair, fancy clothing. Tonight he wore an electric blue vest with a paisley shirt and knee-length coat. His polished black boots reflected the intermittent lighting. I quickly eyed Cam, who was shaking his head at me.

'I ... I think I have a bus to catch,' I said, moving way.

Slade Delaney stepped in my path. 'Ashley, is it?' came his well-known smooth tone. 'Seems you're an acquaintance of both Bryden James and young Campbell here. I'd be delighted if you'd join us at a booth at the back. I reckon a lovely girl like you could liven things up a notch. Let me order you another ...' he bent and sniffed his jacket. 'Piña Colada, I believe.'

If I hadn't been so tipsy, I may have hightailed it out of there.

But the offer of a free drink and a curiosity in spending time with this ageing celebrity delayed my departure.

'You didn't tell me you knew Slade,' I whispered to Cam as we moved away together.

'I only met him tonight. Bryden's the one with the connections.'

I fed my arm through Cam's. 'Stay close, will you? I don't trust that bastard.'

'I did warn you,' he said, blinking through the smoke haze.

28

CAMPBELL

SATURDAY

I peel out of my crumpled clothes and step into the shower. Turning the water on, I bend forward so the fine rainlike spray from the square showerhead hits my aching lower back. If, in the past, I'd taken more notice of my gut instincts I would have saved myself a shitload of pain ... and guilt. I press my forehead against the cool black and white patterned tiles and feel myself being dragged back into hell.

1992

The evening whirled. My twenty-first was being lost in a fog generated by alcohol and lines of coke. Pulsating noise. Flickering lights. Girls coming from nowhere for a quick pash before disappearing just as swiftly. Mouths moving—their words drowned out by the boom of music. Conversations enacted in mime.

I thought we were celebrating my birthday. In fact, Bryden had simply slotted me into his regular Saturday night activities. Then Ashley arrived at the Smooth Cat, drunk and flirty, adding to my confusion.

Ravenous for more than peanuts and pretzels, I searched out Bryden and he led me through a pitch-black hallway to a metal exit door. Pushed out onto a landing, I was at the top of an iron staircase at the rear of the nightclub. Lightning flashed, illuminating bulbous clouds encroaching upon the full moon. Rain looked imminent. I swivelled around and discovered the door had been shut and I was on my own.

I staggered down the stairs, I faced a back alleyway lit solely by a caged wall lamp clouded by insects. Though giddy, it was easy to see there were no food vendors waiting to sell me their wares. Confused, I sat on the bottom step and stared numbly at the brickwork of an ancient retaining wall, its century-old craftsmanship still visible. As unappetising odours wafted around me from an overflowing industrial bin, I wished I'd celebrated my birthday by staying home and eating sponge cake with my family.

I was there only a few minutes when I heard the creaking of the exit door. Craning my neck, I peered above.

'Ah ... birthday boy. Want some company?' called Slade Delaney.

'Sure,' I said, batting away an annoying grey hawk moth. 'You wouldn't have any food with you by any chance?'

He smiled as he descended, his teeth glimmering in a flash of light.

29

ASHLEY

I flirted with Slade to piss Bryden off. Sitting on his lap and wearing his famous hat, I gushed over his celebrity status, stroked his ego, and monopolised his attention until more exuberant afficionados drew him away. Yet, it was difficult to determine my ploy's success because my brain started doing weird things. People's voices see-sawed from ear splitting to whispers, and their movements jerked between fast forward and slow motion like a badly edited movie.

I squeezed my eyes shut and clamped my hands over my ears which helped momentarily, though when I tried to stand, the floor rose in heaving waves and I stumbled against Bryden.

'Someone's spiked my drinks,' I said, slurring my words.

Bryden laughed, suggested I get some fresh air, and gave me directions to the nearest exit.

I snatched my bag and a bottle of cider and wobbled down the darkened corridor to a large metal door. Pushing hard on the panic bar, I stumbled out onto a checker plate landing. The rumble of thunder and cloying humidity added to my nausea and I bent over the edge of the railing, gagging.

A sharp, 'Fuck off!' from somewhere below, shocked me from spewing.

Curious to who had shouted, I held onto the iron railing for balance as I negotiated the stairs in my high heels to a poorly lit alleyway. A gruff voice directed my gaze to two figures scuffling against a brick wall. Thinking I'd walked in on a drunken brawl, I considered going for help until I noticed one of them—dark hair shot with silver—with his hand down the front of the other man's trousers and having a rough fumble around.

Embarrassed by my discovery, I retreated and would have left them to it if the man being groped hadn't objected loudly and lifted his face into view.

My stomach lurched.

Cam's eyes found mine just before his skull was smacked against the brickwork.

I cried out and his assailant spun around. It was Slade Delaney.

'Well, well, the lovely Ashley. Come to join us, have you?'

The fog in my brain cleared as I stared at Cam, now crumpled on the paving, then at Slade. 'What have you done?'

'Not as much as I would have liked.'

'You're a sicko. Wait till people hear about this.'

'That wouldn't be a good idea,' he said, moving into the circle of light coming from a lone bulb.

He seemed to grow in power as he stood centre stage in this horrible scene. I expected him to break into a soliloquy to expound on this warning, but all he did was throw his head back and sneer.

I backed away, jarring my hip against the iron railing of the staircase, and took a step up, then another.

Slade lunged, and I lashed out, striking him over the head with the cider bottle.

He staggered, blood oozing between his fingers as he clutched his scalp. 'Bitch! You'll pay for this!'

I dropped the bottle and heard it smash as I turned to climb upwards. Tugged back by the strap of my shoulder bag, I took Slade with me as I lost balance and crashed to the ground.

I rolled off him and scrambled to my knees only to feel my top grasped from behind. Straining against the pull, I heard a rip and tumbled onto my hands within reach of the shattered remains of the bottle. I curled my fingers around the broken neck and flipped over to find Slade flat on his back clutching a handful of gold material. Blinking away trickles of blood and hissing through clenched teeth, he was no longer the celebrated music guru. He was a monster.

I leapt up and stood over him, thrusting the jagged glass in front of his face. 'One more move and you're a dead man.'

His eyes darted. 'You wouldn't have the guts.'

'You wanna bet,' I snarled.

A clang of a heavy door swinging open drew our attention to the top of the stairs.

30

CAMPBELL

Gaining consciousness, I saw Slade wrestling with someone. By the glint of her top, I realised it was Ashley and I tried to rise, but there was an explosion going off in my head.

More scuffling. Raised voices. A clang, and a figure appeared on the landing of the metal staircase. With his long coat trailing behind, Bryden looked like a caped crusader as he flew down the stairs to reach the pair on the ground.

Before I could move over, Bryden kicked Slade in the ribs and thudded a highly polished boot down on Slade's extended belly, pinning him to the paving.

Ash stood alongside clutching a broken bottle. 'Make him pay, Bryden!'

Agreeing with Ash, I crawled forward and fell on top of the mongrel's writhing legs to hold them still.

Bryden lifted his boot from Slade's stomach, let him suck in a lungful of air, and then stamped on the barrel chest. A gasp shot from the full-lipped mouth.

'You dirty, fucking faggot,' Bryden growled, bending down,

and extracting a small knife from inside his boot. As the blade flicked out, a dark, far off look appeared in his eyes and I feared Slade's outcome.

Before I could warn him off, there came a squeal and a rush of blood as Slade's left cheek was sliced open.

Bryden straightened, and I eased my hold of Slade's legs, satisfied with the punishment dealt. But instead of removing his foot as I'd expected—as I'd hoped—Bryden applied more pressure. Putting all his weight behind it, he bounced. Slade's flabby face darkened. His eyes bulged. His fingers clawed at the boot crushing his chest.

'Bryden, that's enough!' I yelled, getting to my knees, and shoving him off.

He stumbled but righted quickly. 'This is for Julie,' he said, raising his leg again, and stomping on Slade's throat.

A ghastly popping sound. Wheezing. Gurgling. Slade's arms flapped like the wings of an injured bird.

Ash shrieked and tugged at Bryden's leg. Only then did he remove his foot from Slade's neck.

I knelt over the sputtering man wondering how to give aid when the flapping ceased, and the choking stopped. I waited, prayed for a breath to be inhaled through those blood-flecked lips, but it never came.

A clap of thunder and my eyes darted skyward. *Had we enraged the Gods?*

Raindrops sparkled like scattered diamonds as they ricocheted off the paving. A typical Queensland downpour that started slowly and turned into a deluge, rain would soon pound across iron rooftops and soak us to the bone.

I glanced at Bryden who began shouting commands. 'Cam, stop whimpering. Ash, I'll let you out the side gate. Run. Get your car. Get something to wrap this prick in.'

She stared blankly back at him, her face pale, her body shivering as shock took its hold on her.

'Move!' he yelled.

Rushing over to the wire fence blocking the alley from the road, he kicked at a rusty padlock until it released. The gate swung wide and Ash slipped out, vanishing into the wet streetscape.

Bryden ordered me to stay, saying he'd return in a jiffy, and then he too was gone.

Trembling, tasting sweat and blood in the rain on my lips, I locked eyes with a dead man and watched steam drift from his still warm body into the cool air.

31

ASHLEY

I raced along the wet pavement dodging electricity poles, rubbish bins, and groups of strangers. Having dumped my high-heeled shoes and top back in the alley, I ran barefoot, wearing only my black bra and harem pants. Yet no one seemed to lift an eye. Maybe this sight was the norm for a city street on a Saturday night.

My lungs ached and my throat burned. Still, a repeated word kept my feet moving without my knees buckling. 'Shit, shit, shit …' My bag rasped against my hip, but I didn't care. I needed to reach my apartment.

It only took twenty minutes but felt like fifty. Taking the stairs two at a time, I fumbled with the key in the lock and pushed open the door, falling against it as I struggled for air. My heart thumped against my rib cage; its pulse thrummed in my ears. *Had this horrible thing really happened? Or was it just a nightmare.* My memory of the incident was a blur—a dark, fuzzy smear of horror, a crushing, gurgling terror.

Rushing into the bathroom, I vomited into the sink. My reflection in the mirror showed bloody grazes on my face and down one shoulder. I opened a drawer and dabbed on antiseptic cream. *What the hell was I doing? I had to go back. Had to get my car keys.*

I found them in the fruit bowl on the coffee table. Before heading out the door, I returned to the bathroom and ripped down the plastic shower curtain. It would have to do.

I sped out of the car park and realised I hadn't picked up a replacement shirt. A maniacal laugh burst from my mouth. As far as I was aware, there was no dress code for disposing of a body in the middle of the night. Hot tears stung my eyes.

32

CAMPBELL

The rain pissed down—filling gutters, cascading from rooftops, and rushing in waves over the paving. I now waited under the staircase, trembling from the shock of what had just taken place rather than the cold.

After what felt like forever, Bryden reappeared.

'Quick, we gotta move Delaney out of the rain,' he said, coming alongside.

I blinked away rainwater. 'Why? I reckon he's beyond caring about getting his clothes wet.'

Bryden glared at me. 'Out of easy view, you dickhead.' Pointing to where we were standing, I noticed he now wore leather gloves. 'We'll bring him over here.'

I helped drag Slade under the ironwork. He sure was a heavy bugger.

'Where are we going to take him when Ash arrives?'

Bryden sighed and shook his dripping head. 'It's not like in the movies, Cam. The more you try to cover your tracks, the more evidence you leave. Here will do fine. We'll make it look like a mugging. See if Ash has left anything behind, will you?'

I searched in the downpour and found her shoes and torn sequin top. Shoving them under my shirt, I was struck by twin beams of light. My heart jolted. I shielded my eyes and peered through the curtain of water to see a car door open and a figure move towards the gate.

It was Ash.

She pressed her face against the criss-crossed pattern in the wire and I gave her a wave.

I discovered Bryden bent over Slade and rifling through the pockets of his clothing. 'Ash is here,' I said.

He nodded and withdrew Slade's wallet. Taking out gold credit cards and a wad of cash, he tossed the leather Oroton billfold onto the body.

'Don't touch anything else,' he urged, pushing me out from under the stairs.

Ash opened the gate wide. 'I bought plastic for wrapping the ...' She stopped mid-sentence as we dashed out and Bryden shut the gate behind us. 'What are you two doing? You're not leaving him here. We can't—'

'Shut up! Let's just get the fuck out of here!' Bryden demanded, opening the front passenger door, and jumping inside.

The wiper blades madly slashed water from the windscreen as we slowly reversed out, their screech keeping in time with my heartbeat. The torrent had cleared the streets, and people sheltering under umbrellas and awnings were given anonymity. So were we. We stared straight ahead as Ash drove away from the club, the wet bitumen reflecting the red, yellow, and green of changing intersection lights.

'Why aren't we getting rid of the body, Bryden?' she asked sternly. 'Someone's bound to find it.'

'Of course they will. Leaving it there means no trails will be followed. Keep it simple, that's the key. That's where amateurs go wrong. Too much messing around.'

Bryden giving us instructions instead of consolation caused me to wonder, with discomfort, how many times he had done something like this.

We sat in silence for the short drive to Ash's apartment—me with my head in my hands, Ash sniffing and gulping, Bryden tapping his fingers annoyingly on the dashboard.

When Ash parked the car and turned the engine off, Bryden's voice cut through the cloud of tension.

'I need a drink. I hope you've got something stronger than coffee, Ash.'

Wrenching her door open, she leapt out and slammed the door so hard the car rocked.

33

ASHLEY

I faltered at my apartment door for the second time in fifteen minutes. A rush of footsteps and Bryden collected the keys my trembling fingers had dropped.

Once inside, I opened a cupboard in the kitchenette and pulled out bottles of vodka, Bacardi, tequila, and Bailey's Irish Cream and set them in a row on the breakfast counter. Having shed his coat and boots, Bryden sat on a kitchen stool and watched as I removed a six-pack of beer from the fridge and added it to the line-up.

'Take your bloody pick,' I snapped, slamming down a glass tumbler.

Cam entered the apartment, his jeans lined with mud, and his shirt collar streaked with blood from a head wound. The birthday badge hanging from a torn piece of shirt fabric now proclaimed a falsehood—he was no longer enjoying his coming of age. I walked over and ripped it free, tossing it across the room. He didn't protest, he just handed me my shoes and shredded top.

Here we were again—the three of us hiding, not knowing how

our future or even the next hour would pan out. Though this occasion was much worse. All because of Bryden. *Fucking Bryden.*

I stared at him pouring a drink from my stash of alcohol. No sign of death on him, no evidence of having been in a fight. Yet Cam and I looked as if we'd gone a few rounds with Muhammad Ali. I threw my shoes and top on the pile of clothing near the door.

'Where's your bathroom?' Cam asked, his voice shaky.

I pointed down the hall, and he slunk away.

I figured I couldn't dislike Bryden any more than I did. But I was wrong. My hate for him as he loped into the lounge area and flopped onto the sofa soared way off the Richter scale. Stomping over to the counter and snatching up a beer, I heard the welcome click and hiss as I tugged the ring-pull free. I raised the can to my mouth and stopped.

'The cider bottle. What did you do with it?'

Bryden looked up. 'What cider bottle?'

'The one I smashed over Slade's head. I used the broken neck to fend him off.'

His cold, dark eyes narrowed. 'Why didn't you get rid of it?'

'Oh, maybe because I was in shock from seeing a man slaughtered and then sent racing through the city like a crazy woman.

'Shit!' He rubbed his forehead with his glass. 'They'll have your fingerprints. What else did you touch?'

'Touch?'

'In the club. What did you touch?'

'Loads of things.'

'What did you drink?'

Beer frothed from the can as I banged it on the countertop. 'How am I supposed to remember that? I had plenty.' I thought hard. 'A Blue Moon was my last.'

He shook his head. 'Jesus, Ash! They'll match the prints on the broken bottle with the ones left on the glass or anything else you put your mitts on ... connect you to us. We're screwed. We might as well hand ourselves into the cops right now.'

Great! Just when I thought things couldn't get any worse. I rushed over and slapped him, almost busting my fingers.

'Why did you have to kill Slade? Why didn't you just beat the shit out of the bastard ... shatter his stupid grinning face or ... or ... snap a few limbs or something! The sicko certainly deserved that, but ...' a grotesque scene flashed in my mind, one I knew would be impossible to erase '... smashing his windpipe so he choked to death. God almighty, Bryden!'

He massaged his red cheek and casually reached for an apple from the fruit bowl on the coffee table. Resting back on the sofa, he took a large bite.

'What is it with you?' I cried. 'It's like there's a friggin' switch inside your brain that flicks on in the heat of the moment and turns you into a raving lunatic. You've always gone a step too far ... always.' My voice dropped a tone as I added, 'I know that for a fact, don't I?'

His eyes met mine before darting away.

'You're warped, Bryden, and this time you've really fucked up.'

I hurried from the room and heard a thud as the apple hit the lounge wall.

34

CAMPBELL

As the wall shower in Ash's bath rained over my scalp, causing split flesh to sting, I tasted blood—copper, metallic, like sucking on old coins. I looked at my feet where the water swirled pink.

We had killed a man.

Shouting from the other side of the door curbed my heaving cries. I turned the taps off and strained to listen as Ashley argued with Bryden ... no, berated him.

An hour ago, we were celebrating my birthday in the throbbing atmosphere of the Smooth Cat and being enthralled by the outlandish stories told by a famous celebrity. A little star struck and plied with free drinks and drugs—we were having the time of our lives. Now we were at Ash's flat trying to deconstruct in our minds what had happened.

I stepped out of the bath and rubbed the fog from the mirror above the basin. A gaunt face glared back at me—red-veined eyes, new crevasses, freckles stark against pale skin. I leaned closer. Did I look like a murderer?

The bathroom door burst open and I covered myself with a

towel as Ash walked in.

She closed the door, stripped out of her clothes, and stepped into the bath. Turning the water on full, sprays rebounded off her body to join the puddle already on the floor.

'The shower curtain,' she said in a monotone, her eyes meeting mine, 'it's still in the car.'

Seeing Ash naked for the very first time was not how I'd imagined it. In a moment devoid of desire, we were just two zombies eyeing each other blankly.

Ash ducked under the steaming jets, covered her face with her hands and began to sob.

I hurried out.

Adding my soiled clothes to the pile near the front door, I stood in Ash's lounge room with the towel wrapped around my waist and water dripping from my hair. Bryden reclined on the sofa—legs out straight, bare feet pointing upward, the glass in his hand empty of whatever he had gulped from it—while I struggled to breathe.

As the muted bawling of my shattered childhood friend drifted from the bathroom, my chest tightened. My mind raced into the future, then back to the nightclub, then to my wet footprints on the floor.

'Christ, Bryden,' I rasped. 'Why all the shouting?'

Nothing from him. Silence. He didn't move or even acknowledge my presence.

'Hey, shithead! Tell me what the hell just happened?'

Bryden lifted his head, one eye squinting at me. 'Keep your voice down. We don't want to alert the other tenants.'

'Too late for that, don't you reckon?' I said, lowering my voice anyway.

He raised his empty glass. 'Get me another will ya? I'm screwed and so are you, you prick.'

My immediate response was to throw something. It turned out to be a packet of potato chips from the breakfast counter. The bag hit him and split, spilling its contents over his chest and onto the rug.

Bryden didn't flinch. He looked down, fingered a few of the broken chips and popped them into his mouth. 'It seems Ash smashed a cider bottle over Slade's scone before I arrived,' he declared with a sigh. 'Now it's sitting outside the Smooth Cat a few metres away from a dead body with the bitch's fingerprints all over it. We're all going down.' He laughed, and not in a good way.

I cut him off. 'I got rid of it.'

His head twisted around. 'You what?'

'I saw it in her hand. When you both ran off, I found it lying on the paving, so I crushed it underfoot. All that's left is powdered glass.'

Bryden sat up. 'Cam the man! You've saved our bacon.' He laughed again, more joyfully. Then rising from the sofa, he grabbed a beer can and tossed it over. 'Here, you deserve one of these, at least.'

'What about security cameras? We might have been caught on film.'

Bryden shook his head, 'Nah. None in the alley. And in the club only half the cameras actually function. More of a deterrent than anything else. In my line of work, I make it a priority to know these things. There's nothing to worry about now.'

Nothing? That was presumptuous. I stared into space, knocking back the beer. It was only when Ash entered the living area, dressed in jeans and a long-sleeved shirt, that I snapped out of my daze.

'That towel won't do,' she said, throwing an armful of clothing at me.

The T-shirt, track pants, and a pair of jocks were probably

leftover from when a 'friend' visited. I dropped the towel and slipped them on.

Bryden told her about me crushing the cider bottle and Ash went limp, crumpling to the floor. Tears slid from her eyes.

When Bryden rushed forward, I assumed he was going to offer her comfort. Instead, he snatched the car keys from the kitchen counter and headed for the door. As he clasped the knob, he looked back.

'Let's go for a drive ... and bring that mess,' he added, pointing to the pile of clothing.

He was already down the steps when Ash appeared at my side with a black garbage bag.

As we filled the bag together, she gripped my hand. 'Thanks, Cam.' I knew she was talking about the cider bottle.

'No, probs,' I said with a shrug as if all I'd done was saved us from getting into trouble for littering.

In fact, I'd crushed that jagged bottle neck out of rage. Rage for what Slade had tried on me. Rage for Ash having to save me from a situation I shouldn't have gotten into. Rage for Bryden not being able to control his darkness. And rage for my life turning to complete shit with one deathly stomp of a polished boot. Only after, as I hid under the steps waiting for Bryden to return, did I realise I'd destroyed a piece of evidence that could have sent Ash—and maybe the three of us—behind prison walls for God knows how many years.

We found Bryden seated in Ash's car, behind the steering wheel. Ash sat in the back, as far from him as possible, so I took the front passenger seat.

'Where are we going?' I asked.

'Some place where we can safely talk without being overheard,' Bryden said, sharing his plan as we drove out of the city just after midnight.

35

CAMPBELL

Lake Mitchum's picnic area was deserted, with silhouettes of vacant timber tables and unmanned brick barbecues giving it an eerie quality.

Bryden was the first one to open his door. 'Follow me,' he ordered, 'and bring the bag.'

I slid from the car and dragged the black plastic garbage bag from the back seat. Slinging it over my shoulder, I hauled it like Santa carrying a sack full of presents over to Bryden standing alongside a brick-edged fire pit.

'Drop it,' he commanded, and I let it fall at his feet. 'Tip the stuff in there,' he said, shining a torch found in Ash's car into the shallow hole filled with charred remains from a recent campfire.

'No, you tip it,' I argued, stepping back. 'I'm not your bloody slave. You do something.'

He removed a disposable cigarette lighter from his trouser pocket. 'I will,' he glowered, 'but you need to tip that in there first.'

I folded my arms and stared him down.

Ash took over but grappled with untying the bag.

Bryden gave a groan. Producing his small knife he slit the plastic, enabling Ash to empty the contents into the pit.

Then removing his boots from the pile, he dropped them on the grass and lit a corner of his thick coat. It sparked and smouldered, wisps of smoke rising. Shuffling around the brick edge he set the remaining articles alight—my jeans and shirt, and then a piece of Ash's gold top that jutted up from the middle of the pile like a birthday candle. The fire took hold, but a little too slowly for Bryden who threw in the lighter.

A burst of flames made us leap back, with me slipping and falling on my arse. Bryden laughed and so did Ash, which surprised me. I joined in, though it wasn't long before the reality of our predicament descended once more.

Ash and I sat on a log while Bryden rolled up the plastic bag and dropped it into the flames. As he stirred the crackling fire with a slender tree branch, we watched sparks fly, flakes of ash flutter, and the evidence of a murder go up in smoke. It distressed me that the three of us were once again watching a fire burn with our hearts in our throats.

'We should be singing Kumbaya,' I said, straight-faced.

'Well, shit, Cam, that wouldn't be fitting, would it?' scoffed Bryden. 'I think a rendition of Bohemian Rhapsody would be more suitable.' He started to sing the song's first line.

'Shut up, will you,' cried Ash.

He turned to her. 'Well, it's the truth, isn't it?'

I stared at him. 'Why did you kill Slade?'

Bryden threw the branch into the blaze and squatted, stirring the edge of the fire with the knife. He muttered words I had to strain to hear. '... *and do not kill the innocent and righteous, for I will not acquit the wicked.*'

He was quoting the Bible like he used to. Not a good sign.

A touch on my elbow. Ash's eyes were wide as they looked into mine. Uneasy with the trance Bryden had drifted into, we both sat still and silent.

'That fat pig deserved it,' he said, straightening, and enlightening us on Slade's background and sexual perversions. 'There are loads of rumours going around about Delaney's loose zipper. Even though he let women think they had a chance of getting laid by him, he preferred men, the younger the better. Cam, when he went outside tonight, I knew he was going to try it on with you.'

I leapt up. 'You what? You knew what he would do?'

'Yeah. Sorry. I may have jokingly inferred to him that you were gay.'

My blood boiled. I gritted my teeth. 'Why would you say such a thing?'

'Jesus, I didn't know he'd get violent. I just thought it'd be funny. Anyway, you look fit, Cam. I thought if he tried anything, you'd be able to fend him off.'

'But I was high. I could hardly stand.' Why did I have to defend my actions? It was Bryden who'd orchestrated the turn of events. I bit my tongue. Tasted blood. Felt sick.

'That was a shitty thing to do,' Ash said.

Bryden shrugged. 'I know that now. That was before I found out Delaney killed my mother.'

My jaw dropped. Had I heard correctly? 'He did what?'

'While he was with you in the alleyway, one of his boofhead cling-ons told me he knew my mother. Said he'd met her and the bloke she was living with at a rave party hosted by Delaney. It was a pretty wild night with DJs, free booze, and Delaney doling out ecstasy pills like they were Smarties. My mum seemed to be having fun like the rest of the crowd. So the next morning, when this guy heard about her shocking death, he believed she must have been off her head after taking some pretty heavy shit to do such a thing. He said he thought I might be relieved to know it wasn't suicide, like it was reported.' Bryden let out a long breath. 'I wasn't relieved. I was furious.' He wiped his nose on his sleeve and returned his gaze to the flames.

I looked over at Ash. The way she held her head in her hands told me she too struggled with this sad revelation.

Bryden's voice rose again. *'The righteous will rejoice when he sees the vengeance. He will bathe his feet in the blood of the wicked.'* He raised his head, and though his eyes reflected the fire's glow, there was a coldness to their depth. 'I lost control when I saw him attacking you two. That bastard had to be taken from the earth. A life for a life. Now the devil will see to him.'

He spun around and hurled the knife like a dart towards a tree, the blade embedding itself in the smooth trunk. Then he lifted his hands to the sky. *'And do not fear those who kill the body but cannot kill the soul. Rather fear him who can destroy both soul and body in hell.'*

A gust of wind rustled through leafy branches and the mood of our small camp felt heavy with fear.

Ash stood. 'Bryden, you're scaring me with this religious talk.'

'Scaring you? Grow up Ash. We deal with evil every day. *If you harbor it, it will rest easy with you.'*

'But I detest evil,' she said, wrapping her arms around herself.

'What we did wasn't right,' was my attempt to counter him.

'Don't lecture me on what's right,' he snapped. 'You welcome darkness into your life each day. Look at your dad ... the pathetic drunk. Look at your whole family, never letting on that dear old daddy can be an evil prick when pissed. You know how shitty it can get, but you keep it a secret. So what's right, Cam?'

Ash grabbed his arm. 'Stop it! We're fragile. There's no need to add to the hurt.'

Bryden brushed her hand away. 'Fragile? Do you think it's

been easy for me? I'm the only one who stepped up to right the crap that's been going on for years. Delaney's lauded around the country—everyone smiling, slapping that faggot's back—while accusers of his sick actions are lining up. I guess you didn't know that. Now both of you are joining in and saying this needs to go unjudged.'

He wagged a finger at me. 'Have you forgotten it's only been a few hours ago since he was forcing himself on you, Cam? It might have been you who was killed, or maybe Ash. Should we be sitting here crying over each other instead of Delaney?'

Bryden's accusations stung, but his words resonated. It dawned on me that I needed this justification or else I could never forgive my part in Slade's murder.

'But it's never right to kill someone,' Ash said.

Bryden now turned on her, the universe swirling in the black of his eyes. 'Ashley ... dear Ashley, you're no better than me. By whose hand did your baby's life come to an end? *Judge not, that ye not be judged.*'

36

ASHLEY

We were at Lake Mitchum—in the dark, around a fire, emotions running high—when Bryden accused me of murdering our baby.

I reeled back. 'I didn't kill it!'

He stabbed a finger at me. 'But you paid someone the money I gave you so it could be killed. That's the same thing.'

Slumping onto a log and staring at my feet, I swallowed hard. 'I didn't. I never went through with it.'

A groan made me glance up.

With hands locked behind his head, Bryden's eyes darted. 'Don't tell me you had the baby? Were you out of your fucking mind?'

I started to speak, but his rambling as he paced the dirt, tugging his hair, cut me off.

'What did you do? Adopt it out? Holy shit, there's a kid of mine out there. God, what a fuckup.'

I broke down. His anger was too much. The whole friggin' night was too much.

Cam's arms folded around me and I curled into his chest, sobbing.

'You arsehole, Bryden,' he growled, 'she lost the baby. She was going to have it, and love it, and give it a real good life ... but then she miscarried.'

That shut Bryden up.

My cries turned into gasps, then hiccups.

'I'll get you a drink,' Cam said, releasing me. 'There's a bottle of water in the car, isn't there?'

I nodded, and he hurried away.

Bryden knelt in front of me and I flinched when his hands rested on my knees.

'When?' he asked, in a calmer voice.

'Early ... on,' I hiccupped. 'But it was still ... hard. I'd decided, you see ... I couldn't do what you said. You were such a ... a shit.'

He nodded. 'And I'm still a shit. Look at what I've gotten you two into now. Christ, Ash, I've never felt such rage. After hearing Delaney was the one dealing to Mum, and seeing him fighting you, and Cam on the ground, well, I went ballistic.' A tear rolled from his eye and slid down his nose. 'I'm sorry, Ash ... for everything.' He dropped his head into my lap, and I heard sniffing.

This was the Bryden that once stirred my heart—sensitive, hurting, struggling with the crappy hand of cards life had dealt him. Surprised that this Bryden still existed, I didn't know what to do other than sit stock-still and watch a large grey moth skirting the fire, hoping it wouldn't fly too close to the flames.

A wail drew us apart.

Cam stood on the opposite side of the fire pit, fury distorting his features. In his hand he clutched the small knife that Bryden had embedded in the tree trunk.

Bryden leapt up. 'Put it down, mate!'

Cam's chest heaved as he shuffled the knife from one hand to the other.

'C'mon, don't be a dickhead,' Bryden said, edging around the fire. 'Drop the knife.'

Cam planted his feet and thrust the weapon out in front. 'Keep coming you prick.'

'I'm not fighting you.' Bryden raised his hands in surrender. 'Now drop it.'

Cam shook his head, waving the blade around as he spoke. 'You take everything. You don't give a shit about anyone but yourself. It's all about you and your bloody ego. You suss out people's weaknesses, their faults,' he directed his gaze at me, 'their vulnerabilities.'

I cringed, the truth hitting home with force.

He turned back to Bryden. 'Then you slither in and go for the kill. As long as you get your kicks, or come out on top, it doesn't matter who gets hurt in the process. I'm sick of it. I'm not taking your bullshit any longer. I have every mind to go to the police myself and tell them what you did to Slade. How you crushed the life out of him with no hint of remorse. And with you knowing about his dealings with your mother, I'd say they'll charge you with pre-meditated murder for sure. How many years in prison do you get for that, these days?'

The night's stillness magnified Bryden's laugh. 'You're forgetting something, buddy. If you hadn't held him down for me, I mightn't have got him so easily. Add to that all the groping he did with you, and who knows how much material evidence was left behind.'

He spun around and eyed me through the cloud of smoke. 'Same goes for you, Ash. You fought Delaney. Did he scratch you? Maybe you left your blood on him, some fibres from your glitzy clothing. Now me, I hardly touched the mongrel other than my boot, which will see the bottom of this dam real soon. You need me. Both of you do.'

Cam stabbed the air. 'You bastard! You said we had nothing to worry about.'

'Well, maybe I was wrong. With Delaney's high profile, I'm betting they'll be bringing in the best detectives around to help solve this case. So stop mouthing off, Cam, or I'll have to do something about it.'

I sprung up. 'What do you mean by that? You wouldn't dare.'

'Wouldn't I? You heard what Cam said. When push comes to shove, it's about saving my own skin.'

My anger grew, so did my confusion. Had Bryden just played to my weakness to get me back on side? Or was he playing me now, trying to scare me into submission? My brain hurt. I wanted this nightmare to stop.

Cam lunged at Bryden.

But Bryden was too quick. He swung around and grabbed Cam by the wrist before the knife found its mark. Twisting Cam's arm behind his back, he forced him to the ground and wrestled the knife away.

It skidded in the dirt and I rushed for it, not trusting either of them with its possession.

Cam kicked Bryden in the knee. He buckled and collapsed and would have fallen into the fire pit if I hadn't dragged him away. Which, ironically, was quite the opposite of what Bryden had done to me five years earlier.

'Stop it!' I yelled. 'This is not the time to be fighting each other. We should be working together.'

Bryden crawled to his feet. 'C'mon, get up, you idiot. She's right. We should be banding together.' He held out a hand.

Cam knocked it aside and pushed himself up. 'Well, band away. I'm out of here.' Picking up the torch, he strode off.

'Where's he going?' I asked.

'Somewhere to lick his wounds, I suppose,' Bryden scoffed.

Could tonight get any worse? I turned and ran towards the lake.

'Hey!' Bryden shouted. 'Now where are you going?'

I waved the knife. 'To chuck this horrid thing away.'

A sound of a car starting up made our heads twist, and through the trees we saw headlights. Tyres spun in loose gravel as my Mazda sped off.

Bryden jogged over holding a black boot in each hand.

'Will he come back?' I asked, knowing we'd be up shit creek if he didn't.

Bryden gave a sigh. 'I bloody hope so. He'll return when he's calmed down. If you're gonna get rid of that knife, you'd better follow me.'

'Where to?'

'The dam wall.'

The sojourn through the bush brought back memories—odious memories of a youthful prank, so innocent compared to what we'd experienced only hours before.

We reached the cement wall. The railing on the high walkway had been extended since we were last here, with sturdy fencing wire now giving it a precautionary extra metre in height. Bryden might not have been the only idiot to show off by tempting fate.

Halfway along the top we stopped, and with the strong breeze whipping our hair into a frenzy, we stared out at the monochrome nightscape. The dark of the forests defined the edges of the lake, while the expanse of water rippled gunmetal grey. Rolling out from the middle—like a landing strip for aliens, or some fantastical winged creature—a carpet of moonlight stretched up to the dam wall.

Bryden moved to the railing. 'Yep, over here is best.'

I took the knife from the pocket of my jeans and was about to feed it through a gap in the wire, when Bryden snatched it away.

'No, not like that!'

He dropped his boots and took several steps back. Raising the knife above his head like a miniature javelin, he ran forward and pitched it over the top of the fencing. The blade flashed silver as it soared through the air and plunged silently out of view. Then picking up the boots, he hurled them one-by-one over the wire. This time I heard a splash far below.

'They'll sink, never to be found.' Bryden sounded sure of this fact and I believed him. I had to.

I pressed my face against the wire and peered out at the lake. 'Do you think God will forgive us?'

'*For what is evil, but good tortured by its own hunger and thirst,*' Bryden said, coming alongside.

'What's that? Another scripture verse?'

He shook his head. 'It's from *The Prophet* by Kahlil Gibran.'

Gripping the railing and arching back, moonlight illuminated his face. Though shadows dwelt under his eyes and in the hollows of his cheeks, he had an alluring appearance. Lucifer was supposedly the most beautiful of beings before God threw him out of heaven. I wondered if he looked something like Bryden.

'I did a good thing,' he said. 'I know I did.'

'What good thing?'

'When I killed Delaney.' He let go of the railing and turned around. 'I did good ridding the world of him. Think of all those young men out there ... boys really ... who'll be breathing sighs of relief when they hear the news and knowing they'll never have to fear running into him again. I reckon they'll be pretty fuckin' happy. Maybe I should do it again.'

My skin prickled. 'Do what?'

'Help others. Now that I've been blooded, I figure I'm up to doing the world a few more favours. There are a lot of sick fuckers out there.'

I exploded. 'Are you serious? Who the hell do you think you are? Batman? An avenging angel?'

'This could be my new calling.'

I couldn't tell if he was joking. A quote from Charles Darwin came to mind. *'We stopped looking for monsters under our bed when we realised they were inside us.'* Listening to Bryden, I suspected such a monster inhabited him. It may have always been there, hiding in the recesses, playing peek-a-boo, until tonight when it finally broke free of its constraints. Years before we'd stood in almost the exact same spot. Bryden had scared me then. He was scaring me now.

'Cold?' he asked, seeing me shiver.

I shook my head. 'We should go back. Cam might've returned.'

'I guess we should do something with those ashes. The fire would've died down by now.'

When we arrived back at the fire pit, we found Cam using my torch and a stick to sort through the embers.

'Where have you two been?' he said, without looking up.

'Getting rid of the knife and the boots,' I said. 'Bryden threw them into the dam.'

Cam nodded. 'I've picked out stuff that didn't burn completely. Some buttons and the zip from my jeans. Your top melted into a solid gold nugget of plastic. I got that out too and hid all the bits in packets and food containers inside the bins. I'm pretty sure council garbage collectors don't search through rubbish.'

'Thanks, mate,' Bryden said.

Cam raised his head, and I saw fresh grazes on his face from being tackled. Ignoring Bryden, he threw the keys to me. 'It's after three. I need to get home. Mum'll be shittin' bricks.'

I drove this time. Cam lay on the back seat while Bryden sat next to me, flitting annoyingly through stations on the radio. We kept to ourselves until I took Cam home first.

'I'll be in touch,' Bryden said, as Cam stepped out of the car.

'Don't bother,' he said, slamming the door.

Bryden leaned out of the window. 'Remember, you need me buddy. You won't get through this without me.'

Cam stormed off. Kicking one of his father's garden gnomes like a football, it flew across the front yard and smashed against fence palings.

Bryden uttered similar words to me when we arrived at his swanky high-rise unit block close to the city CBD.

'I'll give you a call in a few days and see how you're travelling.' He slowly undid his seatbelt. 'I meant what I said back there. I really am sorry.'

He stared at me for a moment and I had a feeling he was about to say something else, but then he opened his door and got out.

I reached home just before dawn and went straight to bed. Struggling to sleep, a revelation came to me. It wasn't Cam and me who needed Bryden, it was Bryden who needed us. Our friendship was the key to his salvation.

37

CAMPBELL

My father greeted me at the door. 'You're looking worse for wear, birthday boy.'

'Yeah, it's been a big night. How come you're still awake?' I asked, hoping he hadn't heard me kick the shit out of one of his stupid garden gnomes.

'Had to get up for a piss. Don't make too much noise. Don't want to wake your mother.'

I moved straight to my room. Shutting the door, I sat on the end of my bed in the dark, my head swirling with thoughts.

A gentle knock and a sliver of light shooting across the room drew me from the horrors replaying in my mind.

'Cam?' came a whisper through the door's narrow opening.

'Hi, Mum,' I said.

She entered and sat beside me. 'How are you? I've been a little worried.'

'I'm good,' I reassured her. 'Sorry I disturbed you.'

She stayed for a time, tapping her fingers on my knee, and

listening as I gave her a very sanitised version of my birthday celebrations—no mention of drug taking or, of course, murder.

'You reek of smoke. Get some sleep,' she said, then slipped from the room.

All that was good about that moment—my mum's reassurance, the quiet house, the safety of my room and its familiar surroundings—added to my knowledge that what had transpired over the last few hours was so terribly wrong. So foreign to all I had been taught. I lay back on the mattress, and as a stillness settled over me, I drifted off to sleep. But not for long.

A rapping on my window woke me. I rolled over and peered out to see Bryden motioning me outside. He looked like that kid from all those years ago who came late at night with an invitation to join him in some mischief.

Sneaking out of the house through the rear door, I found him crouched in the back yard.

'Shit, Bryden, it's almost daylight. What is it? I've got to get some rest. I'm rooted.'

He stood and whispered, 'Cam, I wanted to assure you that I was dead serious when I said I'd protect you from all of this. It was entirely my fault and I'm sorry you were involved.'

I studied his hunched shoulders, furrowed brow, and eyes shimmering with moisture. He was genuine. Here was someone asking for forgiveness.

He continued. 'I know we could end up in some serious shit. Unless we think this through, we could all be ... well ... screwed. If the cops come sniffing, I'll have to get in touch with Francis.'

He went on to explain that if help was necessary, it would be legal argument that would open the door to our freedom.

'Cam, I don't want to throw my life away ... especially not for Delaney ... but if we have to use the justice system, then I'm not opposed to it.'

I didn't want to contemplate getting caught, but Bryden had a way of offering solutions that made sense. Justice resonated with me. Fighting evil was reasonable. I would need to cling onto these lifelines to stave off doubt and guilt.

He clasped my shoulders. 'Cam, if you need to talk, or come stay with me for a while, that's fine. Take time off work if you have to. Do whatever will help ... and remember ... I've got your back, buddy.' He surprised me by leaning in and giving me a hug. 'I'll call you soon.'

Then he dashed to the side of our house and jumped the fence.

As I returned to my room, I heard the distinctive sound of his EH Holden starting up a street away, and its deep rumble as it raced away.

Unable to fall asleep, I changed into my own clothes and crept from the house. Releasing the handbrake, I let my car roll backwards down the driveway and onto the road before I turned the key in the ignition. Swinging by Macca's, I returned to Ash's apartment.

38

ASHLEY

A loud noise. A door banging shut.

I woke with a start, my heart pounding, my eyes seared by beams of morning light shooting through the venetian blinds. The bedroom looked odd until I realised I'd slept the wrong way round with my feet at the top of the bed. Then I remembered. *Oh God!*

I staggered out of the room with a pneumatic drill hammering inside my head, and discovered Cam seated at the breakfast counter.

'How'd you get in?' I croaked.

He spun around on the stool, munching on a burger. Wiping his mouth with the back of his hand, he smeared a glob of mayo across his face. 'The door wasn't locked.' His eyes widened. 'Hey, isn't that my old T-shirt?'

I glanced down at the shirt I'd worn to bed with a pair of pyjama shorts, the cassette recorder print now faded and stretched out of shape. 'Yeah ... I never did return it.'

Cam licked the corner of his mouth. 'I couldn't sleep. My nerves are shot, and I wouldn't have survived my folks asking more questions about my birthday bash.' He pointed to a brown paper bag resting on the counter. 'I got you a Big Mac and a chocolate thick shake for breakfast.'

I removed the burger from the bag, unwrapped it, and peeled back the top layer of the bread roll. 'Pickles,' I groaned. 'You know I hate pickles. And I drink vanilla not chocolate.'

Cam slammed his hand down on the counter, crushing his empty paper bag. 'How was I to remember? It's been a zillion years since we shared a Macca's meal. Christ! You're lucky I even got you something. My brain isn't running at full capacity right now.'

I flicked a pickle at him. 'Yeah, that's for sure.'

'Hey, I'm not the monster here, Ash.'

'No,' I said, taking a tentative bite from the cold burger. 'He's probably sitting at some fancy restaurant tucking into bacon and eggs and hitting on a giggling waitress.'

Opening a cupboard drawer, I pulled out a packet of painkillers and downed three capsules with a mouthful of chocolate shake. Cam helped himself and did the same.

'If you're hanging around, I think I'll get dressed,' I said, leaving him to eat all the fries.

I changed into a denim skirt and another T-shirt. *How were we to get on with our lives after what we'd done? How were we supposed to act normal?* Glancing in the mirror, I noticed my shirt was emblazoned with an image of a skull with roses for eyes, and quickly replaced it with a white lace top.

Cam now sat on the sofa flicking through TV channels. I flopped down beside him. 'What are you looking for?'

His eyes met mine.

'Oh ...' I said, with realisation.

Relieved at not finding any news about a local killing, we watched a replay of an episode of *Friends* and tried not to think about what happened hours before—or what might now be happening in a certain part of The Valley.

I must have dozed off because I was woken by Cam tapping me on the shoulder. I lifted my head from his lap and wiped dribble from my cheek.

'I need to get out of here,' he said, 'I'm going stir crazy waiting. Where can we go?'

I pointed upwards.

The sun warmed my skin as I peered over the brick edge of the rooftop terrace at the usual Sunday traffic. People of all shapes and ages walked the footpaths or ambled into nearby New Farm Park to place picnic blankets and eskies in the shade of sprawling fig trees. Couples huddled, while kids kicked footballs, threw frisbees, and chased runaway dogs. Such a pleasant morning. Who could imagine that a murder had been committed only hours before and only a couple of kilometres away?

I studied Cam as he took in the view: jaw clenched, crinkles appearing at the corners of his eyes as he frowned.

'Weird isn't it?' he said. 'Here we are freaking out, wondering what the hell we've turned into, and they're all down there having jolly fun without a care in the world.' He faced me, chewing his bottom lip. 'Thanks for turning up when you did ... last night ... in the alley. If you hadn't ...'

I lifted my hand and smoothed the creases from his forehead. 'It's okay. It was time I protected you for a change.'

He gave a weak smile and held my hand. 'I don't know what will happen to us, Ash. But while I have the chance, I want to tell you I've always—'

The scream of a siren cut his words short.

We looked down to see a police car weaving through the traffic. It came closer and closer until it stopped in front of the apartment building.

Cam squeezed my hand, crushing my fingers, and I held my breath, my body rigid.

Moments later, the car moved away, its blue light flashing, its siren blaring as it travelled down the street and around the corner.

I fell against Cam, my heart almost bursting from my chest. 'God, I thought they were coming for us.' Burying my face into his shirt, I was reminded of my father. Cam had the same smell about him: Black Suede, the only Avon product Dad would allow Mum to buy him. My father's presence, if only in this familiar scent, gave me a sense of security and I inhaled deeply. 'So, what were you going to say before?'

Cam lifted my chin and I watched his lips part. 'Just that I ...' He frowned again and arched his head back.

I did the same as a staccato of noise grew louder, came nearer. The sound of rotor blades.

We clamped our hands over our ears when the Channel 7 News helicopter thundered overhead and moved to hover over The Valley and the vicinity of the Smooth Cat.

'Oh, shit!' Cam cried, his eyes wild.

39

CAMPBELL

We were caught in a whirlpool of anticipation.

Nervously taking in the view from the rooftop of Ash's building—and desperate to tell her what I had been feeling for years—our world suddenly exploded in a rush of noise. Racing down the stairs, we retreated behind closed doors.

Ash slumped onto the tub chair in the lounge room—her head in her hands, her long crimped hair falling around her like wrinkled curtain—while I rushed to the window and searched the sky for more helicopters. Finding no others, I paced the floor until I demanded Ash find something to relieve our agitation.

I thought she would line up a row of bottles on the breakfast counter. Instead, she dragged me to her bedroom. I didn't protest. I was up for anything. As she knelt on all fours on the carpet, I hesitated in the doorway, unsure of what she expected of me. Then, reaching under her bed, she pulled out a box of old comic books and we mindlessly flicked through Mad magazines and Marvel comics while the number of helicopters whirring overhead increased to three.

The noises eventually faded, and I dropped off to asleep. Waking sometime later, I found Ash curled up beside me, her head on my shoulder, one arm draped across my chest. A wet patch on my shirt showed where she'd drooled.

I shook her awake. We still hadn't heard from Bryden.

Returning to the lounge room, we switched on the television. And there it was.

'Breaking News. Slade Delaney was found dead earlier today outside a Fortitude Valley nightclub. Evidence at hand indicates the well-known celebrity died in the vicinity of the Smooth Cat late last night after a vicious attack by persons unknown. Ruled a homicide, the area has been secured and police are continuing their investigations.'

Homicide. That terrible word spoke volumes. Video clips of Slade Delaney's contribution to the entertainment industry began to roll across the screen and both Ash and I jumped up, eager to turn the TV off.

A knock on the door had us exchanging anxious glances.

The door opened and Bryden appeared.

He told us the club manager had called him in to the Smooth Cat. Being one of several regulars known to be in attendance during the evening, he was questioned by the police. He stated that he had been partying with Slade Delaney at one point but had assumed Slade had gotten lucky, or moved on to another group, or even gone to another venue. After a staff member confirmed Bryden's story that he was with her around the time of Slade's disappearance from the club, he'd been allowed to leave. It turned out while Ash was getting her car, and I was safeguarding a dead body in the rain, Bryden was enjoying a quick shag in a stairwell.

'Only to create an alibi,' he assured, with a sly grin.

He then informed us that the police were examining footage

from the working security cameras, though he was confident nothing would be discovered that could incriminate us.

'Remember, it was crowded and dark inside the club, and there's no camera in the alleyway. I wouldn't have sent you down there if there was.'

This eased my concerns but heightened my irritation. If Slade had seriously attacked me, there would have been no proof of what actually occurred, and it would have been my word against his.

'What about the staff?' Ash asked. 'Wouldn't they have seen Slade hanging around with us? Known who he was buying drinks for?'

'He schmoozed with loads of people last night. That's what he did. He liked the attention, the ego-boosting. We weren't the only ones he lavished his money on.'

'What do we do now?' I said, still unconvinced of our safety.

'Go home. Act normal. Get on with things. First, I'm going to grab a feed and have a lie down.' He looked over at Ash and winked. 'Want to join me in the sack?'

She threw the TV remote at him and he deftly seized it as it glanced off his shoulder. 'Bugger off, Bryden! I'll be happy if I never see your face again.'

He laughed and headed towards the door. 'That's what you say now. You'll be begging to see me soon enough.' Then he left.

'What an arsehole,' Ash growled.

I agreed, to some extent.

40

ASHLEY

An aching back drew me from a haunted sleep. Unfurling stiffened limbs, I remembered it was Monday. *How in God's name was I going to front up to Dusty's after what we'd done?*

It was an effort to walk those few steps to the bathroom. My reflection in the mirror disturbed me: hair a rat's nest, eyes bloodshot, cheeks lined with crusty grazes. I needed caffeine—and lots of it.

After staring into my third mug of coffee, I decided on a change of scenery. Throwing on running gear, I ventured outside and jogged to the park. To unleash nervous energy in a much safer way than smashing glassware or punching walls—as well as purging the knowledge that I had aided in someone's death, someone's murder—I ran hard.

I raced along bitumen paths, through fragrant rose gardens, past buttress-rooted fig trees, and beneath a flowering arbour until —legs shaking, lungs burning—I slowed and trudged towards a Federation-style rotunda. Built as a bandstand, and now frequently used as a wedding venue, I found it vacant and flopped onto a step to catch my breath.

Did I feel better? I was no longer agitated—exercise had taken care of that—yet with remorse still suffocating me, I wondered if I would ever find release.

A breeze picked up, causing leaves to drift from branches and twirl in the air, along with discarded food wrappers. A page from a newspaper danced past, catching on thorny stems in a rose bush beside the rotunda steps. I fed my hand through the balustrade to tug it free and cringed at the image on the front page of the morning paper. Above the headshot, in large bold type, were the words *SLADE SLAYED*.

Was this how it would be? Reminders leaping out at odd times, poking invisible fingers in my face, and screaming MURDERER. How was I to survive a guilt-ridden existence? How was I to even live with myself?

And then I read the small print. *Paedophile ... drug dealer ... victims celebrate ... justice served.*

I considered all those saved from hurt because Slade was dead. Had what Bryden said the other night been the truth? Had we done a good thing by ridding the world of such a man? The weight on my shoulders lessened as a sense of validation formed, and clinging to the notion we were possibly heroes, not villains, I jogged leisurely back to my apartment.

I returned to work that afternoon and discovered the nightclub abuzz with theories concerning Slade's death. Joining in to appear interested, I removed myself whenever the discussion delved into ascertaining the killer's identity.

Over the next fortnight, I kept myself busy at Dusty's and occupied my time at home binge-eating and watching videos. Sleep did not come easily without medication, and a cocktail of alcohol and Benadryl was my substance of choice. Cam hadn't returned any of my missed phone calls, and Bryden had made no further contact. We were obviously trying to deal with things in our own way.

One lunch time, my feet led me through the arched doorway of a historic city church. Quiet and classical, the hallowed ambience was seen in the gothic architecture and heard in the sound of my footsteps bouncing off high sandstone walls. Feeling very much a sinner, I sat alongside a pile of hymnbooks on a timber pew and eyed my surroundings.

A stained glass window nearby showed Jesus, robed in white, and a woman with her arms wrapped around his legs, tears dripping from her eyes. Who was she? Mary Magdalene? Mary his mother? The woman caught in adultery? Whoever she was, her action touched my soul. I closed my eyes, breathed in smells both old and new, and opened up to the only one I could trust with my guilt.

My confession tumbled out in a mess of words and tears, and I experienced relief in sharing my pain with someone other than Cam and Bryden. Rather than receiving a Godly rebuke, strange warmth flooded over me. It was like being enveloped by a blanket of love.

A noise burst this heavenly bubble.

I twisted around and gasped. Jesus was sitting in the pew right behind me.

'Hello,' he said, his full lips forming a smile.

I took a second look at the bearded young man with soft brown eyes and shoulder length hair, and noticed his loose white shirt, blue jeans, and rubber thongs.

'The name's Andy.' He held out a hand.

My fingers trembled as I shook it. 'You scared the crap out of me. I thought you were—'

'I know,' he interrupted, with a shrug. 'It happens a lot. But I can assure you, I am definitely not the Son of God. Son of Barry, actually.' He laughed, and I liked the easy tone of it. 'Are you okay? I heard you ... you know ...'

I jolted. *Heard me?* What did he hear?

'Don't worry, crying's quite the norm in a place like this,' he said, offering up a box of Kleenex. 'I come here often. It does one's heart good to be in God's presence.'

I tugged a wad of tissues from the box and blew my nose.

He laid a hand on my shoulder and I didn't flinch. His touch was gentle and reassuring. 'You want to grab a coffee? My shout. There's an awesome cafe near here.'

I frowned. 'You're not the minister, are you? I'm not religious.'

'Hell, no. Just an average guy with a sneaking suspicion that someone, or something, greater is out there who doesn't mind giving a helping hand when needed.'

I liked this Andy. I accepted his offer of a free coffee, and we chatted for ages, making me so late that I skipped going back to work.

We ended up meeting regularly to discuss the meaning of life and our purpose in it and even attended several Sunday church services together. This led to us dating. Though we became close, I never told Andy about Slade Delaney or the part I played in his murder. I had no need. God had forgiven me.

Three months later, we stunned everyone by ditching our jobs and eloping to tropical North Queensland. My new life—far away from destructive memories and influences—had begun.

41

***

CAMPBELL

On the Monday after the horrors, I wheeled the cash tins out of the bank strong room and stopped to loosen my tie, the constriction around my neck adding to my physical discomfort due to lack of sleep and a head swirling with conflicting emotions. The stark news of the nightclub murder filled every conversation I overheard, and the stuffy air—heavy with shock—set my nerves on edge. I patted sweat from my forehead with the end of my tie and jumped when my name was yelled.

The manager blocked my path. Beady eyes peered over thick-rimmed glasses. 'Don't tell me you've turned up to this prestigious banking establishment partly toasted?'

'No, Mr Laycock. Could be the beginning of a cold, sir,' I lied.

He bent close, his mouth against my ear, his halitosis as stomach-churning as ever. 'That's bullshit, boy. Get your pickled arse out of my branch and piss off home.'

I offered no protest. I willingly handed over my keys and exited the building just before the doors opened for the start of trading.

Glad to be released from the confines of the bank, I headed straight for the bus stop. Passing the newsagent, I stumbled when I saw the day's lead story clearly displayed. *'Slade Delaney Dead'*. Startled, I caught the first bus to arrive. Sitting on my own, without distraction, I pondered Bryden's idea of taking time off work.

I could go away ... but where? Where would I find a suitable hideout? In the mountains ... at the beach ... in another state ... another city ... or maybe some dying country town where no one would think to come looking for me. Nothing seemed right. I felt like a hare chased by wild dogs, zigzagging across a field not knowing which direction to take.

As the bus approached Spring Hill, close to the city, I sighted a painted sign that spoke to my heart. Alighting at the next stop, I found the Buddhist meditation centre. Peace, wherever I could briefly find it, might be in there.

Exotic incense smells reached my nostrils as I inched my way through the large wooden doors. As I was led down a long hallway, the heady aroma of sandalwood was strong yet calming. I spent three hours sitting cross-legged on a mat with the only sounds being the occasional high-pitched tinkle of finger cymbals and the resonating tone of a gong drifting in from some other area. Yet my time there was not meditative, it was simply an escape from reality.

The following day, I made a second attempt to return to work. But when two police officers entered the bank and approached my section of the counter, I began to panic.

They removed their caps, tucked them under their arms and deposited a pile of papers in front of me.

'Good morning. Constable Jackson and I would like to ...'

The blood pounding in my ears muffled his words. Gripping the edge of the counter, I watched his lips move while a bead of perspiration trickled down my face.

'Excuse me!' the voice commanded, slicing through my fear.

I blinked. 'Sorry?'

The constable gave a sigh. 'I said, we'd like to open a banking account.'

The taller police officer pushed the papers further towards me. 'Today would be good,' he added sarcastically.

That moment spooked me into asking another teller to assist. Feigning sickness, I exited the bank and returned home to the relative sanctuary of my bed.

My life imploded from this point. As my drinking progressed in line with my father's example, the ensuing weeks were a blur of intoxication and sleeping off hangovers. Calls from Bryden updating me on the progress of the murder investigation didn't at first reassure my chaotic thinking. Sensing my confusion, he elaborated on what was unfolding.

From what I gleaned, Francis Bryden had his ear to the ground regarding this case. In the past he'd followed the covert legal proceedings concerning Slade's predatory sexual behaviour and was now keen to see where the investigations would lead. He revealed to Bryden that out of court settlements procured by notorious public defenders—Laboni and Piper—had saved Slade from serious prosecution but had inflamed the ire of true justice seekers. This, as well as the interest shown by many underworld figures in Slade's financial affairs, suggested his killing was due to payback.

I had some knowledge of this as it had also caught media attention, with new facts and rumours being reported daily by various news outlets.

'The longer time rolls out, the better it will be for us,' Bryden remarked.

Days turned into weeks, and weeks turned into months. With

additional claims of sexual assault coming to light, and the media transforming the shocking killing into a more complex and sordid case, public sympathy turned against the once-loved celebrity. Whether this collective apathy led to police investigations not being meticulously carried out, we'll probably never know. But as time clicked by, the truer Bryden's prophetic words became.

Even so, my paranoia continued until my inattention and level of absenteeism ended my banking career. I then moved into factory work where repetitive processes were a respite for my troubled mind. I cold-shouldered my family and once again distanced myself from any friendship with Ashley and Bryden. Fully aware our bond of secrecy would keep us linked to one another, I no longer desired to nurture the relationships. Ash running off with some guy and getting married up north was barely a blip on my radar. Though I hoped in doing this, she'd find the peace that I too craved.

My initial foray into Buddhism stirred me to search out mindful practices and I became a student of Tai Chi and alternative therapies of healing. I soon found myself in groups chanting meditation mantras, practising yoga, and using laughter therapy, each experience adding a little more resilience to a terrible secret that would ultimately be judged.

III

CRASH AND BURN

42

ASHLEY

1993

Body parts littered the shallow seabed: bleached skeleton fingers, dull green brains, hair dancing wraithlike from sandy scalps. Snorkelling over a coral reef affected by global warming, I dwelt on how perfectly it symbolised the state of my marriage—colourless, dying. When the blue, crinkled lips of a giant clam parted in a fleshy, silent scream, I felt like joining in.

It turned out that Andy and I were too dissimilar. Our life at Airlie Beach consisted of him bumming around, painting landscapes, and attempting to sell his artwork at local markets, and me working six days a week for a travel agency bringing in a regular wage to pay for rent and food and basic living. He seemed to have hardly a care in the world—trusting in God to meet our needs—while I worried about the bills, panicked about the future, and fretted about the past. Peace of mind had been brief and absolution temporary, with guilt becoming a burden I couldn't shake no matter how many prayers I uttered. Unable to share the truth with Andy—for obvious reasons—I retreated into myself, with work as my only respite.

That day in May, I was sampling a reef tour offered by a new company seeking recommendations. Earlier, I had mentioned I'd give the tour four stars if they dropped me off on a deserted island and left me there for a month. They assumed I was joking, but I was deadly serious. Now, flipping onto my back to loosen my mask and ease the headache building from the tight rubber seal, the snorkel suddenly dipped beneath the waves and I inhaled seawater. Choking, I righted and trod water to clear my lungs while several swimmers, oblivious to my plight, flippered past, their black neoprene backsides and tubes of plastic bobbing above the ripples. I finally coughed up a glob, refitted my mask, and ducked below the waterline.

Drawn to a shoal lit by sunlight, I discovered coral in every colour of the rainbow. A clown fish playing catch-me-if-you-can with a disc-shaped butterfly fish darted between the tentacles of pink anemone. I followed them as they frolicked in and out of swaying purple seagrass and red ferns growing from brain coral like an Indian chief's headdress. It was magic. I wished I could remain here forever—a mermaid with no responsibilities, and no remorse to darken her thoughts.

Days later, I was forced over the edge and prompted to end a relationship I believed had only been a means to an escape.

When Jonathan Clay first strutted into the agency office, I was so aghast at his resemblance to Bryden that I almost booked a flight to Kathmandu for an elderly couple rather than a bus trip to Kakadu. This new team member's appearance and cocky attitude disturbed me, and I avoided him as best I could.

Sensing my coldness over the ensuing week, Jonathan

cornered me at the pub frequented by staff after work on Fridays and confronted me about my snobbish behaviour. He accused me of seeing him as a threat, afraid he might steal my clients away. Annoyed by the absurdity of this assumption—and being at my lowest ebb—I told him if he thought so highly of his abilities, he should go fuck himself. His shove sent me crashing against a table, upsetting the silverware, and jarring my back. I lost my temper, picked up a fork and stabbed him in the arm. Consequently, I was relieved of my position with the agency.

Informing Andy I was finished with Arlie Beach, I also declared I was finished with our marriage. He didn't try to persuade me to stay or run after me once I'd left. Apparently, he'd already disengaged from our holy union and was happy to follow the heavenly winds of change.

Ashamed of how my life had transpired, I didn't return to Brisbane but took a diversion to Hervey Bay where I found employment with a Whale Watching Tour company.

43

___

CAMPBELL

Tina was my last client for the evening, a slight, well-tanned girl with long, brown hair twisted into a bun and held in place by a bamboo chopstick. While she took her place on the massage table, I slipped a CD into the player, chosen to help restore harmony and aid relaxation. As the rich deep sounds created by Tibetan singing bowls drifted around the room, I lit two lemongrass incense sticks and waved the citrus smelling smoke towards her to ease anxiety and alleviate stress. Asking Tina to roll onto her stomach, I then dripped sweet almond oil onto her toned calves which fit easily into the palms of my hands as I worked my magic. Later would come the massaging of her scalp while listening to her moans of delight as the tension released its hold on her body. For a finishing touch, I would caress her earlobes, which always saw her leaving with a smile.

More mind-numbing jobs had replaced my factory work— labouring in a worm farm, driving a council bus, and at one point selling flowers on a city street corner— until this restlessness, and an inner search for peace, led me into therapeutic massage. Utilising these new skills at a health centre frequented by university students, the quiet rhythm and aroma of fragrant oils often enabled psych graduates to openly share their intellectual philosophy. I quickly countered their thoughts with my own studies of astrology, Reiki, and Taoist thinking.

There were side benefits to this casual work. The conversations, the philosophy and the drinking of herbal teas instilled in me a gentle nature appreciated by women, such as Tina. In the past, hanging out with Bryden provided opportunities for me—struggling with shyness—to break into situations I normally wouldn't get involved in. Now, with a better sense of self-worth, and a realisation that my sensitivity had a place in this world, I was a more confident person.

However, it did little to mask the ache that dwelled within from what had transpired that rainy night in the alleyway. My mind found a strength to resolve the conflict, but not my heart. I discovered, soon enough, that hurt, regret and guilt are time travellers.

A recurring nightmare would arrive on its own schedule and leave me unsettled for a day or two: me travelling on a tram; Slade engaging me in banter with both of us laughing and joking; him standing too close. Next, the scene would change to Slade lying on the tracks and me screaming for the tram to stop. I wake when the tram's iron wheels crush his skull and sever his head.

And then there was Bryden. As much as I attempted to lessen contact with him, he had a knack of appearing without warning and then disappearing just as quickly for lengthy periods. His conversation naturally gravitated to 'the case' and where it had been drifting. Each visit left me edgy with fresh revelations and the knowledge that evil lurked in areas society trusted. Recoiling from these meetings, I would immerse myself in burning incense and caressing the bodies of strangers.

His last meet-up revealed a disturbing story. After mentioning he'd secured a job in a music store and was selling hi-fi gear to 'toffee-nosed deadbeats', he'd drifted into talk about his grandfather who still keenly followed the Slade Delaney case. Bryden suspected this was due to Francis Bryden—one of several men of influence and stature Slade had befriended—ensuring his private matters remained confidential.

Bryden went on to share his belief that the cocaine habits of many members of the legal fraternity would startle the heaviest of users, and that a good number of Judges in the High Courts—and by extension politicians—were associated with paedophile rings. This prompted Bryden to question Francis's own involvement in 'the fraternity'.

He also speculated that Slade had been a cog in the wheel of this activity, hence the slow response of the investigators and the persistent legal manoeuvrings to delay the coroner's report. Yet more sinister was his idea that a network of henchmen from the police force stood guard over all this.

Bryden's revelation of conspiracy was truly startling.

'Who do we trust? Who do we turn to for justice?' he offered. 'Cam, we did no more than chop one of the heads off this beast.' Then, as a parting thought, he'd added a quote. '*All of us growl like bears and moan sadly like doves. We hope for justice, but there is none. For salvation, but it is far from us.*'

That afternoon, as I waited in the airport departure lounge on the way to a temp job two hours from Brisbane, I pondered his theories. Reaching down beside my chair, I unclipped the small lock of my carry-on luggage and removed a folded paper bag. From habit, I unfurled it, tipped it sideways, and shook out the contents. Once again, I watched with a mixture of excitement and revulsion as three burnt fragments of fabric slid into my hand. One bore a dull gold glint.

44

―――

ASHLEY

1996

A blackboard chalked with the words *Wayne & Stephanie* inside a love heart informed me that I had taken the correct path through Brisbane's City Botanic Gardens.

It had been three years since I'd seen Stevie when she'd visited me at Airlie Beach. There I was regretting my decision to marry and bagging the whole idea of love, and she was buzzing with a new relationship. I was floored when she told me she was going out with Windy Winslow—or Wayne, as he preferred, now he was an adult and a successful structural engineer. I couldn't believe that after all her travels, and all her liaisons, she'd fallen head over hills with a boy from school. In the end, each had found their soul mate, and I was delighted for them. Maybe there was such a thing as true love.

Yet, I'd deliberated for weeks before accepting the wedding invitation. The thought of meeting up with old school friends was a little terrifying. My life filled with disappointment and drama led me to fear the small talk required at such an event, and the possibility of running into Bryden or Cam who I hadn't had contact with since heading north with Andy.

I soon rounded a lily pond where I found rows of white chairs adorned with large purple-ribboned bows and, in front of a massive weeping willow, a lace-covered table. Careful not to sink my stiletto heels into the manicured lawn, I stepped closer, searching the clumps of wedding guests dotting the lawn for recognisable faces. I spotted Wayne standing in the shade with two unfamiliar young men—work mates or relatives—and Stevie's mother and brother helping some oldies find a seat in the front row of chairs. People around my age chatted with one another but no one turned and signalled me over, so rather than interrupt their conversation, I took in the spectacular view of city skyscrapers rising above the treeline.

A gust of wind whipped the skirt of my yellow chiffon cocktail dress into a frenzy, and my struggling to keep my satin undies out of view caused a shoe heel to imbed itself in the ground. Attempting to tug it free, the heel snapped clean off. I stumbled and would have landed ungraciously on the grass if it weren't for a helping hand—or should I say a helping backside. Falling forward, I grabbed onto whatever was in reach, which happened to be a man's bum. He spun around and caught me in his arms, saving us both from tumbling.

Blue eyes stared down at me from a tanned complexion. 'Ashley,' he grunted. His fair hair was long, resting on his shoulders, and he had a neatly trimmed beard that suited him.

'Cam,' I squawked.

A shapely girl with glistening olive skin appeared at his side, a large flower pinned in her dark curly tresses. She fed her arm through his, holding onto him in a clear manner of possession.

I opened my mouth, but Shania Twain's 'From This Moment On' drowned out my comment. Resembling a game of musical chairs, guests scrambled for seats as a purple entourage of bridesmaids sashayed down the path.

After dithering around, I chose a seat across the aisle from Cam and his 'plus one'. Peering over my shoulder to witness the bride's entrance, I saw my stiletto heel still stuck in the lawn like a white golf tee waiting for its ball. I would have retrieved it except Stevie appeared on the arm of her father, the strapless, mermaid-style gown showing she still had a figure that could turn every male head on the planet.

Halfway through the ceremony, movement to my far right indicated a late arrival. My eyes widened as I sighted the person slouching beside a flowering camellia shrub.

It's funny how you morph a person you haven't seen for a while into either the biggest demon or the brightest saint. Then when you meet them again, you realise the thoughts that disturbed your dreams and invaded your waking hours were just fantasies, blown way out of proportion. In the stark light of reality, people are often a shadow of your imagining—average humans with neither horns nor halos—and you wonder why you wasted so much energy on silly pondering. This was how I felt as I studied Bryden. His expensive looking suit did little to hide his gaunt features: dark shadows under his eyes, pale skin, unshaven face, and stringy hair. All clues to a lack of wellbeing. I noticed Cam frowning as he also watched Bryden.

During the rest of the ceremony I caught Bryden fussing with his hair—styled in a kind of reverse 'mullet'—and jigging from one foot to another as if busting for a pee. This was not the Bryden I remembered. He seemed edgy, flustered. I wondered what had become of his customary bravado.

· · ·

Afterwards, while the photographer did his thing, the guests moved to the reception venue for appetisers and pre-dinner drinks. Fortunately, The Sheraton Hotel was in easy walking distance, and I didn't need to hobble on a broken heel for too long. I picked out Cam and his girl in the procession's midst, but Bryden was absent.

As soon as we entered the hotel, Stevie's younger brother cornered me. At twenty, Jason was as tedious as he was at thirteen. Having no other option, I listened to him rabbit on about his obsession with a video game called 'Resident Evil'. Though I nodded in response, I searched the crowd for a means of escape.

My gaze landed on Bryden waiting at the bar, rubbing his hands over his trousers, gnawing his bottom lip. His head jerked robotically as he scanned the room. It wasn't a hot afternoon, so when he wiped sweat from his face with a paper serviette, I presumed it was nerves he was dealing with. He sculled the drink placed before him and took a second glass with him when he exited through a side entrance.

He returned ten minutes later. Calmly swaggering into the room through the same door, I noticed his shakes and jitters had disappeared. Walking by and giving me a wink and a 'Hey Ash', his glassy eyes and heavy lids proved he'd just knocked back something stronger than alcohol. Alarm bells rang in my head. Bryden was now in control of himself.

I had a brief, polite conversation with Cam before we were invited into the ballroom to find our places at the decorated tables. Seated with some of Stevie's friends from the department store where she worked as a cosmetic consultant, I enjoyed the delicious meal and girly chitchat before the formalities got underway.

The speeches went as expected until the MC made the big mistake of asking if anyone else wished to add something. My heart kicked up a notch when Bryden stood up from his table at the back where he'd been placed with other past students from our school years—including Cam and his lady friend.

Bryden cleared his throat. 'On behalf of the fellow school students of both Stevie and Wayne, I would like to offer a hearty congratulation.' His remark was greeted with applause, so he continued. 'Who would have guessed that old Windy and the charming Stevie would one day hook up and then go the whole hog and get themselves hitched? Not me, that's for bloody sure.'

Laughter followed. Not from me, I was cautious. I had a niggling feeling things would not end well.

Bryden held up a hand to settle the giggles. 'Stevie, you've chosen a top bloke. A great sportsman, a good mate, and millionaire in the making, I hear.'

Cheers burst from the crowd, and a banging on the table in the middle of the room suggested it was seated with Wayne's work colleagues.

'Windy ... sorry, Wayne,' Bryden smirked. 'You've scored yourself one hell of a girl. Wouldn't you agree, fellas?' He nodded to those seated at his table. 'Actually, come to think of it, I think we all might have scored a taste of Stevie at one time or other.'

Only a few sniggers this time, and a couple of gasps. I glanced at the bridal table. Stevie looked far from happy.

'Johnno,' Bryden went on, 'wasn't it at Angela McCarthy's sixteenth birthday party? And Tony, correct me if I'm wrong, wasn't it in the back seat of your Valiant ... or was it the Toyota?'

Some coughing and loud murmuring followed this comment. I felt sick. Bryden was relishing being the centre of attention. *Please God, let someone stop him.*

'Russ, me old buddy,' he said, slapping the shoulder of the guy on his right, 'weren't you the lucky one to get the first touchdown in grade eight, behind the sports equipment shed?'

The sound of a chair leg scraping the tiled floor. A flash of movement from the front of the room.

'As for me,' Bryden stabbed a finger into his chest, 'the first time Stevie let me get into her—'

Wayne's fist smashing into Bryden's face halted his next words, and they both crashed to the floor.

The room erupted with shouts and screams. People rose from tables—some rushing over to watch the fight, others to break it up. Me, I just stayed where I was, gulping down mouthfuls of wine in quick succession.

45

CAMPBELL

1996

I stood apprehensively next to the red postal box, tapping the small envelope in my hands. Then, as I watched the wedding acceptance card disappear into the slot, I considered the wisdom of reuniting with old school friends at the celebrations. Solandra had convinced me we should attend Wayne and Stevie's nuptials. She was part Spanish and loved the drama of life.

We had met a few months before over a discussion about karma and how it weaves through life like a great tapestry. As our reflections led us to more intimate moments, and we agreed that our karma should be explored and savoured, she confessed her life's quest was to grab every moment and live in its immediacy. I shared a little of my serious adventures and she was enthralled by how I had been dragged along by those circumstances.

'See,' she said with excitement, 'life has set these moments for you. Your biography is written in the stars. It takes courage to ride the wave.'

I had not revealed my darkest secret. That would have sent her into raptures about destiny, past lives, and how in this life we get to be the victim if in the last we were the aggressor.

Stevie and Wayne's wedding had Solandra intrigued as to who would be there to karmically reconnect with. I knew Bryden would be attending. He had phoned unexpectedly the week before to guffaw on the idea of Stevie getting married ... and to Windy Winslow.

He had crassly commented, 'Stevie has screwed her way around the world and landed back with a guy who lived two streets from where she grew up. She could have saved herself a few kilometres.'

I could handle meeting up with Bryden. It was the possibility of seeing Ashley, and the three of us being together after so long apart, that had me anxious. Ridden with guilt and unresolved anger, would we be able to keep our secret intact?

Solandra had been correct about 'the ribbons of life' the instant Ash practically fell into my arms while we wandered the parklands before the ceremony. The Gods had orchestrated a broken shoe and there she was, a stumbling yellow flower grateful for my well-timed catch.

The wedding skipped along, and it was during the reception at The Sheraton Hotel that Bryden greeted me and introduced himself to Solandra. When he edged his way into the group I was speaking with—hand on my shoulder and arm around Solandra's waist—I could tell he was already wasted.

'Campbell Druery, you sly dog.' He paused and breathed heavily as he turned to my Spanish companion. 'My beauty, if you are with Cam, you are a deserved woman. He's a good guy, a good heart ... and a good root.'

Bryden wasn't just pissed, he was souped up on one of his

preferred uppers. Yet Solandra soaked up his bravado and smiled at his flirtations.

'Campbell is a darling and has charmed me, as gentlemen do,' she calmly retorted.

'He's a killer, darling,' Bryden responded.

My heart stopped.

'Don't be conned by the boyish face hidden under that beard. He was a raver in the bank. Women fell off desks for him.' He laughed raucously and winked at me.

My pulse regained its rhythm. Bryden's carefree demeanour was proving troublesome. It took him only forty minutes to confirm my thoughts when he rose from his chair to offer a speech during the wedding formalities.

I cringed at his willingness to goad everyone with his remarks, especially the bride and groom. His round up of Stevie's conquests —at least the ones seated in the room—was thankfully cut short when Wayne launched himself and collared Bryden. Solandra was in her element watching this curious play unfold, and her rapid patting of my leg under the table indicated she was fully engaged.

I did my usual thing of escorting Bryden out of the vicinity to ease the tension. His bloodied smile showed he enjoyed the spectacle, and his dabbing of the cut with a pocket-handkerchief was mixed with tiny grunts of pleasure.

'Geez ... don't know what all the fuss was about,' he shrugged. 'What I said was all true.'

'Windy might prefer to shag his wife tonight without those images, mate,' I whispered.

Solandra arrived and offered Bryden a glass of water. 'You have a way with words that remind people of their vulnerabilities.'

'Right you are, Sol.' Bryden already had a nickname for her. 'The truth is solely for the strong. It does not need to be defended.'

This quip from Bryden captured her imagination. 'Destiny

brings its gifts for the prepared and the under-prepared,' she nodded.

Bryden smiled knowingly. *'Watch therefore, for you know neither the day nor the hour.'*

This innocent exchange ignited something in Solandra, and in that instant, I felt our relationship melt away.

46

ASHLEY

The cutting of the wedding cake was delayed due to Wayne needing to tidy himself up. He suffered no visible injuries, yet I wasn't so sure about Bryden who'd been shuffled outside and hadn't returned. I hoped he'd done a runner, the best thing under the circumstances.

More than a little tipsy, I ditched my shoes and took a plate of cake onto a quiet balcony overlooking the park. Eating only the thick white fondant, I dropped the remains over the railing and watched it break apart as it hit the paving below.

A cough startled me, and I whirled around to discover a figure seated on a stone bench between two potted palms.

In the diffused light, Bryden didn't look too badly done over, though his bottom lip had a nasty gash and drops of blood stood out on the collar of his pale-blue shirt.

He saluted me with a slender-necked bottle. 'Been a long time, hey, Cinders.'

I cringed and shortened the distance between the sliding door and me. 'You were such a dick back there. That wasn't cool.'

He gave a shrug. 'I guess it wasn't. But wedding speeches can be as boring as cat piss. A real drag. I thought I'd liven things up a bit.'

'You don't air someone's dirty laundry at their wedding. That's cruel.'

'I was just telling some home truths.'

'Well, your timing was crap. You never did know when to stop stirring.'

'Why should I? There's no fun in toeing the line, remember?' He smiled, then winced, and touched his lip.

With the dull lighting accentuating his gaunt appearance—jutting cheekbones and hollows under the eyes—I felt emboldened to ask, 'How are you Bryden? Really.'

He took a swig of beer and placed the bottle on the floor between his feet. 'Trying to live the best I can.' He rubbed his hands on his knees. 'I own a music store now. Did you know that?'

'And how's that working out for you? You look like death. What drugs are you into these days?'

His eyes became slits. 'What's it to you?'

'How deep in are you? Are you dealing?'

I jolted as his heels snapped together and the bottle skittered across the tiling.

'Shit, Ash! I hear fuck all from you for four years and now you show concern.'

'You know what it was like. I needed to get away ... make a new life for myself.'

'And did you? Are you happy now?'

I looked away, unable to answer. Life had eased somewhat since leaving Andy but, with the failure of my marriage adding to my guilt, I wasn't settled by any means. Maybe I would never find real happiness. Never find peace.

'Well, whether you're happy or not, you're looking hot, girl. You've matured nicely, like a fine wine. Can I have a sip?'

Though hairs stood up on my arms, I stood my ground and glowered at him.

Bryden patted a place on the bench beside him. 'Let's chat about the good ol' days. The fun we got up to.'

The fun? He had to be joking. The sweetness on my tongue turned sour. 'I'd rather eat razor blades,' I snarled.

'Geez, Ash,' he whined, feigning a sulk. 'I thought you liked me.'

'That was ages ago. You don't need reminding, a lot's happened since then.'

He slapped his thigh. 'And you got married. I didn't receive an invite. I was utterly crushed.'

'No invitations. We eloped.'

'So,' he made a show of looking around, 'where is the hubby? I'd like to meet him. Compare notes and stuff.'

I gritted my teeth. 'We're divorced.'

'Holy crap, that was quick. What went wrong? Did you pick a dud? Wasn't he exciting enough for you?'

I glared back. There was no way I would admit how close he was to the truth.

'Well then, you're footloose and fancy free, like me. We could make a night of it.' He slipped a hand into his trouser pocket, removed a set of car keys, and jangled them in the air. 'Your place or mine?'

I stared at this shell of a man. It was hard to believe he once set my pulse racing with desire. Revulsion brought bile to my throat. 'You've got to be fucking kidding. You're delusional as well as pathetic. You make me want to puke.'

Leaping up and grabbing me by the shoulders before I could race away, he leered at me, those feline eyes dark, wild, and familiar. 'We're connected forever, remember?' Then he wrenched my arm up to his mouth and licked the burn scar.

I shoved him away.

'What's going on?' came a voice.

'Wouldn't you know it,' Bryden said, sitting back down as Cam stepped onto the balcony. 'The protector arrives right on cue. The knight in rusty armour comes to rescue the sullied maid.'

47

CAMPBELL

Ash looked flustered when I came upon her and Bryden tucked away on an outside balcony. I'm not sure what I interrupted, but Bryden seemed agitated by my arrival and I let his sarcastic remark slip by. Recognising his mood for baiting people, I chose not to play.

The uncomfortable silence between the three of us stretched on until it was too much for Ash, and she escaped back into the buzz of the ballroom.

Bryden raked his fingers through his hair and shrugged. 'Women!' His red-veined eyes studied me. 'They weaken men, Cam. Don't let Sol baffle you with her ceaseless cosmic bullshit. She's just trying to scramble your brain.'

He'd always carried a big spoon to do his 'shit stirring', but he also had powerful observational skills which helped him pick the right time to stir. His comment about Solandra agreed with me. I had grown tired of looking for the mysterious in every act of life. It no longer suited my need to seek peace in gentler moments—

staring at flowers, listening for undergrowth rustling during forest walks, or gazing up at brilliant blue skies.

I sat next to him and placed my hand on his shoulder. 'How are those demons?'

'Constant,' he sighed.

'What helps you keep them quiet?'

He dropped his hands between his knees and rubbed his palms together, as if trying to scrub them clean. 'A coloured pill or two. We're forever surrounded by dark forces, so you've got to be on your toes.' Then he turned his face to mine. 'I could give you some uppers? They work like a charm. Or some weed. Have you ever tried that hydroponic shit?' I shook my head. 'Don't,' he strangely counselled. 'It opens up your paranoia, and that's when you're really fucked.'

Tempted to ask if he heeded his own advice, yet fearing a rebuke, I held my tongue. Still, he launched into a rant.

'We have to fight the stupidity. The brain-dead existence that is being played out in there.' He pointed to the ballroom. 'Those sheep inside getting pissed, getting married, getting so caught up in rituals. It's all bullshit, Cam. They'll root like rabbits, multiply, pretend to listen to each other, screw their kids up with parrotlike views just like their parents ... more sheep, more rabbits. Then someone will fuck off, leaving them to deal with the mess.'

'Yep, sometimes it's hard to get off that treadmill,' I said, hoping to quell the tirade that Bryden's bitterness for life and its hypocrisies had fuelled.

'It's not treadmill stuff. It's power. Those who have it shape the lives of others, and when you have enough dim-witted, hollow-headed numbskulls complying, you have a nation of zombies.'

'Well, maybe Windy and Stevie will bonk their way free of the bondages. Or maybe bondage will be part of it for Stevie,' I smiled, attempting to make light of the conversation.

'Has anyone told you you're a dickhead?' Bryden said, grinning and pushing me off the seat.

He left the reception soon after though not before apologising to Stevie and Wayne and planting an inappropriate kiss on Stevie's lips which resulted in Wayne frogmarching him towards the door.

I offered to call him a taxi, but Bryden shook his head and said he was going in search of real food. Giving me an awkward hug and patting me on the bum, he was gone.

I'd lost track of Solandra, who was no doubt karmically re-engaging somewhere else. So, when the wedding reception wound down, I headed to the hotel we'd booked into for the night alone.

48

ASHLEY

Once Stevie and Wayne had made their departure, I left the festivities and drove to The Park Royal Hotel. Well over the alcohol limit, I was glad I only had to travel a short distance.

When I stepped out of the elevator on the fifth floor, I was surprised to find Cam waiting to get in. Turns out, he was staying in the same hotel and only a few doors up from my room. He didn't give a reason for needing to go down to reception. Actually, he didn't say much at all, not even a mention of the encounter on the balcony at The Sheraton.

'Well, see ya around,' he said coldly, getting into the lift.

Turning the key in my door, I glanced over my shoulder and caught him standing in the open elevator, glaring at me. Just because he'd had some airy, fairy spiritual awakening didn't make him any better a person than me. I knew he still carried a monkey on his back. He might get away with faking that peace and love and karmic crap with others, but I could tell by looking at him that our shared history continued to gnaw at him.

I dropped my overnight bag on the bed and headed over to the mini bar. Before I chose my first drink from the assortment of tiny bottles, there came a knock, and I opened the door. Surprised to see Cam standing there, I threw back my shoulders, steeling myself for the expected scolding for stuffing up my life even further. Instead, he calmly asked to come in for a chat and brushed past to flop into the lone armchair.

I enquired about Solandra. He said she'd shot through and had probably taken a taxi home. I didn't have the heart to tell him I'd seen her walking away from The Sheraton arm-in-arm with Bryden. My guess was they were rampantly creating mind-body connections in the Botanic Gardens, but I kept that thought to myself. Over a mix of whisky, Bacardi, and Creme de Menthe, the iciness thawed between us and we caught up on the last few years.

An hour or so later, I was drifting off and Cam said he should leave. He suggested we keep in touch and I gave him one of my business cards, telling him I'd show him a 'whale of a time' if he ever ventured up to Hervey Bay. He laughed and went back to his room.

Running the shower and undressing, I caught Cam's reflection in the bathroom mirror. I whirled around. 'How'd you get in? I locked the door after you left.'

He held up a hotel key. 'Seems I took yours by mistake.' Eying me half-naked, he added, 'Fortuitous, I reckon.' Then he unbuttoned his shirt and unzipped his trousers.

I briefly considered turfing him out. This was madness. It could totally wreck our friendship.

Back at the wedding reception—before the speech fiasco—I'd bumped into Solandra in the ladies' toilet and she'd told me she could see my aura. Curious, I asked her what it looked like. She said it was bright red, which indicated high energy, passion, and determination. Taking my hand in hers, she giggled and said that someone was going to get lucky tonight. I told her she might need more practice because it certainly wasn't going to be me, unless Brad Pitt or Matthew McConaughey walked into the celebrations. She commented that there was enough desire pulsating through me to satisfy both actors. I laughed loudly. I didn't tell her that if the opportunity did arise, I hoped I would remember what to do since I hadn't had sex in a very long time. When Bryden propositioned me on the balcony later on, I thought Solandra must have gotten her wires crossed and mistakenly picked up on his intentions.

Now, as Cam stripped and stepped into the steaming shower, beckoning me in, I believed she truly did have a gift.

49

———

CAMPBELL

I watched the number five light up and the elevator door slide open. About to enter, I stepped back when a woman exited. Long legs. Shoeless. Yellow chiffon. An enticing figure. A familiar face.

'Ash!'

She looked just as surprised. 'Cam ... what are you ... is this level five?'

'Yep,' I said, eying the over-sized key tag in her hand. 'Your room's straight across. I'm down a little way.'

She nodded. 'Great. Where are you off to?'

'Down. Reception.' No need to mention I was checking to see if Solandra had left me a message.

Ash moved aside so I could step into the lift.

I watched—my foot keeping the elevator door open—as she glided across the red oriental carpet, her hair bouncing, hips swaying, toned arms carrying her shoes and overnight bag. I was still watching when she turned her key and peered over her shoulder, catching me staring. Pressing the 'close door' button, she disappeared from view.

My heart pounded as the lift descended, and I did something that would have made Solandra proud. Destiny and karma had delivered Ashley to me, and I intended to catch the wave and ride it as far as it would go. I hit the level five button and waited to be returned. When the lift opened, I rushed out and knocked on her door.

The words came effortlessly—the Gods speaking through me. 'I know you must be tired, but I'd like to hear how you've been doing.'

Her scowl had me worried. She poked her head out through the doorway and viewed the empty hallway. 'Will Solanjee be joining us?'

I gave a groan at her mistake. 'No, *Solandra's* not here.'

We finished several small bottles from the mini bar as we sat on the bed and talked. I queried Ash on her travels. Between tears and used tissues, she opened up about the failure of her marriage and the struggles and fears she'd had since departing Brisbane following the Slade incident. We laughed through some of our shared dread of one day hearing a banging on the door and being escorted into oblivion—a scene that could still play out for us.

Ash snuggled close and rested her head on my shoulder. 'Cam, there are days when I am so scared, I can hardly breathe.'

I held her, feeling the coolness of her skin through the fabric of her dress. 'You're cold. Do you need a blanket?'

'No, just hold me tighter,' she whispered, feeding her fingers between the buttons of my shirt, and stroking my chest with her nails.

'When things don't work out, you've got to be honest and be true to yourself, and you've had the courage to do that, Ash. Now don't freak out, but sometimes God puts us in situations from which to grow.'

She pulled away. 'Don't you start throwing Bible verses at me.'

'No, I mean life often includes experiences that test where our strengths lie.'

'I don't understand,' she said, replacing her head on my shoulder.

'Well, most people pray for love, peace, romance ... whatever. But the universe doesn't just plop them into your lap and say, *Here you go. Here's some love or justice or forgiveness to help you on your way.* The angels send circumstances to draw out the compassion, mercy or whatever that you've always had. In some ways I think the whole Slade thing was about us learning good from bad, finding inner peace when churning with guilt, forgiving ourselves, and becoming better people who stand up for what is right. And you, Ash, are so full of decency and goodness.'

'I am?'

I nodded and breathed in the scent of her hair.

After a few moments of quiet, I realised Ash was falling asleep.

'I better go,' I said, peeling her from me. 'We both need to get to bed.'

We promised to catch up, and I hugged her before leaving.

Standing outside my room—still feeling Ash in my arms, smelling her perfume on my clothes—I wished I hadn't left so soon. When I struggled to unlock my door, and realised I'd taken her room key by mistake, I knew I'd been offered a second chance.

I slipped into her room, thinking she'd be curled up in bed. Instead, I discovered her in the steamy bathroom, naked and grinning—as if expecting my return. *Had she cunningly switched our keys earlier?* I didn't care. I knew I had to have her.

Ash helped me out of my clothes and I eagerly followed her into the hot shower. As she turned to adjust the heat, I wrapped my arms around her and pressed our bodies together.

The warm water rained down, spilling over my shoulders,

cascading over her breasts. It created reservoirs where our skin met and slid through crevices where it did not. Ash squirmed against me, and I gritted my teeth, fighting for control, not wanting this moment to rush to its end. My hands roamed over her, my fingers revisiting the places of my dreams. Brushing hair away from the back of her neck, my mouth found the inked heart and devoured it. Ash bucked and shuddered and moaned. Entwined and lost in riding the wave, the world could have stopped spinning and I wouldn't have given a shit. In that instant, I was complete.

In the quietest of voices I murmured, 'I love you.'

It was immediate—the stiffening of her body, the lifting of her head, the intake of air. With those words, I had broken Ash from her ecstasy and back to reality. My pulse skidded to a stop. *Had my nirvana come to an end?*

Twisting around, she stared up, blinking water from her eyes. Then she kissed me.

50
____

ASHLEY

Cam lay on his side away from me, the coverlet crumpled at his feet. Sex with him had been good—very good. Our bodies had easily acquainted themselves with one other, and we'd taken turns at being the conductor of a physical song borne of desperate passion. Now sated, he snored gently while I was too hyped up to sleep.

In the soft dawn light, my fingers followed Cam's contours—not touching, but hovering over each dip and rise. The short, awkward boy, and then lanky youth, had transformed into a tall, broad-shouldered, athletic man. Not stocky like a footballer, more lithe like a swimmer. My eyes were drawn to a small shadow on the calf of his left leg: a dent, an old wound I'd forgotten.

Sometime back in primary school, Bryden had thrown a dart at Cam. It had embedded in his leg and the injury had gotten infected and taken ages to heal. I glanced at my scarred arm. Bryden had left his mark on both of us—visible and unseen—results of his wild and reckless behaviour. He would never hurt us again. We were now made of much stronger stuff. I bent and brushed my lips over Cam's scar. Together we would prove a powerful force.

I slipped from the bed and tiptoed to the bathroom. Collecting our strewn clothing from the floor, I shook Cam's trousers free of crumples and noticed something slip from a pocket. I picked it up. It was a small envelope, like one used for a gift card. On the front was written: *'To Wayne & Stephanie'*. I flipped it over. Scribbled on the back in a different hand, and with a different pen, was: *'Hey Cambo, here's some of that quality shit I was telling you about.'* It was signed with a large letter *'B'*. Inside, I found a handful of coloured pills, and it wasn't difficult to guess who'd passed them on. I flushed the pills down the toilet and scrunched the envelope up, dropping it into the rubbish bin.

My hands trembled as I dressed. *How could Cam get caught up in this crap?* I'd been wrong about him. He was going to end up just as screwed as Bryden. I couldn't deal with this. I needed someone in my life with direction and strength. Not someone who constantly required dragging up from the gutter. *Shit!*

I gathered my belongings. Before I could sneak from the hotel room, Cam woke.

'Screw you!' I yelled, throwing my broken shoe at him.

He deflected the white missile and leapt from the bed with a pitiful look of shock on his face.

'Ash! What the hell's the matter? What's happened?'

I shrugged off the hand that gripped my shoulder. 'It was a mistake. You're a friggin' loser, Cam. I thought you'd changed, but no … you're still as weak as piss.'

He rubbed his eyes. 'What are you talking about? What have I done?'

I shoved him aside and grabbed the door handle. 'Why don't you grow some balls and stop being led by your nose!'

I tugged the door open and Cam yelped as it snagged his foot.

Rushing across the hall, I found the lift doors ajar. Without glancing back, I jumped in, hoping Cam wasn't following. For one thing, I may have slapped him stupid. Another, his being naked could have caused a stir if anyone popped their head out of their room to see what the ruckus was about.

'You mad bitch!' I heard as the door slid shut.

Tears streamed. The hope of a bright future as a united force crumbled along with my heart.

51

CAMPBELL

Ashley's despicable walk out at The Park Royal Hotel had broken something in me. After she'd gone, I'd swigged the contents of four small bottles from the room's mini bar, crashed onto the bed, and slept like a dead man. This manner of sedation became the only way I could cope. Even meditation and rituals involving incense and singing bowls could not ease the gut-wrenching pain of Ash's rejection, and after three weeks of turmoil, my brain totally snapped.

As a child, Bryden idolised a comic book hero, The Shadow. When mucking around with me, he would often quote the known catchphrase, *'What evil lurks in the heart of men? The Shadow knows.'* So, deferring to my dark side, which I never really knew existed, I decided to show Ash the capabilities of my shadow. Planning childish actions that I would later regret and wish could be erased from history with a click of my fingers, I used the information from Ash's business card to track her down in Hervey Bay.

Her tour company office was easily found, and I sat in wait, eating fish and chips, and reading the local rag. When she appeared, finished for the day, I discreetly followed her home to a block of three flats in Torquay. I rented a caravan a few blocks away and set about observing her comings and goings as she worked on the tour boats around the bay.

It started innocently enough. One morning, I punctured a rear tyre of her car and watched her exasperation as she kicked the deflated rubber and wildly looked for other means of transport to travel to work.

The next day, after she'd set off, I clambered underneath her flat and pinpointed the living area. Dressed in overalls and looking like I was doing a little maintenance on the property, I hoped not to draw attention to my schoolboy prank. Having purchased a large flathead, some timber, and a few nails, I hammered the dead fish onto the crossbeams under her floorboards. Once the extra boards were nailed in place—sealing the fish in—I knew time would take care of the rest, with the odour from the rotting flesh being nearly impossible to locate.

I followed this by stealing her mail and, on another occasion, turning off the power to her flat and letting the heat of the day do its work on her defrosting foodstuffs. These immature acts of mischief eased the hate that had festered inside me since Stevie and Wayne's wedding.

Solandra, with her breezy approach to all things, slid out of my life less dramatically than Ash a few days after the nuptials.

'We've drunk from the cup and now it's empty ... our journey and destiny call us in other directions,' she'd said with a gentle kiss and a wave goodbye.

Discovering Bryden had humped Solandra in the Botanic Gardens the night of the wedding, gave me more disdain for the hurt that accompanied Ash, Bryden and me whenever we got together. Like a boy playing with a wing-plucked fly, I enjoyed the torment unleashed on Ash. Her tears meant nothing to me. Her frustration in dealing with her daily dilemmas was reward enough for my efforts.

After a week, and realising I only had a day left of my secret holiday, I planted the most devilish of pranks. In a large envelope, I enclosed a message written via cut out letters from a newspaper, just like in a classic television crime drama. *'WE'RE COMING BITCH. BLOOD FOR BLOOD'*. I slipped it under her door, ready for her return from work.

Driving away from the sun-drenched and sleepy bay that afternoon, I was content knowing that she would have to deal with the 'bogie-man' and possibly run back into the arms of the one guy who could hurt her the most.

52

ASHLEY

Bryden's music store was bigger than I'd imagined. Jam-packed with racks of records, cassette tapes, and CDs, it also sold a wide choice of Hi Fi equipment and musical instruments. A busy Saturday, people jostled for room, and some sang along with the Backstreet Boys as their hit song pumped from ceiling speakers.

The last thing I wanted was to seek Bryden out, but who else could I turn to? Not Cam—he was definitely not an option. Not the police. So that left Bryden. The only person who might be able to shed light on the weird happenings of the recent week that had frightened me so much I'd thrown in my job with the tour company and gotten the hell out of Hervey Bay. Now, here I was, my pulse racing and my hands trembling as I waited to speak with one of the three attractive female assistants and ask to see Bryden.

A cheery blonde informed me he was unavailable at present. I told her it was urgent that I see him and gave her my name. A moment later, she ushered me into a room furnished with—among other things—a leather chesterfield, a state-of-the-art stereo system, and a Foosball table. The herbaceous and musky odour of weed was thick in the air.

I thought I was alone until a head popped up from behind a timber desk littered with paperwork and stacks of folders. 'What are you doing here?' Bryden sneered, his face showing even more strain than the last time I'd seen him.

My stomach twisted at the sight of him, but I pressed on. 'I need to talk with you.'

He crossed his arms. 'About what?'

I closed the door, then changed my mind, and opened it a crack for ease of escape if needed. 'I'm being stalked ... and threatened.'

'Threatened? By who?'

I lowered my voice. 'I think it has to do with Slade.'

The scowl slipped away, and he hopped up, motioning me to sit on the sofa. Wheeling an office chair out from behind the desk, he sat across from me. 'Tell me,' he said, leaning forward with a distinct interest.

I slid a stash of music magazines out from under my backside and related the events of the past week. I told him about the deflating of my car tyres, the mail going missing, the strange feeling that someone was watching me, and the horrid planting of a dead fish under the floorboards of my apartment.

'A neighbour told me she saw a maintenance man working under the house and thought the landlord had sent him. Then I received a note threatening payback. It said, *Blood for blood.* Surely it has something do with Slade. Someone must know I was involved in his death. What about you? Have you had any threats?'

He rested back—his hands meeting at chest height, fingers clasping—and closed his eyes. Silence.

Muffled music drifted through the door gap. As I waited for Bryden to say something—anything—I recognised 'Wannabe' by the Spice Girls. Answering their lyrical question, what I wanted, what I really, really wanted was for Bryden to bloody well open his eyes and tell me the same thing had happened to him!

I was about to shake him out of his dissociative state when his eyelids fluttered. Staring back, he shook his head.

My fear spiked. 'You're saying you haven't been targeted like me?'

He shrugged. 'Nope, I haven't. Not like that.'

I gripped the armrest of the sofa, my nails biting into the upholstery. 'Why just me, then? I wasn't the only one there, Bryden. I didn't finish Slade off. Why aren't they threatening you, for God's sake?' My mind shifted. 'You sick bastard! You were the one stalking me.'

I lunged for him.

Bryden gripped my arms by the wrists and thrust me back onto the sofa. 'Stop it Ash! It wasn't me. I didn't do any of that shit.' He slumped into the office chair and tucked his hair behind his ears. 'I haven't been threatened, but I suspect I'm being watched all the same. Sometimes I hear footsteps following me. Yet when I look around, there's nobody there. Then there's the odd clicking sounds on my phone.'

'You're being bugged?' I peered at the telephone quietly lying on top of a pile of papers. It looked harmless enough.

'I now only use pay phones for personal calls. Strangers watch me. They don't approach, just watch ... like spooks. I'll be in a shop, or walking down a street, or on the train. When I catch them staring, they quickly turn away or return to reading their book or something. It's fuckin' eerie.'

'Who are they? The police? People from the club scene?'

Bryden pushed up from his chair and moved to a filing cabinet. Tugging open a drawer, he removed a large brown envelope.

'What's this?' I asked, as he handed it to me.

'Open it,' he said, pacing back and forth.

I raised the flap and hoped it didn't contain little coloured pills, or zip-lock bags bulging with white powder. Peeking inside, I saw copious amounts of scrap paper. I tipped the envelope and watched as pages ripped from a spiral notebook, newspaper clippings, and photographs fell into my lap. A quick examination revealed pages covered in scribbled notes and diagrams, and clippings on police corruption, unscrupulous judges, and paedophile rings in political circles.

I frowned. 'I don't get it.'

He lifted a photo from the pile and held it up. 'I'm pretty sure he's behind it.'

My eyes flicked over the black and white snap. 'Your grandfather?'

He nodded and the intensity in his gaze showed he was serious.

'You believe he's caught up in this?'

'I'd bet my life on it. I reckon the sanctimonious bastard has more than his finger in the pie. He's had too keen an interest in the Delaney case for it to be a healthy one. My guess is he, along with plenty of others, hopes it remains a cold case. If Francis suspects my involvement in Delaney's death, he's not letting on to me or the cops.' He moved his fist in a circle. 'Stir a pot and shit rises to the surface. He doesn't want that to happen. None of his legal fraternity do.'

He flopped down beside me, and I instantly tilted my body away from his nearness. 'That's why I'm being followed,' he said. 'They're keeping a close eye on me. For the time being, I'm not doing anything to upset their apple cart.'

'The time being?'

He stared for a long time before speaking. 'Can you keep a secret?'

I raised my eyebrows. 'Do I honestly need to answer that?'

'Guess not. Francis was questioned regarding the Anton Wilkes killing.'

My jaw dropped. *Anton Wilkes.* Everyone knew of the journalist's murder. It had made national headlines. Two years ago, after writing articles on paedophile judges and exposing judicial bribery, his body was discovered in bushland north of Sydney. He'd been beaten, tied up, and shot in the back of the head. A small lead weight from a vintage set of scales was found wedged in his throat, and it was labelled a 'justice' killing. Nobody had been charged with his murder.

'You're kidding me,' I gasped.

'The questioning didn't go anywhere, but it sure rattled the old man. I'm conducting my own investigations, and I reckon one day I'll have enough evidence to lead the cops straight to Francis's fuckin' front door.'

Was this all true? Or was it just another of Bryden's conspiracy theories? 'Do you think Francis arranged someone to scare me because of my connection to you?'

'Sure. It's a power thing.' Bryden rubbed his hands together. 'A game. I am a pawn and by association, so are you ... and Cam. Has he had any trouble?'

I studied my hands. 'Er ... we don't keep in touch.'

'Really? I could have sworn I witnessed some sexual tension between you two at Stevie and Windy's wedding.'

I winced. 'What? Don't be stupid. You must have seen Cam since then. You would know if he's had trouble.'

'Nope, haven't seen him.'

Yeah, right. What about the drug dealing? I was on the verge of challenging Bryden about this when the door opened wide.

'C'mon Barbie, let's go party,' flooded in, accompanied by a buxom blonde in a tight, black Van Halen T-shirt.

'Bry, honey,' she crooned through glossed lips, 'you're needed out here. Some guy's asking about an order for a Fender Stratocaster and we can't find any record of it.'

'Give me a minute,' he said, waving her away.

I jerked when the door slammed shut and Bryden laid a hand on my knee. 'Be careful, Ash. Don't do anything foolish.'

I brushed his hand away. 'Like what?'

'I don't know.' His gaze darted to the door. 'Were you followed?'

Shit! I hadn't considered that. 'Not that I'm aware of.'

'Where are you staying?'

'With my parents ... until I work out my next move.'

'Tasmania.'

'What?'

'Go to Tassie,' he commanded, stuffing the pieces of paper back into the envelope. 'There's bugger all down there. Head into the wilderness. Lie low. No one will find you there.'

Then he jumped to his feet and spread his arms wide. '*He found him in a desert land, and in the howling waste of a wilderness. He encircled him, He cared for him, He guarded him as the pupil of His eye.*'

Pulling me up from the sofa, he pushed me towards the door. 'Send me a postcard and I'll be there in a blink. We could disappear like a pair of Tasmanian tigers and never be heard from again.'

The idea of living the life of a fugitive in the wild freaked me out. I wouldn't be going to Tassie, and I certainly wouldn't be sending Bryden an invitation to join me, wherever I ended up.

53

CAMPBELL

For all the self-development workshops I'd participated in, there still comes a strange and deep satisfaction from having the upper hand: the taste, the sense of control. For most of my life, I had been at the mercy of circumstance, powerless over events that swamped me. But now at a local Coffee Club, with Bryden having sought me out with news that Ashley was back home after being spooked by threats, something empowering filled a space within my being.

I showed my concern—hands cupping my face, mouth slightly agape. Inwardly though, I felt a mix of shame about what I'd childishly done to Ashley, and a sense of euphoria as I watched Bryden flitting between each thought, trying to piece together his theories of why this manipulation was in play.

'The sick bastards put fish heads under her house,' he said, shaking his head.

I copied his gesture. 'The bastards.'

'What about you? You okay?'

'I'm good. No shit like that happening to me ... yet,' I grimaced and took a sip of my cappuccino. 'So, what are you thinking?'

'Buggered if I know. Maybe they're just keeping us on our toes, keeping us running.'

I imagined Bryden's mind whirling, searching for answers, as he wrapped his hands around his mug and gently blew across the coffee, separating wafts of rising steam.

In the past I'd listened to his suspicions regarding his grandfather and the coke-fuelled courtrooms; judges handing out justice while their after parties were rife with the same ill-gotten gains that had sent others to prison. 'They're untouchable,' Bryden would claim.

He eyed me, unblinking. 'What would you say if I told you Francis was involved in the murder of Anton Wilkes?'

I stared back. This was a big call. Every man and his dog had heard about Anton Wilkes's death. As far as I was aware, his murderer—or murderers—had not been found. 'What do you mean? What do you know?'

'Not a great lot. I'm still working on it. I assure you, though, one day Francis will get his comeuppance.'

'So what do we do now?' I said, trying to snap Bryden out of his crazed thoughts.

'Ash is nicking off to Tasmania to lie low, keep safe.'

I bit my tongue with the shock of this news. My God, what had I done? 'But, if they tracked her down at Hervey Bay, couldn't they just as easily find her there?' I queried, playing along.

'It depends on how clever she is.' Bryden grinned. 'She's not that clever though, hey, mate?'

In that moment I couldn't see the humour.

'She wants me to join her in the Tassie wilderness somewhere,' he added, 'once she's settled.'

That hurt. I'd initially wanted Ash to run to Bryden for consolation, an opportunity for him to give her a little more sting.

But the idea of them hiding away together rattled me to the point that I finally confessed to my stupid pranks on Ashley.

'That was you?' Bryden's shock turned into admiration, and he bowed before me. 'I've taught you well, grasshopper.'

'You can't tell her,' I urged.

'Why would I? Keep her running scared, I say.'

Then he clapped me on the back and laughed until his eyes watered.

54

ASHLEY

1996

I didn't run off to Tasmania. I travelled west to Cunnamulla, 750 kilometres out from Brisbane, as far removed from the inner-city chaos as one could get. This country town—known for its wool production, and pig and kangaroo hunting—was also a tourist destination for those wanting to experience life 'beyond the black stump'. A pretty good place to hide out, by my account.

Rob and Stella Palmer owned Kilberry Homestead, a bed-and-breakfast situated on a former sheep station. They wished to expand their tourist appeal and, though I was under-qualified, I applied for the position of promotions manager. Out of necessity they offered me the job. Out of desperation to distance myself from my past, I accepted.

The Palmers were a couple in their sixties—welcoming, salt-of-the-earth people with a real drive to further their retirement dream. While the property comprised a large late 19th century homestead with guest bedrooms, and a low building—once the shearers' quarters—now being remodelled into backpacker accommodation, I was allocated a one-bedroom cottage. This suited me fine. The serenity of the countryside and the friendly, laid-back nature of its people eased my fears from the first day. This was a place of safety.

Employed to get the news of the recently renovated B & B out to the public—take photographs, produce brochures, advertise in newspapers and magazines—I also provided suggestions regarding design and décor. Rather than modernise the shearer's quarters, we retained its rustic charm but with modern comforts. To utilise a huge, unused machinery shed, I urged Rob and Stella to hold regular bush dances and weekend barbecues with performances by local musicians.

One afternoon several months after my arrival, the Palmers had family visiting, and the sight and sound of children on adventures had me feeling strangely melancholic. Retreating to my cottage, I found an intruder in the bedroom. His mop of black hair swayed like waterweed as he spun around from facing the dressing table. Amongst a sea of freckles, two dark eyes widened. He was a kid around six or seven years of age.

'What are you doing in here?' I growled from the doorway.

His cheeks turned a rosy pink, and he dropped his head. 'Nothin' ... just looking,' he said, in a high, thin voice.

'Just looking at what?'

'Your stuff.'

I stepped closer. 'And what's so interesting about my stuff?'

He lifted his eyes to mine. Bony shoulders protruded through his T-shirt as he gave a shrug. 'Dunno.' He sniffed and wiped sweat from his face with a grimy hand, leaving a dirty smear across his cheek.

'What's your name?' I asked, softening my tone.

'Marty.'

'Marty ... that's a real nice name.' I held out my hand. 'I'm Ashley ... or Ash.'

His smile, as he shook my hand, revealed two missing top teeth. 'You have nice hair. It looks like it's on fire.'

I laughed and tucked wild strands behind my ears. 'I guess it does.'

'What did you do to your arm?' he asked, pointing.

I stared at the ridge of scar tissue. I couldn't tell him I'd been pushed into a bin of burning rubbish by a friend. So I went with, 'Happened while cooking marshmallows over a fire. Some fell off the stick and burned me.'

'Big marshmallows?'

'Yeah. Pink ones as big as beach balls.'

He grabbed my hand. 'You're funny. I like you.' His grip tightened and his eyes narrowed to slits.

My heart skipped a beat. I saw Bryden in those eyes. I saw Cam in those freckles. It was as if they'd transformed into one person, and that person was a little kid.

'Yoo hoo! Are you there, Ashley?' called a voice from outside.

Marty dropped my hand, and I walked out into the sunlight.

Stella stood on the porch steps fanning her heat-flushed face with a straw hat. 'Are you busy? My son wants to hear your publicity ideas.'

'Sure. I was just talking with ...' I glanced over my shoulder, but Marty was gone. I guessed he didn't want to get into trouble for snooping.

After only three years, Kilberry Homestead appeared in a prestigious magazine as one of the top twenty holiday destinations for Western Queensland for that year, and we were thrilled. Life in Cunnamulla went along smoothly until things took a turn in 2001, around my thirtieth birthday.

It was a crisp winter's night with an unpolluted sky, dotted with diamonds that sparkled against the black velvet backdrop. The crescent moon smiled down at me. By heading out here, I had been reborn. I'd shrugged off my troubles like an old skin and taken on a new identity—an independent one capable of living productively.

As I sat on a hillside above my cottage, experiencing an overwhelming sense of gratitude, Marty appeared on the path below. I waved my torch, and he loped up to join me. He was now a lanky eleven-year-old, and as he flopped down beside me, he drew his bony, denim-clad knees up to his chest.

'Whatcha doin', Ash?'

'Thinking.'

'About what?'

'I'm turning thirty tomorrow.'

He pulled a face. 'Thirty? That's really old.'

I mussed his hair, still long and shaggy and plenty of it. 'Yeah, I suppose it is.'

Most of my school friends would be up to their eyeballs in nappies and baby food and the demands of young children by now. Single, enjoying each day, and saving heaps, I wouldn't have swapped my existence for quids.

I glanced at Marty. Being the same age my lost child would have been, I'd gravitated to him in a big way. Catching glimpses of two other boys in his actions and features, I enjoyed him shadowing me, trying to help out where he could, and annoying me with his constant questioning. It was silly, but my heart would break a little each time he left.

As Marty and I studied the sky, my thoughts slipped back to when I was not much older than him. I recalled a conversation

Cam, Bryden, and I had while walking home from the local cinema after seeing Robocop.

It was dark, and we were peering up at the evening sky, picking out the constellations. Cam said he wanted to be an astronaut and travel to another planet, capture an alien like E.T. and bring it home as his friend. I said I liked watching for falling stars and making wishes before they disappeared. Cam asked what I wished for, but I didn't tell the truth—that I wanted to be kissed before I turned thirteen—so I told him I wished for things like world peace. Bryden informed us that when we looked at stars, we were looking into the past and that most of the stars were already dead. We later found out this wasn't quite true, and discovered, to our own detriment, that Bryden made a habit of turning something fun into something sad.

'What's the baddest thing you've ever done, Ash?' Marty asked, shuffling closer for warmth.

I didn't dare share what that was. I didn't want to frighten the crap out of the poor kid.

'Keeping secrets,' I said.

He frowned. 'Is keeping secrets a bad thing?'

'Sometimes,' I replied, taking his hand in mine.

'Not keeping a surprise a secret, like a present you got someone for their birthday.'

I smiled. 'Did you buy me a present?'

He grinned.

'No, that kind of secret is okay. I mean secrets you keep so you won't get into trouble, which is sort of the same as telling lies.'

'Will I go to hell if I do something bad?'

I wrapped an arm around his flannelette-covered shoulders. 'No, never. Not you.'

Maybe me, though.

I jumped as a tawny owl screeched overhead, its wings

flapping noisily as it searched for prey. I shivered. Was it from the cold or from fear?

We headed back down the hill, and after saying goodnight to Marty, I got ready for bed.

A rapping at my door came just before my body hit the mattress.

Stella handed me an envelope. 'Sorry, luv, forgot to give you this earlier. It arrived for you in today's mail.'

I thanked her and shut the door, leaning against it as I ripped open the envelope and lifted out a postcard bearing a picture of a Thai beach. Flipping it over, I trembled as I read, *'Welcome to your thirties, Cinders.'* It was signed with a letter 'B'.

How the hell did he know where I was?

My sleep that night was disturbed by dreams I hadn't had for years. Rather than waking refreshed and excited about my birthday, I felt miserable and restless—and scared. If Bryden was able to discover my whereabouts, so could others more dangerous.

After a celebratory lunch with the Palmers, I drove into town and got so drunk at the pub that I marched into a tattoo parlour and demanded artwork to cover the scar on my arm.

Flicking through a folder, Santo, the wrestler-sized tattooist, pointed to an intricate design. 'That one should get rid of your bad memories,' he said, knowingly.

I was soon gritting my teeth as something more beautiful and symbolic of my new life—two stylised butterflies on a leafy vine— obscured an ugly reminder of a painful event and soured friendships.

Yet, the restlessness grew, and the nightmares continued. Six months later, when my mum was diagnosed with emphysema, I returned to Brisbane.

55

CAMPBELL

Jupiter's majestic journey through the heavens takes twelve years to complete. It is the astrological king of planets, the great overseer, and its return generally signals a revisiting of past events.

The years since the wedding 'reunion' and Ashley's departure had seen the three of us lose contact with one other—well sort of. Bryden reappeared at random, though his infrequent visits were endured by me rather than enjoyed, and each time I would note how his continuous battle with inner demons and abusive use of stimulants weathered his once youthful appearance. He now lived part time in Thailand after a holiday escape saw him forming a relationship with Jalar—a local girl from Hua Hin—and blending into the life and culture of that exotic location.

I'd taken a less escapist approach than the other two and remained relatively close to Brisbane. Working in hospital administration on a contract basis, I moved from one region to another picking up employment. The work was mundane but, given what had rolled out in previous years, I appreciated the boredom and anonymity that enveloped me.

The only trouble I encountered was getting caught without a ticket after a mad dash to catch the train when running late one morning. Copping a fine from the inspector didn't faze me. Having to pay a penalty of seventy-five dollars—or any monetary amount for that matter—was no comparison to the day I dreaded, when a surprise visit from those dark-suited officials would see me locked up for twenty to thirty years.

Relationships came and went. If mighty Jupiter was watching overhead and judging, then volatile Mars—and its two-year rotation—seemed to govern the beginning and ending of these intimate liaisons for me. No doubt, a psychologist could probe my inner workings and discover the reason for my inability to make a relationship stick. Maybe it was my stories of fires and associated mischief that had women doubting my suitability.

Bryden once reassured me, 'Relationships are for people who fear being alone in the dark ... and besides,' he added, 'who wants to shag someone who ends up turning into their mother?'

While I attempted to soothe the guilt through meditation and spiritual discussion, I still felt like a half-squeezed lemon, with more juice to be extracted. My search for peace drew me to more arduous physical pursuits. I discovered that strenuous activity released calming hormones, and the resultant pain provided penance for my sins.

It started simply enough by jogging along suburban streets and glimpsing the different lives in each of the houses I passed. To remove more filth from deep within, I developed a sweaty three-runs-per-day routine. Between catching pyjama-clad elderly men collecting early morning newspapers from their lawn and smelling home-cooked dinners wafting through open kitchen windows in the late afternoon, I crammed in a quick twenty-minute sprint at lunchtime.

One Saturday had me running deep into a park reserve that led into a state forest. The densely wooded area swallowed me up as I ran alone, my legs aching from traversing the undulating gravel pathways. This cocooned world of tall eucalyptus and silent trails, pervading with the fresh fragrances of nature, triggered in me a drive to push myself further. With each kilometre added to my daily run count, my endurance level increased, and I could go for hours. The fatigue that followed offered satisfaction and comfort, and I was hooked.

I expended the necessary outlays for backpacks, breathable activewear, the best in athletic shoes, and a cap with a fabric flap at the back that fluttered in the breeze as I ran. I entered cross-country marathons of up to 200 kilometres which took four to five days to finish. My exhaustion at the completion of these torturous endeavours left me in agony, though triumphant. The aching hips, parched throat, sunburnt skin, and dry patches around my eyes and nose proved that penance had been successfully attained. As my body became lean, and my indifference was replaced with stoicism, the everyday efforts rallied me for yet another incursion against guilt.

While the physical punishment dulled the memory of that terrible event in that back alleyway, one cold morning in June I found myself studying my battered feet—the assorted plasters circling blistered toes, the odd blackened toenail, the hardened flesh on heels. As I picked at a small piece of loose skin near my little toe, a thought slipped from the recesses of my mind and forced a way through the armour shielding my emotions.

How many more kilometres did I need to endure before I forgot about Ashley?

56

—————

ASHLEY

2006

I saved enough money during my time out west to buy a home in Paddington, a hilly suburb overlooking inner-city Brisbane. A traditional early 1900s Queenslander—high-set timber house with a corrugated iron roof, wide wrap-around verandah, and cast iron lacework—I bought quality antique furniture and vintage ware, complemented by country style decor. Turning the six-bedroom home into an upmarket bed-and-breakfast guesthouse, I offered visitors yesteryear charm with easy access to the city. Successful marketing and four-star reviews generated activity, and it soon became a popular venue for interstate visits and romantic getaways.

While organising this, I helped my family as my mum struggled with her health and my dad settled into new employment outside of the defence force. Marty visited occasionally, and I enjoyed listening to his adolescent babble about boarding school, his desire to become a humanitarian aid worker and, of course, girls. I did not renew contact with Bryden or Cam, and they showed no interest in touching base, which suited me fine. Then one night in my fifth year running the B & B, a booking made by a Frank Bowden caused my world to churn once again.

On his arrival, I realised that the aged, well-dressed gentleman standing at my door was, in fact, Francis Bryden. *Had I misheard him when he phoned to book, or had he used an alias?* In his mid-seventies, his hair was now fully grey and his face criss-crossed with lines. Yet those dark, narrow eyes—so much like Bryden's—remained unsettling, even though he didn't seem to recognise me as I welcomed him inside.

Leading him to the master suite—the more expensive of the five available bedrooms—I answered questions about the history of the house and directed his attention to the photos taken by past owners, now displayed on the walls. I cringed when he stopped to study an Award for Hospitality I'd received the previous year.

'Ashley McCabe.' He cocked his head. 'Have we met before?'

'I don't think so,' I mumbled, opening the door to his room.

'Are you certain? I could have sworn—'

'I've come from out west,' I interrupted, taking his suit bag, and crossing the floor to the carved mahogany wardrobe.

He followed close behind. 'Really? Where out west?'

'Cunnamulla,' I said, hanging the suit and breathing in wardrobe air still tainted by decades of mothball use.

'Oh ... Cunnamulla,' he sighed in the same tone I imagined him using if served tinned tomato soup instead of a bowl of lobster bisque. 'No, I wouldn't have met you there.'

I caught his reflection in the wardrobe mirror. He was tapping his chin and frowning, as if racking his brain for a memory.

I rushed into my standard dialogue. 'The en suite is through that door. Fresh towels and toiletries are supplied. Feel free to make yourself at home in the living areas or wander the yard. We have lovely spots to sit in the garden and on the verandah. Brewed coffee can be located in the dining room, along with an array of French pastries. Breakfast will be available from six-thirty till eight-thirty. If you expect to return late from your evening activities, please phone ahead as the front door will be locked at eleven pm. I hope you enjoy your stay.'

Then I was out of there.

Leaning against the wall in my own quarters, off from the kitchen, my heart pounded. *What if Francis remembered me? What if he already knew and pretended he didn't? What was his real motive for being here?*

Fortunately, I was busy settling in a couple from Alice Springs when Francis left for his dinner engagement and ensconced in my study going through paperwork when he arrived back at half past ten.

I didn't speak with him again until he found me in the morning, setting out breakfast on the buffet in the dining room.

A waft of woody aftershave followed by a voice over my shoulder. 'I've worked it out. I know where I've seen you before.'

My hand trembled as I placed the lid on a serving dish of scrambled eggs and slowly turned around.

Francis held a travel magazine up for me to see; the pages were splayed open to reveal an article on whale watching in Hervey Bay. It included an interview I recalled giving—with accompanying photos—on the tour company I worked for. A chill swept over me. In a matter of hours, Francis had gotten his hands on a magazine issue printed almost ten years earlier. That showed determination.

'How did you find this?'

'I have my ways.' He grinned, exposing a perfect set of dentures.

I was sure he did ... and a league of flunkies eager to do his bidding.

The pair from Alice Springs entered the room and I escaped into the kitchen to collect stewed plums and yoghurt to go with the muesli they had ordered.

When I returned, I found Francis deep in conversation.

'Oh no, I'm no stranger to Brisbane. I visit quite regularly. My grandson lives here. Unfortunately, he's unwell at present and getting treatment at a specialised clinic. Costs a pretty penny, but then you do whatever you can to help family, don't you?'

His eyes meeting mine as he said these last words convinced me my connection to Bryden was known. *But did he know our secret?*

An hour later, Francis was out the front door and catching a taxi to the airport.

As I dwelt on his visit, I wondered what had happened to Bryden. I also reflected on my stalking at Hervey Bay and Bryden's fearful theory regarding Francis and his cohorts.

That afternoon, a high-profile barrister made a booking. Then a week after, a retired supreme court judge and an ex-police commissioner. Soon, a number of powerful figures from the legal fraternity were regularly meeting behind the closed doors of my spacious parlour. I quickly suspected these gatherings were conspiratorial, and that Francis Bryden turning up on my doorstep had not occurred by chance. Whether he understood the true facts about Slade's murder or not, I knew I was being used.

It also dawned on me that in accepting their money, and allowing these influential men to utilise my rooms, I was an accomplice to whatever illicit plans were being made under my roof. This horrified me. If I wanted to free myself from this quicksand, I needed to form a plan of action.

57

CAMPBELL

2006

I'd continued my studies in alternative therapies and expanded my understanding of the 'events behind events' in the movement of the planets and their astrological interpretation. With great precision, Bryden came knocking in the week I had been noting the crossing of Jupiter on my chart's rising/ascendant point.

More creases etched his forehead, and deeper lines travelled down from the corners of his grinning mouth. His unshaven face, sunken cheeks, and brushed back stringy hair made him look like a vagrant. Still, those slitted eyes darted, vigilant to everything around him.

'Cam, the more life experience Ash gains and the older she gets, the more she proves to be a dim-witted, bend-over-backwards dullard who thrives on stupidity.'

'What are you talking about?' I said, surprised at the sudden outburst that introduced Ashley into our conversation.

The cigarette wedged between his fingers created a cloud of

smoke around him as he gesticulated. 'That dumb redhead has become some sort of host for the most depraved, power-infused bastards that ever existed.'

'Mate, I've got no idea what you're on ... or on about.'

'She now runs a guesthouse in Paddington. The goss is she's become friendly with Francis and his cronies. They've set up a convenient spot at her place for colleagues from all around the country to meet regularly. And I'm bettin' they're not just getting together for tea and scones.'

Bryden's theory on high corruption in the courts had been forefront in his mind since his convinced 'cover up' by Francis of the incidents surrounding Slade Delaney's death. Rather than being thankful for the murder investigations drying up, he viewed it more as a power game that would eventually return and bite us all.

'That stupid bitch has willingly been roped in and is playing with fire,' he added, 'and those sparks are gonna spread.'

As usual, I listened uneasily while Bryden relayed his thoughts and theories. If there wasn't enough to reassure me that my astrological readings had a ring of truth to them, a distant thunderclap heralding a storm brewing in the western hills conjured up an image of Juno issuing his warning and displeasure.

'Bryden, I really don't understand any of this ... or your issue with your grandfather.'

I felt some loyalty towards Francis Bryden seeing he'd recently organised lucrative employment for me within the Aged Care industry; one that offered plenty of scope for career growth. Death in this age group was common, and I coped with the passing of those I'd bonded with by trusting that there was an afterlife—one in which a person could find the peace they had not attained while living.

At first, Bryden had reacted with disdain for my accepting his grandfather's help, but as the job did not directly necessitate Francis's involvement, he let his concerns slide. Yet, while I enjoyed my new role, I was slightly suspicious of why Francis had sought me out and fast-tracked my application. I doubted it was solely his generosity that provoked such an action. Maybe it was his way of keeping close tabs on my movements, and therefore Bryden's. Or possibly, by having me in his pocket he had control over where my allegiance lay. Still, I believed that as long as I behaved myself—which I had every intention of doing—there was little for me to fear from him.

My agitation grew. 'Let's just leave this, and anything to do with Ash, alone.'

Bryden shook his greasy hair. 'We have to make those rats scatter. Disease spreads when too many of them feed at the same table.'

'Let it go,' I urged. 'If it's as you say, then you're stirring with an awfully big shit stick.'

The cigarette cartwheeled from his fingers as he flicked it away, as he always did, in some defiant act against the anti-litter campaign. Then with a huff, he raced off.

Disheartened, I watched as he sprinted across the road through a gap in the traffic and merged into the streetscape. The darkening sky matched the mood that settled over me. In Bryden's mind, my childish pranks on Ashley in Hervey Bay may well have intertwined with his conspiracy obsession, driving him to inflict more injury and pain upon her. Feeling somewhat responsible, and certain that Bryden's action of retaliation would be swift, I needed to hurry if I wished to put things right with Ash.

Apart from sending random Christmas cards, I'd had no reason to contact her. Those haphazard festive greetings were a sign—to me at least—that my past anger had cooled, yet Ash always gazumped me by not responding. So I now found myself doing what Bryden so expertly did to me—arriving on her doorstep unannounced.

Her cold greeting was no surprise. My visit was obviously as welcome as a fart in an elevator.

'Yeah ... sorry to intrude, Ash. I need to talk. It's important. It's to do with ... you know ... Bryden.'

I tried to sound earnest, but my nerves were on edge. Not only was I delivering a dire warning, I was toying with the idea of admitting to my period of insanity and the dumb stunts that had sent her fleeing. Added to that, the sight of Ash after nine years stirred a range of emotions. She looked good—a little rounder, in a healthy way. Her floaty floral dress, smart ankle boots, and lace scarf gave her a country-meets-city chic. So did her hair, piled high on top of her head, and stabbed with a sprig of lavender that exuded a scent I could smell from where I stood.

'Everything seems to be important when it comes to you and your mate,' was her sarcastic response.

'Yep, you're right.' I squirmed, feeling highly uncomfortable at having this conversation out in the open.

'Is he still staying at the clinic?'

I cocked my head. 'What clinic?'

She blinked. 'I heard somewhere that he was getting some help.'

'Was he? That's news to me.' I spoke the truth. Bryden had mentioned nothing of this. But then why would he? 'He hasn't been around much. I gathered he'd gone overseas for a bit. Look, can I come in? It's rather urgent.'

She glared at me. 'I'll give you ten minutes to spit out what it is and then you're out of here.'

As I followed Ash into a spacious sitting room, my eyes were drawn to the tiny tattooed heart on the back of her neck. Memories jumped me like muggers in the dark and I had to hold on to an armchair to steady myself.

'You're dripping on my furniture,' she said, and walked out.

While she was gone, I lifted my shirt to dab the sweat trickling down my face and discovered, by the pungent smell emanating from my armpits, that my new brand of deodorant had failed me.

Ash returned with a hand towel, which I used to mop my torso before draping it around my neck. As she stood with her arms folded, my eyes were drawn to the tattoo hiding her burn scar. Her time away had hardened her—or maybe she'd hardened herself to the past.

'Go ahead,' she commanded.

My feet shuffled awkwardly on the expensive looking antique rug. 'I'm only trying to help you. It's Bryden and his hell-bent quest to right wrongs.'

She sighed and rolled her eyes. 'I've heard this shit before, Cam. Don't bring any of this back into my life. I've had enough of you two arseholes to last me a lifetime.'

'Well, that may be the case, but it's not going to stop what might be coming.'

A heel of one of her boots tapped the floorboards. 'Get to the point, will you?'

'Bryden's upset that his grandfather visited you here. His conspiracy theories include Francis and his group of legal buddies, and he reckons you're aiding them.'

Though she dropped her arms and laughed, I picked up on the alarm in her eyes and the way her fingers gripped the skirt of her dress.

'Bryden's last comment to me was that he was going to scatter the rats.'

'Meaning?'

'Haven't a clue, but it made me sick when he ran off. He's determined to do something.'

Ashley chewed the corner of her mouth. 'What's he got planned?'

'Like I said, I have no idea. I just wanted to let you know ... warn you.' I sucked in a deep breath. 'Also ...' I searched for the courage to reveal my idiocy in Hervey Bay. If I was asked to comment on a philosophical argument and I'd respond in a flash, but in Ash's presence, and knowing how badly she would receive my confession, I was tongue-tied.

'What?' she snapped impatiently.

The interruption of a telephone ringing had us both looking to the hall.

'You're both bastards. Get out,' she snarled, pushing me out of the room. 'I hate what you've dragged me through.' Shoving me out the front door, she tugged the towel from my neck, 'Tell your screwy friend I think he's a gutless wonder.'

Then she slammed the door in my face.

58

ASHLEY

Cam's unexpected visit had me shocked and then spooked. Sinewy, tanned, and dripping sweat all over the place from his soaked sportswear, his edginess had me wondering if he was hyped up on energy drinks. When he ranted about Bryden's threat, I lost it and turfed him out of my house. I didn't need this intrusion. I couldn't bear another dark cloud smothering me. If Bryden intended on acting out his warped sense of recrimination, like Cam implied, I wasn't taking any chances.

According to my records, neither Francis Bryden nor any of his cohorts had made reservations for the month. So Bryden would be disappointed if he hoped to catch any evildoers arriving at my door anytime soon. Still, I needed to plan my defence just in case. *Circle the wagons ... raise the drawbridge ... man the barricades!*

That evening, I did the rounds of the house—locking doors, fastening windows, drawing curtains—and checked the outdoor security lights worked before keying the deadlock on the front door. It felt like a preparation for an attack by a band of ransacking rebels—not a solitary man with a mind brimming with demons. But then again, it was Bryden, who was capable of anything.

I considered notifying the police. Yet, what evidence did I have other than Cam's fears? How could I explain the reason for Bryden's threats without the chance of incriminating myself, or spilling the beans on what took place fourteen years earlier in an alleyway outside the Smooth Cat? A confrontation with Bryden might be the way to go. I could try to persuade him to steer his manic energies elsewhere. No. I rejected that idea in a heartbeat. Finding the sharpest kitchen knife, I hid it under my pillow and drifted off into a semblance of sleep.

The next day panned out without incident. I visited the market to buy fresh produce, dropped into a store to collect an order of new linen, and reached home in time to welcome two ladies from the Gold Coast for the night. It was in the afternoon, after I'd cleared the letterbox and sorted through the mail, that my anxiety returned. Amongst the usual business correspondence and junk mail was an unaddressed envelope. 'Ashley', being the only word scribbled on the front.

I ripped it open and discovered no warning letter inside, merely a piece of paper marked with cartoons similar to a newspaper comic strip. Entitled *The Adventures of ABC* it included four boxes of line drawings—a storyboard.

The first box showed three characters holding hands: a boy wearing a skewed baseball cap and a T-shirt bearing the word Handycam; a long-haired girl in a bathing suit with a sash draped over her shoulder printed with Trash McBabe; and a muscled superhero with a cape and face mask, his costume emblazoned with a large letter B.

The second box in the story had the three characters standing in front of what looked like a school building. The third, a hand lighting a match. The fourth, the building in flames while the trio laughed.

I didn't have to be a forensic analyst to know that, if dusted for fingerprints, Bryden's would be found all over this piece of paper. He hadn't ruffled my feathers as he'd surely hoped; he'd only proven he was stuffed in the head. That was until the following day when I received the second envelope.

Once again, a comic strip involving four scenes in a story: the first scene pictured the same three characters drinking beer; the second, Handycam blowing out a 21 candle on a birthday cake; the third, a military-style boot. The fourth had the trio standing alongside a tombstone and grinning. Chiselled in the stonework were the words 'RIP Slade'. I was on alert once more.

My nerves kicked into overdrive when a third envelope arrived. It creeped me out imagining Bryden sneaking past my house and dropping them into my letterbox. Yet, it eased my mind that all he had in his armoury were these stupid, childish jottings. I tore the envelope open and gasped at the vulgar nature of this offering. The comic strip pictured B-Man having sex with Trash McBabe, then Handycam having his way with her, followed by a sordid 'threesome' between the trio. A ball of anger formed in my stomach as I viewed the fourth scene where Trash McBabe had her legs wrapped around a man wearing a Ku Klux Klan hood.

So, Bryden believed I was sleeping with the enemy. Maybe he was right, but it was due to naivete not necessity. I had to tell Francis Bryden, in no uncertain terms, that he and his cronies were no longer welcome in my guesthouse. Working up the courage to phone Francis, my call was answered by a recorded request to leave a message. So I did, informing him, clearly and strongly, of my decision.

The fourth comic strip delivered to my letter box bore a cartoon of a whole mob of hooded Klan members arriving at Trash

McBabe's house and being let inside. The third scene showed a hand on the plunger of an old TNT detonator—Wile E. Coyote style—and fourth, the house exploding.

I didn't sleep at all that night. Frequently peering through parted curtains and listening for any odd noises from outside, I felt more alone than ever before. Who could I turn to for help? Not the police. Definitely not my parents. I balked at asking Cam. What could he do, anyway? I tried contacting Marty, but he was unavailable.

Armed with my mobile phone and a pruning saw, I snuck out and hid in a corner of the verandah with a clear view of the street. I remained there until sunrise and returned again with a cup of tea to wait the rest of the morning. In all that time, not one person ventured close to my house. However, I searched the letterbox, finding it empty except for a dead ghost moth covered in ants. The cartoons had been a scare tactic, that's all.

Two days passed with no horrid surprises and I was convinced that Bryden had simply been playing a pathetic game of cat and mouse and had given up. Then a fifth envelope appeared.

This comic strip was entitled *Handycam Goes Fishing*.

Scene 1: Handycam sitting in a dinghy, holding a rod, and reeling in a fish.

Scene 2: Handycam outside a house.

Scene 3: Handycam under the house and nailing the fish to the floorboards.

Scene 4: Handycam behind a bush and laughing as Trash McBabe runs out of the house pinching her nose.

I shuddered. *Was Bryden telling the truth?* Had it been Cam playing a trick on me in Hervey Bay and not some thugs trying to scare me off about Slade?

So afraid by those strange events, I had moved to the-back-of-beyond to hide from whoever wished to see me destroyed, only to now discover it was some juvenile prank orchestrated by an imbecile for being found out he was a pushover. That was worse than fearing my house may be blown to smithereens.

I had to get out. I had to confront Cam. But first I needed to find where that shithead lived.

One brief phone call to Dot Druery and I had the answer.

59

CAMPBELL

Pounding on the door of my rental flat woke me from an afternoon nap. I jumped up from the worn couch and slipped into the Thirsty Merc T-shirt I'd only half an hour before shrugged off.

I opened the door to an angry red face and a fist raised from battering the timber panelling.

'Ashley?' I grimaced. 'What the hell's going on?'

She struggled to release words that seemed to be jammed in the back of her throat. 'You ... you ... ugh ... ARGH!'

Then she slapped me.

I reeled back clutching my face. 'What the fuck was that for?'

'Fish!' was the first word she spat from her mouth. 'Stick!' was the second.

My eyes smarted from the stinging pain. 'Fish stick? I don't get it?'

'Dick!' she yelled. 'I called you a dick!'

Fish dick? Still didn't make sense. She was batshit crazy.

'Bryden ... t-taught you well,' she stammered. 'You're a ffuckin' loser. I hate you.' She punctuated this last statement by stomping on my foot.

I groaned and hopped on one leg while she threw a ball of paper that bounced off my chest and landed at my feet. Her hair whipped my arm as she turned and rushed back down the stairs.

I dropped my aching foot to scoop up the paper wad and unfurl it. As I viewed the comic strip, the physical pain dealt by Ash's outburst was eclipsed by the fury I felt at Bryden's betrayal.

60

ASHLEY

Arriving home and feeling like an idiot, yet no less angered, I discovered a swarm of people milling outside my house. Some had video equipment. I froze. It was a camera crew! *What the hell had happened in my absence?*

Parking on the roadside, I jumped out and rushed into my front yard.

'That's her!' someone shouted.

'Ms McCabe!' came a male voice from behind.

I looked over my shoulder and had a fluffy-headed microphone poked in my face.

'Is it true your so-called guesthouse is, in fact, a brothel?'

I batted the microphone away. 'A what?'

'A bordello. A house of disrepute. A sin—'

'I know what a brothel is,' I snapped.

'So, Ms McCabe,' said a female, waving a microphone tagged with a Channel 10 logo. 'You admit to running a whorehouse, right here in suburbia.'

'No!' I cried. 'It's a guesthouse. A house for paying guests. Visitors who wish to stay overnight.'

'And you cater for every need?'

'I do my best.'

'And what needs do you cater for,' sneered a vaguely familiar man on my left. *Which show was he from, Today Tonight, The 7.30 Report?*

'Not those types of needs. Now get away. Everyone! You're on private property.'

I shoved at the wall of bodies and saw the female reporter trip over and land on her arse.

'Assault!' she cried into her microphone from the ground. 'I've been physically assaulted by Ashley McCabe, brothel owner.' She pointed to a cameraman. 'Did you get that, Phil?'

I took the steps up to the verandah and turned to the crowd, noticing it now consisted of a few nosy neighbours.

'Listen. I run a perfectly reputable and legal establishment here. It is a guesthouse for ordinary people visiting Brisbane. I offer only food and accommodation. No sex. No drugs. Nothing of a sinful nature. Now will you please bugger off before I call the police.'

As if on cue, a police car screeched to a halt in front of my yard.

Thank God, I thought, moments before two uniformed policemen pushed through the sea of flesh towards me.

'Ms McCabe?' one burly cop asked.

'Yes. I'm so glad you're here. This is crazy. I don't understand what's going on.'

He removed his cap and frowned. 'Ashley McCabe, we have reason to believe you are operating a house for prostitution, illegal gambling, and drug trafficking. We ask that you come to the station for further questioning.'

I jolted back. 'No way!'

He nodded towards the noisy mob. 'I'm sure you don't want to do it here with that lot watching on. We could go inside if you like.'

A sound of smashing glass.

I spun around. A rock had shattered a window.

'No, I'll go with you,' I said, my voice shaking.

Escorted back through the jeering throng, I was ushered into the police car.

As we pulled up away from the kerb, I recognised another face in the crowd. It was thinner and more aged than I remembered, though the narrow eyes and tousled hair were the same.

I showed him my middle finger. 'Fuck you,' I screamed, hoping Bryden could at least read my lips if he couldn't hear my shout through the window glass.

Returned home six hours later—no charges laid—the incident appeared on the evening news and reported in the morning newspaper. Even though it was proven to have only been an allegation, my reputation and that of the guesthouse remained questionable.

After two months of negative attention and lack of bookings, I sold up. At least I was no longer involved in whatever Francis Bryden and his fraternity were up to. Yet, the relief was minor compared to the disappointment I felt in Cam and the contempt I harboured for Bryden.

After a stint at my parents' place, I travelled overseas in an attempt to shake off my depression. Touring Europe in a blur of self-pity, I came back home and bought a much smaller house in a new estate close to my parents. Still, the ball of pain sat heavy within. And with the added worry of my mother's deterioration, there were days I lacked the energy to even put one foot in front of the other.

61

CAMPBELL

Watching TV on the night of Ash's angry visit, I sat open-mouthed as a local news channel reported on the discovery of an illegal brothel being run from a home in Paddington. I recognised the house. I recognised the woman being escorted by police through a raging mob and roughly placed into a cop car.

I phoned Bryden.

'What the fuck have you done?' I screamed, before he'd even gotten a word out.

'Well, that's a nice howdy-do. You mean the Ashley fiasco, I take it.'

'You bet I do.'

He gave a snort. 'It wasn't me.'

'Don't give me that. You say you're going to do some crazy shit and then this happens. You're in it up to your eyeballs.'

A laboured sigh. 'I admit to being there when they dragged her away, but it wasn't me who dobbed her in.'

'Bullshit! Who was it, then?'

'You tell me, dickhead. Use your brain for once.'

'You mean Francis? Holy shit, Bryden. When are you ever gonna get over that conspiracy crap? It's all in your head, you fuckwit.'

'Oh ... so I'm the whacko, am I? Who shoved dead fish under Ash's flat? Not me.' He laughed sharply. 'Is that the best thing you could come up with? A stinking mullet or two? You're such a weak-arsed pussy, Cam. I don't know why Francis bothered to take an interest in you. You're a dead set disappointment. You've even dropped your game where Ash is concerned.'

I rubbed my forehead where an ache had formed. 'What are you talking about?'

'Well, where was Cam the protector in all this? I told you something was about to go down. But where were you? Not at her side, shielding her from what was to come. No, you'd buggered off with your tail between your legs.'

Though my hands curled into fists and I had an urge to visit him and punch his bloody lights out, I knew he had a point. Like a switchblade, the truth twisted under my ribcage and into my heart.

It so developed that all three of us hated each other. Ashley detesting Bryden and his ability to crush her private life, Bryden abhorring my gutlessness and Ash's connection with—in his suspicious mind—the wicked and depraved, and me loathing Bryden for being the one to reveal my lovelorn vendetta against Ash which had her despising me even further.

IV

SMOKE AND MIRRORS

62

———

ASHLEY

SATURDAY

Marty has answered my call and dropped in. Unlike previous visits, he doesn't look happy to be here.

'You're not much fun today,' he says, pulling a face similar to when he was a little kid. He is taller than me. Broad-shouldered, good-looking, and smart, he is also kind-hearted. At twenty-six he has the world at his feet, and I am so very jealous.

'Sorry, I'm going through some pretty heavy shit, right now,' I say, without giving further details. 'I just wanted to see your smiling face.'

I've never confessed my dark past to Marty and, though he knows I have secrets, he has never pushed me to share them. He wraps me in a hug I never want release from. Yet I am forced to break the embrace at the sound of a car pulling into the driveway.

One peek out the living room window and my stomach squirms like a hessian bag filled with snakes. *Bloody hell!* Marty makes himself scarce while I steel myself and open the door before Lauren raises her hand to knock.

'Oh ... Ashley! Have you looked in the mirror today? You look crap.'

'Hello to you too,' I say, pressing flat against the door to allow my sister to brush past in a cloud of Calvin Klein's *Eternity*.

She thrusts an empty lasagne dish into my hands. 'Just dropping this off from Dad. He's going through his old army photos with Brett, so I thought I'd pay you a quick visit.' Her smoky eyes wash over my bare feet, track pants pilled from frequent wear, and wrinkled shirt. 'Not heading out, I see.'

I, in turn, study her high leather boots, skinny jeans, and pristine linen blouse. An angora pashmina slung around her shoulders gives an impression of careless thought, which I know wasn't the case.

'Nope, not today,' I shrug.

She looks around. 'You should open the curtains, it's as dark as a crypt in here.' Her sculptured nose crinkles as she sniffs the air. 'You could do with opening windows too. The place reeks of garlic and onions.'

At least I still cook my own food. I go into the kitchen and put the dish on a shelf.

Lauren pokes her head in. 'Do you have green tea? I could do with a cuppa.'

There's a box in my pantry, but I'm not wasting it on her. I shake my head and watch as her eyes spy the half empty gin bottle and used glass on the bench near the sink.

'Drinking again?' she scowls. 'Is that wise? You are aware of the dangers of consuming alcohol while on medication.'

Of course I am, you sanctimonious bitch. 'I know what I'm doing.'

'Do you? Got to keep that black dog from nipping at your heels.'

I wish I had a dog to set on you. I walk into the living area. 'What do you want, Lauren?'

She follows and sits at the mahogany dining table. 'Horrible news about Bryden James.'

Ah, the real reason for her visit. 'Yes, it is,' I say, crossing my arms.

'Dad said you were shaken up.'

'Yep, it was a shock.'

'Was it?'

I cringe. 'What do you mean by that?'

'Well, Bryden was a jerk. Had quite the reputation. A bad seed even back then.' She smiles in a way that always irks me. 'He was your first, wasn't he?'

How does she know this? I swallow hard. 'How did you—'

'You told me in a game of truth and dare.'

I certainly did not. I would never have let slip what happened between Bryden and me that night at his place. Never! Lauren has to be lying.

She taps her chin with a rose red nail. 'It was at a party wasn't it? During a game of Spin the Bottle?'

'Oh ...' My tension eases. 'That's right, my first kiss was at our Grade 7 break-up party. But it wasn't—'

'What you expected?' She gives a knowing, older sister nod. 'I bet he used his tongue. He looked like a guy who'd do that first up. Not like in the movies Mum and Dad allowed us to watch. Remember how we'd practise on our pillows ... or on our arms ... or on my poster of Kevin Bacon?' The accompanying giggle sounds bizarre coming from the mouth of a forty-eight-year-old woman. 'You had a crush on him, didn't you?'

I drop into a chair beside her. 'Kevin Bacon?'

'No ... Bryden James.'

I laugh, hoping it doesn't sound as fake to her as it does to me. 'No way … never.'

'I heard what you two got up to later on. Pretty saucy stuff.'

My heart falters. 'I have no idea what you're talking about.'

'Rumours spread like an epidemic at high school. I didn't believe them, of course. You were such a prude at school.'

Those bloody rumours. 'How come you never said anything about them?'

'I didn't want to embarrass you. Anyway, I was busy forging my own love life. Then there was the school fire, and you being hurt and getting into trouble with Mum and Dad, and it paled into insignificance. At least you were well rid of Bryden after he got sent away to juvy or wherever.'

'Yeah,' I lie. 'I never saw him again.'

'That's something to be thankful for. Imagine if you'd hitched up with him?' She throws her head back and cackles. 'Just think how much more stuffed up your life would be.'

I don't laugh. I check the wall clock. Lauren's been here far too long.

She removes her pashmina, revealing a new gold chain hanging from her neck. A sapphire droplet rests between her breasts. Brett earns enough to buy exquisite jewellery for his wife, send both kids to private schools, and pay off a three-storey house at Hamilton by the Brisbane River. Perfect family. Perfect life. I hate them all.

Her defined eyebrows arch. 'I guess you know the details of his death. It was in this morning's paper.'

I shift in my chair. 'I don't get the paper delivered.'

She lifts her hand and folds all but one finger and her thumb. Holding it to her head, she cries, 'Bang!'

Ice runs through my veins.

'Shot dead. Beaten to a pulp, tied up, then a bullet to the head at close range and dumped in the lake. They discovered his car in the bush, torched. My hunch is a drug deal gone wrong. Or he owed some crime syndicate a truckload of money. Maybe it was payback for doing the dirty with the wife of someone rich and powerful. Whatever, it couldn't have been above board.'

The chair scrapes as I push up from the table. I need her gone. Now.

Lauren's phone pings, and she eyes the screen. 'It's Brett. I have to leave.'

Thank God! I don't have to kick her out.

She rises and wafts her way to the front door. 'Get properly dressed and go out, Ash. No sense being maudlin over a dickhead from your past. He's not worth the angst.'

I don't watch her leave. I shut the door and check my mobile.

There is an email from my agent regarding my soon to be published book, *Better B & Bs*. After writing several well-received articles for magazines and running a successful blog, I've written an entire book, with pictures, offering helpful advice to others in the field. With the launch looming, there's talk of a television appearance on a lifestyle programme. Yet, I can't come at reading this email. Cam's response to my texts is what I'm eager for.

Changing into shorts and a sweatshirt, I race out the door.

Twenty minutes later I am climbing the fence of Thornleigh State School and walking across deserted playing fields devoid of noisy, smelly children and whistle-blowing teachers.

I struggle to find my bearings until I realise they'd extended the rear fence line to acquire more ground when constructing the swimming pool complex. Fortunately, the tennis courts are in the same position, and I use these as a guide as I pass an air-conditioned auditorium—something we only ever dreamed of—and pull up in front of four prefab structures. New builds. Where is the brick building that replaced the fire-damaged block decades ago? Where are the classrooms in which we'd gained knowledge, and the playgrounds in which we formed friendships? Gone forever.

I slouch on a bench in the shade of a spotted gum and gaze disappointedly around the facilities. This Saturday ghost town offers nothing to fuel remembrances. So, like worn film reels, my school memories are left to play within my mind alone as I close my eyes and slip back to another time. Cat Stevens pops in to provide the music score and I hum along as he sings 'Remember the Days of the Old School Yard'.

My phone sounds a single bleep and I tug it from my pocket. At last, a message from Cam. He wants to meet up tonight.

63

CAMPBELL

SATURDAY

I wince as sunshine sticks needles in my eyes. Dropping my sunglasses down from the top of my head, I pick up a rolled newspaper from the lawn. It's not mine, but I unfurl it anyway, my stomach gripping when I see Bryden's face splashed across the front page. What shocks me further is they've used a photo I recall taking.

Years before, Bryden and I had gone for an impulsive afternoon drive up Mount Coot-tha to take in the panorama of Brisbane city and the surrounding suburbs. But once there, he'd been more interested in the television towers that blinked their red lights from the heights. He reckoned he was going to knock on the doors of every TV station on the hilltop and ask to be filmed doing some crazy stunt, such as climb one of the towers.

'Just like fuckin' King Kong,' he'd spouted.

With some coaxing, he'd changed tack and joined me at the lookout to study the view and let me photograph him leaning against the coin-operated telescope. He liked the pic so much he kept it in a frame on his lounge room wall.

'I look so friggin' wistful,' he'd said, 'like I know the secrets of the universe.'

I thought he looked off his face, which he was at the time.

The newspaper trembles in my grip. Next to this front-page headshot is another photo, a crime scene beside water—police tape, suited-up forensic team, and a body covered by plastic sheeting. Bryden's body. I give the report a quick scan. Words rise from the print. *Murdered. Gunshot to the head. Dumped in the lake.* My heart thrums in my ears. I roll the paper back up and chuck it over the fence to Mrs Dabiner's where it should have landed if the crap delivery boy had been doing his job properly.

The garage door rolls up with a whine. I get into my car and insert the key in the ignition, give it a twist. Nothing, other than a pitiful click. I slam my hand against the steering wheel. *Shit!* Just what I needed.

I check my watch. If I run, I'll still be late to meet up with Mum for her birthday.

I get out, search amongst the shadows, and find my dusty bike. The tyres feel firm enough. Shaking my bike helmet free of creepy crawlies I slap it on, fasten the chinstrap, and peddle out onto the road, swearing the entire way to the shopping centre.

'Campbell! You didn't run here, did you?'

I shake my head and give my mum a peck on the cheek. 'Happy ... birthday,' I pant, removing the price sticker from the hurriedly purchased bunch of flowers and handing them to her, along with a slightly crumpled and sweat-moistened birthday card.

Her frown turns into a smile as she opens the card and reads my heartfelt scrawl. 'That's lovely, Campbell. Thank you.' She waves the T2 gift voucher in the air. 'This will certainly come in handy. Can never have too much tea.'

I drop onto the cafe seat opposite her and wipe my dripping face with my sleeve. Mum passes me a neatly ironed and folded hanky and I mop sweat from my forehead. As I pass it back, she grabs my hand.

'How are you, luv? You didn't answer my calls. You had me worried.'

I shrug. 'I'm okay.'

'Are you? Poor Bryden. So sad. I can't believe it. Such a troubled soul. A victim of circumstance. And now this.' She sighs. 'I'm so glad you ceased contact with him. You were always such an impressionable boy, and the likes of him could have so easily led you astray.' She pauses before asking, 'Have you spoken with Ashley?'

I flinch and tell her I haven't.

She looks at me with eyes of disappointment, her typical version of a clip over the ear.

Lifting the laminated menu from the table I skim the list of available meals, not reading a word. 'What do you want for lunch, Mum? Order whatever you like, my shout today.'

'You always pay, dear,' she says with a chuckle, taking the menu from me. 'What's on special?'

As she peruses what is on offer, I fight the gnawing in my gut that is not due to hunger, but from knowing what I must do.

64

ASHLEY

Once again, Bryden has forced our hands. Dropped off by the Uber driver, I'm standing outside the tavern, waiting for Cam's appearance. If I were a smoker, I'd light up a cigarette to steady my nerves. Instead, I inhale deep breaths of cool evening air and repeatedly check my watch.

Twenty minutes pass and I move inside, choose a seat at the bar, and buy a bottle of cider. As I take my first sip and feel the icy liquid moisten my dry throat, I survey the room in case I've missed Cam's arrival and he is lurking in a corner, eyeing me from a distance. I don't see him in any of the faces glancing up at me and wonder how much he has changed. Will I be able to recognise him? Will he even recognise me?

A figure walks through the entrance. His loping stride—so different to Bryden's confident swagger—gives him away. With his hands hidden in the pockets of a military-style jacket and his shirt stretched in the middle there are hints of a slight paunch. A knitted beanie hangs low over his forehead, covering the tops of his ears. I wave to grab his attention, and he nears, I catch dark circles under his strained, blood-streaked eyes. Has he slept as little as me?

'Hi, Ash. How are you?'

I laugh weakly. 'Great. Never been better.' He frowns and I add, 'Geez, Cam, what do you think?'

He orders a drink and we choose a table.

Sitting in an uncomfortable silence, I watch him take a gulp from his glass—his hand shaking, eyes darting, reminding me of a war vet struggling with PTSD. He looks his full forty-six years in the lines creasing his face and the glints of grey in his stubble.

I pull the pale blue envelope from my bag—the one I'd removed from the camphor wood box when searching for Cam's Christmas card—and place it on the table. 'I gather you received something similar.'

He stares at it without saying a word. So I open the envelope and lift out the note.

'*I need your help,*' I read. '*I'm in big trouble. Meet me at my old home in Thornleigh. TUESDAY 1900. You'll want to be there. B.*'

Still no response from Cam.

'I didn't find it until Wednesday,' I say. 'It was amongst a pile of junk mail my father planned to throw out.'

He squints. 'Bryden left the note at your dad's place?'

'He mustn't have known my current address. I only found it because I was doing a little tidying. Anyway, you didn't answer my question. Did you get a note from Bryden?'

Cam fidgets with his drink coaster, tapping each corner on the table. *Is he hiding something?* I guess we are both playing our cards close to our chest. Finally, 'Yeah. But I didn't open it. Chucked it away.'

I ask him when he'd last seen Bryden.

'Dunno. A while back. A couple of years, maybe.'

'How was he? How'd he look? Sick? Sane?'

'The usual. You know ... rambling ... edgy ... gaunt from that shit he's into. So, normal for Bryden.' He eyes me coldly. 'What about you? When did you last see him?'

A chill scoots over me and I reach for my drink. 'I can't remember.'

'Really?' His smirk looks sinister in the dimmed lighting— a gash of suspicion. He slams his glass down. 'Want to go for a drive?'

'What, now? Where?'

'Thornleigh. Percival Street.'

My pulse races. I swallow hard and grudgingly agree. 'We'll have to take your car. I got an Uber ride here.'

65

CAMPBELL

The chilly night air has me sucking in icy breaths as I anticipate yet another confrontation. Locking the door of my mum's old Toyota Corolla hatchback—she insisted I borrow it until I get a new starter motor for my car—I walk towards the tavern.

I'd grown weary of fearful events resulting from my friendships with Bryden and Ashley. With Bryden lying cold and lifeless in a morgue somewhere, I thought this would be the end of my torment. But as I enter the warm and crowded interior, and see Ash standing at the bar in the exact spot where my father used to sit swilling down his favourite bitter and shooting the breeze with his old mates, my emotions collide and mesh.

How many times had I found Dad here, propped up on his elbows, gums flapping, head swaying? Being sent to fetch him home, I often had to force him from his similarly drunk audience and steer him outside. In the early days, I'd save him from playing Frogger with the traffic by leading him safely across the road and through the neighbourhood while he warbled bawdy tunes at top volume. Later, when I had my licence, I'd bundle him into my car and drive him back with the radio on full blast to drown out his raucous singing. Now as I step closer, I consider having a memorial plaque made up and fixed to the bar. 'Raise a glass in remembrance of Phil Druery, our most regular patron,' it could say.

Ashley's long black coat swirls as she turns and spots me, her mouth forming a brief half-smile. Her shoulder length hair falls like a curtain over one side of her face—a face in need of makeup to add life to the pallid cheeks and hollow eyes.

There is no greeting from her other than, 'Let's find a seat away from the noise.'

I order a rum and Coke—realising at the last minute it was Bryden's drink of choice—and leave Dad's ghost at the bar.

As we sit at a table in a dim corner, we both seem at a loss for words. I watch Ash pick at the moistened label of her cider bottle with a nail-bitten finger. She glances up and our eyes meet.

'So ... here we are,' she says.

I nod and rub a sweaty palm over my thigh. 'Yep.'

'You were at Mum's funeral. I saw your name in the attendance book.'

I catch her questioning look. 'Couldn't stay ... work,' I lie. Actually, I didn't stick around after the service because it hurt too much seeing Ash again.

She lets out a sigh. 'Thanks ... anyway.'

Ice rattles in my glass as I lift it to my mouth and I quickly lower my trembling hand before Ash notices.

'It's made front page of the newspapers,' Ash says.

She's not talking about her mother's death. I blink away a vision of Bryden's plastic-covered body.

Ash tugs something from her coat pocket and slides it across the table. 'Did you receive one of these?'

I stare at the pale blue envelope and feel a stab of pain between my shoulder blades. 'Yeah, I did. A few days back.'

'And?' A pause. 'What did you do?'

'I didn't open it if that's what you're asking. I knew it was from Bryden. Gathered it was some more mindless shit and didn't want to get caught up in more of his stupid games. I was done with him.'

Ash takes back the envelope and removes a slip of paper. After reading out the message from Bryden, she says. 'Yours probably said a similar thing. So, you didn't go, then?'

The plastic creaks as I stretch back in my chair. 'How could I if I hadn't read his note?'

She scowls. 'Why did he want to meet up at his old house at Thornleigh?'

'No idea,' I say, taking another quick swig from my glass.

'Who lives there now?'

'Beats me. I never venture past my mum's place.'

Ash sucks in a lip, gives it a chew. 'Who would want Bryden dead?'

I laugh. 'Are you for real? There'd be a line-up of people.' I count on my fingers. 'Francis Bryden for a start, or the whole friggin' legal fraternity. Any number of druggies or dealers. The police force itching to solve a cold case. Shit, even Stevie and Wayne, for all we know.' I lean forward over the table. 'And of course, there's you.'

She pulls back, eyes wide. 'What do you mean?'

'You can't deny that Bryden made your life hell.'

Expecting her to lash out, I'm surprised when a tear slips down her cheek.

'Look, Ash, I'm as pissed off as you. I'm sick of all the guilt ... the sadness ... all the crap that happened. And just when I think it's all been left in the past, I get drawn back in.' My eyes sting. With a catch in my voice I add, 'I am so fucking tired of it all.'

Ash wipes her face. 'Cam, we need to discover why Bryden was so desperate to see us.' I'm apprehensive, but she insists. 'We have to pay a visit to Percival Street.'

ASHLEY

Cam parks his mother's Corolla on the roadside. The house in Percival Street is in darkness—not because no one is at home, or the occupiers have called it an early night. The residence looks to have been abandoned months ago ... maybe even years.

I stare out the car window at an overgrown yard littered with rubbish, the driveway sprouting weeds through cracks in the concrete. The house itself is a decaying corpse, with paint peeling from the chamfer boards like skin off a burns victim. Rusted guttering sags, and most of the windows look as if local kids with stones or shards of cement have used them for target practice.

'Fuck,' Cam says, opening his door. 'I wasn't expecting this.'

I step out and view the street, noting the neatly kept post-war houses that are now home to a new generation of families. 'It's as if we're standing outside a house from a horror movie.'

'Yeah ...' he nods. 'A normal suburb except for that one freaky place.'

'Do you have a torch?' I ask, not wanting to search a deserted property in the dark.

'Look in the glove compartment.'

I lean into the car and shuffle through the glovebox, finding a penlight torch under a travel pack of tissues, a bunch of cassette tapes. and three packets of jelly snakes—one open.

'Geez, your mum sure has a sweet tooth.'

'Er ... they're not hers.'

'Yours?' I grin.

He looks a little embarrassed. 'Yeah ... mine.'

'And she keeps a stash for you? What a spoilt brat.'

'I guess I am,' he says, with a shrug.

The gate creaks when opened, then suddenly breaks free from its rusted hinges and falls amongst the dried foliage of a hydrangea shrub. A dog barks from a yard nearby and we hurry over to the front steps.

'You stay here while I check the back,' Cam says, and disappears into the night.

I climb the stairs. The door opens at the first push and a musty wave of six decades of inhabitants greets me. I duck as something small and black flits over my scalp on its way out the doorway. A micro bat? I turn the torch on and shine it around, noticing the bare lounge room strewn with detritus from takeaway meals. There's a dark stain on the beige carpet. I touch it. Dry. When I lift my fingers to my nose, I smell blood. Not a good sign.

Raising the light, I scan the graffiti scribbled walls. Brown moths, their wings patterned with wavy purple markings, congregate in clumps in the corners. They're Granny's Cloak moths, and I'm no stranger to them, having been swooped plenty of times by the ones that roost in the carport under my dad's house. I move the torch over the water-stained ceiling, and it spotlights an old domed light shade—milky glass with art deco detailing. *A spaceship.*

Memories knock me sideways.

I hear The B52s and the crackle of Styrofoam beans. Feel the vinyl bag hindering my escape, and a burning between my legs, deep inside. See a vein pulsing above two slits for eyes. I reach for the wall to steady myself and start to retch.

'There's nothing outside,' Cam says, entering the room, 'I had a good look but ... are you okay?' His phone torch blinds me. 'You're not going to spew, are you?'

I raise my hand to shield my eyes and shake my head. 'This room ... the memories.'

Cam lowers the light and grips my shoulder. 'What memories?'

'This is where it happened ... right here.'

'What happened here, Ash?'

'We ... he and I ... Bryden ...' The circle of light illuminating our feet shakes. 'This is where Bryden raped me,' I say, tasting bile.

I hear Cam suck in air. 'Raped? When?'

'When he got me pregnant.'

'Oh shit ... Ash ... I didn't know. I always thought ...'

He lifts his hand to stroke my cheek, but I back away. 'I can't stay here.'

Rushing out the door, I clutch the porch railing, battling the need to flee this repulsive home infused with pain. My breath comes in gasps and my knees buckle.

Ground your anxiety. Use your coping technique.

I open my eyes to acknowledge five things around me: one, a white cat lurking on the steps; two, a ceramic pot lacking a plant; three, the wrought iron railing bubbling with rust; four, a glint in the rose bush below the porch. *What is that?* I reach for it, tugging it from a thorny branch and turning it over.

A cry catches in my throat and my mind reels. *What does this mean?*

'Ash!' Cam calls. 'I've found something.'

CAMPBELL

The first spot that has me transfixed at the Percival Street house is the backyard. Once the storage area for discarded beer bottles—whose contents had kept Bryden's dad in a constant state of anger and frustration—the moon gives light to the tall grass that has reclaimed this place.

A breeze brushing over the tops of the stalks creates a soft rustling—a consoling whisper—that eases my tension until I recognise a timber post that once supported a basketball ring. Now splintered and broken to half its height, it was here that Bryden revealed how quickly his playfulness could turn to selfish desires. My remembrance of a dart thrown at my leg turns morose as I ponder how life has eventuated to this day. Bryden's youthful exuberance, his need for adventure, his incisive mind all channelled into destructive pursuits, suspicion, and the capacity for deadly revenge.

I climb the rear stairs and enter through the unlocked door. My phone's torch lights up the kitchen, revealing newspapers glued by age to the floor, broken electrical sockets, and counter tops thick with dust. I shudder. Formerly infused with life, ghostly echoes from the past now fill this empty house.

I venture down the hall and into the lounge room, discovering Ash has already entered. Bent double, gagging, it seems a memory for her is also being stirred. She rejects my offer of aid and tells me the truth of her sexual encounter with Bryden. Related to me by both parties at the time, and believing Ash was a willing participant, I am shocked by this revelation.

When Ash rushes out the door to puke over the porch railing, I explore other rooms, Bryden's old bedroom in particular. Here I find a mess of junk food wrappings right where his childhood bed had once stood. I kick the rubbish aside and spy a break in the wall's skirting board. Another memory rolls out: a game of Operation and Bryden telling me about hiding money in his bedroom wall in case of a quick escape. I tug at the piece of wood and it bends, exposing a cavity in the plasterboard. Aiming my torch inside, I jolt back when a large brown moth flutters from the recess and attaches to my arm. I shake it off and gingerly ease my fingers into the hole, feeling something solid, yet light. I lift it out.

'What's that?' says Ash, from the doorway.

She comes alongside and we both stare at the audio cassette case in my hand. The cover image tells us it is Rocky Burnette's album, *Son of Rock and Roll*, which includes Bryden's theme song, 'Toein' The Line'. But when Ash takes the case and cracks it open, we discover there is only a TDK recordable tape inside. Sliding it out, we see the sticky label has writing on it, and scrawled in black marker are our names.

Our eyes meet. A startled look passes between us.

I grab the cassette and sprint out of the house, reaching Mum's car only seconds ahead of Ash.

'Where are we going?' she asks, eyes wide.

'Nowhere.' I open the driver's door and slip inside.

Ash opens her door and flops onto the passenger seat. 'I don't get it?'

I point to the dashboard.

The old Corolla has never been refitted with a CD player. My mother hadn't seen the need as she still enjoys music from her cassette collection—mostly Michael Bolton and Barbara Streisand.

'Well, put it in,' Ashley urges, pointing to the tape player.

I insert the key into the ignition and turn it to accessories. Feeding the cassette into the player's slot, I sit back.

Some initial rustling sounds come through the car speakers. Then Bryden's voice, as clear as day, sounding like he is right behind us in the back seat rather than lying lifeless in a morgue fridge. A shiver sneaks up my spine.

'*Cam and Ashley ... well maybe it's only one of you listening. Clever boy, Cam, remembering my secret hole in the wall.*' A small laugh follows. '*I'd hoped you guys would've turned up to see an old friend, but you obviously had better things to do.*' The sound of him sucking back on a cigarette comes before he adds, '*Thanks for that, you pricks.*'

He exhales, and his tone turns from sarcasm to sadness. '*I needed your help.*' There is a pause, and I notice Ash squirming in her seat. '*I've never asked for much. You'd think long-term friends would at least show their loyalty by turning up to find out what was wrong with their mate. Even animals look after their own.*'

The words, 'Screw you,' shoot from Ash's mouth.

Bryden mumbles words I can't understand. I adjust the volume, my fingers trembling as I turn the knob. The sound of movement: tapping of fingernails, wind interference. A crow caws in the background.

'*I know I've fucked up in the past. I had my reasons for doing other stuff that I know you guys don't understand. Anyway, here's the deal ...*

my health is rooted. Hepatitis A or B or C ... can't remember which. And I'm exhausted from always looking over my shoulder. I'm pretty sure they know where I live. They think they're as clever as shit, but I've seen them watching me from their cars parked on the street. They keep phoning me and hanging up as soon as I answer. It probably won't be long till they put a needle in my neck ... or a bullet in my brain.'

I look at Ash, who is busy chewing her thumbnail.

'Hey, remember Cam's twenty-first? That big, bad night? Maybe they've always known ... biding their time ... until now, when I'm too weak to fight. And this is where I thought my good mates might offer some protection. But they were elsewhere. By the way, did I thank you for that? I may have. You guys are the closest thing I have ever had to family, so your no-show was a kick in the guts.'

The crow now caws close by, its raucous 'uk, uk' progressing to an extended 'aaark', and Bryden tells it to *'f-a-a-rk off'*. A flapping of wings as it flies away.

'Where was I? Ash, if you're listening, I'm sorry you didn't have the baby. What age would he have been now ... or she? Twenty-four? Twenty-five? Reckon it might have helped me to have had a kid to give solid counsel to, you know, how to keep out of trouble and all. I've certainly had some experience in that.'

Ashley groans and I press the pause button. 'Do you want to stop?'

She shakes her head. 'Why's he acting all righteous?'

We wait for Bryden to finish coughing before he starts up again.

'But then again, perhaps it was for the best. My bad DNA shouldn't be passed on.'

Ash nods strongly in agreement.

'Oh ... *guess what?*' Bryden's voice heightens with excitement.

'I've got me a new friend.' There is another lull, and then odd, muffled noises.

We both frown then lurch back as a blast explodes through the speakers. A gunshot.

Ash shrieks.

'*Holy shit!*' yells Bryden. '*This old bastard sure has some fire power.*'

My mind convulses and I quickly open the car door and vomit onto the road. The sour stink rising up causes me to retch, and as I fight against spewing more, I barely listen as Bryden rambles on about his financial woes, trouble in Thailand, and how the world is in chaos.

'*It's time to put a few things right,*' he announces dramatically. Then nothing, just the whirring of the tape.

I press the eject button, and the cassette pops out halfway. Leaving it in the player, I recline my seat as far as it will go and focus on the roof upholstery, hoping my stomach will settle. As I try to make sense of it all, Ashley is also silent, possibly overwhelmed by her own thoughts.

The cream vinyl overhead suddenly lights up.

I blink hard as the interior of the car fills with blinding flashes of red and blue. Sitting up and twisting around, I peer out the rear window. Apparently, someone has reported our evening house visit.

68

ASHLEY

Cam swears and quickly brings his seat upright as a police car pulls in behind us.

'I saw him,' I say, clutching his arm.

His head twists around. 'Who?'

'Bryden.'

'What do you mean you saw him?' His frowning face flickers red and blue, and then a startling white as the flashing patrol car lights are switched off.

In the beam of LED headlights, I see his mouth gape when I state, 'A few days ago.'

A sudden rap on glass diverts our attention to a uniformed policeman giving a hand signal to roll down the driver's window.

'Evening folks,' he says, bending down. 'Out for a drive, are you?'

Cam blurts out a swift, 'Yes.'

The light from the cop's Maglite torch whips over the Corolla's interior. 'Not disturbing the neighbourhood?'

Cam shakes his head. 'No, not at all.'

'Great,' the cop nods. 'You see, we've had a complaint. It seems a couple of people have been seen lurking around this house, just here.' He indicates Bryden's old home with a nod of his head. 'Now I'm aware it isn't really up to scratch ... more a renovator's delight, as they say. However, there's been a recent spike in break and enter incidents in these parts of late. Some car theft too.' The torch beam hits me in the eyes and then travels to my feet before coming back to Cam. 'By the looks of you two, I reckon you wouldn't be up for that kind of mischief. Am I correct?'

'Of course,' Cam offers.

'Certainly,' I say.

The cop snickers. 'Yeah ... you're not the typical age for gallivanting about at night, skylarking, testing each other's fear factor. So, what is your purpose for being in this street, may I ask?'

While I quickly try to come up with a clever lie, Cam jumps in with, 'I used to live in this neighbourhood when I was a kid.'

'Go to Thornleigh State School, did you?'

'That's right. So did my friend. He lived in that house. Thought I'd check it out for old time's sake.'

The cop smirks. 'A little reminiscing, hey?' His grin vanishes. 'In the dark ... on a Saturday night?'

'What's wrong with that?' I snap, sounding annoyed, which I am. *Let us go, you over-zealous pig.*

Cam warns me with a firm grip on my thigh.

The policeman squats to eye us more closely and suddenly scrunches up his nose. 'What the hell?' he barks, aiming his torch at his feet. Bolting up, he leans against the car and lifts his leg to examine his boot.

'My spew,' Cam whispers to me. 'He's stepped in my spew.'

'Remain here,' the policeman growls, and hurries back to the police car.

'Don't tell me you can get a ticket for vomiting on the road,' I say, 'or soiling police property.'

'Stay cool, Ash,' Cam advises. 'We can't afford to ruffle any feathers. Especially cop feathers.'

The policeman returns with his partner, who is brandishing a breathalyser kit.

'Would you mind blowing into this please, sir?' asks cop #2, looking too young to be wearing a proper police uniform without Velcro tabs.

Cam pulls away from the mouthpiece thrust in his face. 'Why? I'm not drunk.'

Who's showing their irritation now?

'Well we don't know that, do we, sir? We're just doing our job. One long breath, please.'

He does as he's told.

Cop #2 waits for the reading, while cop #1 skirts the Corolla, shining the torch under and over the car. *What is he searching for? Bombs? Contraband? Hostages? Next, he'll be asking us to open the boot.*

'Okay, all good,' announces cop #2, stepping away.

Cop #1 pokes his face through the window. 'Is this your vehicle?'

Cam clears his throat. 'Not quite.'

'And what does that mean?'

'It's my mother's.'

The policeman gives another smug smile. 'Your mother's car. May I see your licence, sir?'

'What's this about?' Cam's voice breaks, like when he was going through puberty. 'I said I was only visiting a friend's old house. The car's in good nick, too.'

The cop holds out his hand. 'C'mon, mate. Give it here.'

I notice a trickle of sweat snaking down Cam's cheek as he

leans sideways to tug his wallet from the pocket of his jeans. He's freaking out. So am I. He drops the licence into the waiting palm and the policeman hands it to cop #2, who takes it and the breathalyser kit back to the patrol car.

Cop #1 stays with us, drumming his fingers on the car's roof as he hums a vaguely familiar tune. I prick my ears and recognise the chorus of Elton John's, 'Saturday Night's Alright for Fighting'. I know Cam has also twigged to the song. He's grasping the steering wheel, his arms rigid and shaking, as if struggling to control his rage.

Cop #2 returns and mumbles something to his partner.

Cop #1 leans in through the window. 'Folks your age should be watching TV, or enjoying a coffee somewhere, not traipsing the streets like bored teenagers. Do us all a favour, will you, and mosey on out of here.' He offers Cam's licence back.

Cam snatches it and grunts, 'Gladly.'

We drive off in silence with the police on our tail until, a block from the house, the patrol car peels away and disappears.

Cam skids the Corolla to a stop beside a park. 'What the fuck, Ash. Where did you see Bryden?'

69

CAMPBELL

Ash turns her face to the passenger window.

I follow her gaze outside to the park and poorly lit playground. Gone are the iron burn-your-bum slippery slides, shoulder-wrenching monkey bars, squash-your-fingers seesaws, and splinter jabbing swing seats. In their place are colourful made-to-safety-standard fibreglass cubes and cylinders, and swings and slides with rubber matting to cushion a fall. Kids aren't built tough like in our day.

'I saw Bryden on Tuesday afternoon,' Ash says quietly.

My jaw clenches. I lean in to hear her better and she turns around.

'I was driving home and had to stop at the traffic lights at Thornleigh School while a group of kids crossed the road. The lights took ages to change to green, and I noticed a man standing at the main gate hugging a backpack. It didn't take long to recognise him, but I was shocked, Cam. He looked so old. Gaunt, bony, hair long and streaked with grey. His mouth kept moving, and at first, I thought he was chewing gum, but then I realised he was talking to himself. I wondered if he was mumbling scripture verses.'

'Probably,' is all I can muster.

'Then he glanced at me and I nearly peed my pants. I slid down in my seat, but I shouldn't have worried because his stare was ... I don't know ... vacant. Remember his eyes, the way they seemed to penetrate your soul? How his presence demanded attention?' She shakes her head. 'Gone. All gone. I felt sad, then I got angry that the Bryden I once knew, the person I was once infatuated with, had lost his way so completely.'

'Did you pull over ... approach him?'

A lengthy pause. 'When the lights changed, I drove off. Drove home.'

'What was he doing at the school? Recalling better times?'

'He kept looking over his shoulder, scared like. Made me wonder if the backpack held drugs or money, and he was waiting to make a deal.'

'Maybe it held the Browning.'

Ash leans in. 'The what?'

I rest back against my seat and breathe in deeply. 'A semi-automatic handgun. That's what I reckon we heard on the tape. My father had an old Browning pistol, a gift from a friend, ex-army. One day when we were kids, Dad took Bryden and me to a firing range to watch him shoot. When Dad died and we were sorting through his stuff, we found the metal box the gun had been kept in, but it was empty. My brothers assumed he'd surrendered it in the gun amnesty after the Port Arthur massacre. But I had my suspicions.'

'That Bryden stole it? When?'

'No idea, but he was often at our place as a kid. Bryden visited the bank when he came back from Sydney that first time, you know, when he got you ...' I swallow my words and move on. 'He asked for a safe deposit box. I was a bit sus about what he needed it for, but being a good bank employee I never peeked inside the box. It only dawned on me, years later, that it may have contained the pistol.'

'If Bryden had it in the backpack, who was he intending to shoot?'

It suddenly feels hot in the car. I wrench off my beanie and claw my fingers through my hair ... hair that I notice Ash is startled to see is now totally grey.

'Jesus, Cam,' she groans. 'You're a godawful wreck.'

'Well you're a heartless, crazy bitch!' I snap.

She looks pained, and then sighs. 'You are so right. I'm batshit crazy. I have an imaginary son, for fuck's sake.'

I jolt back, hitting my head on the window glass. 'An imaginary what?'

Ash unclips her seatbelt and picks my beanie up from where it dropped on the floor. 'Bryden's certainly done us over, hasn't he?' She replaces the beanie on my head, her hands trembling as she adjusts it to fit right. 'He had to pay for what he did to us.'

Our eyes lock and my mouth loses all moisture.

'I understand,' she continues, 'I really do. God knows, there have been plenty of times I've wanted to.'

'Wanted to do what?'

'Murder Bryden.'

My vision blurs at the edges. I feel like I'm being sucked into a black hole.

'You killed him, didn't you, Cam?' Her voice trembles as she adds, 'Did you shoot him with the Browning?'

I glare at her. Laughing through gritted teeth, I remove a small knife from my jacket pocket. A Victorinox. Ash gasps and reaches for her door handle. I lunge, but my seatbelt locks, keeping me tethered as she opens the door and leaps out.

70

ASHLEY

I sprint into the playground. Dodging a bright yellow slippery slide, I pass between a pair of swings and hurdle a rocking horse on springs. My ankle twists as I land, and I stumble. I right myself only to be tackled around the waist and forced to the ground. Wrestling together in a sea of bark chips—kicking, biting, punching—Cam rolls me onto my back and sits on me, pinning my arms out by the wrists. I'm too exhausted to fight any further.

As we both struggle for breath, my mind backtracks. Cam must have read the letter from Bryden. The tape recording mentioned neither of us visited as requested, so Cam must have arranged another meetup after the tape was hidden.

'What happened?' I rasp, spitting out a chip of tree bark. 'Where did you meet him? Lake Mitchum? Did you fight? Did Bryden pull the gun on you? Did you wrestle it from him and shoot him instead? Or did you take your own weapon .... that knife. Beat him up. Then you shoot him. Is that how it played out?'

Cam releases his grip and slides off. 'I didn't kill Bryden. Sure, I despised the sick bastard, but hate him enough to murder him?

No way. Up until a short time ago, I thought it was you who lured him out to the dam and had done away with him.'

I scramble onto my knees. 'Me? Lure Bryden?'

'You're the one with more motives to kill him.'

'You're the one with the knife. How did you find that horrid thing? I could have sworn Bryden chucked it in the dam the night Slade died.'

Cam sits up. 'It's not the same one, you idiot.' He pulls the knife out of his pocket. 'Look. Brand new. I lied when I said I hadn't opened Bryden's letter. Along with a note similar to yours, was this knife and a PS saying he had a job for me. I didn't want to be roped into any more crap, so I never went to the house. Stuff him and his wacko bullshit.'

My mind whirls, thoughts colliding, ricocheting. 'Bryden mentioned at the end of the tape he would put things right. What did he mean?'

Cam stands and brushes bark from his clothes. 'Maybe he decided to face off with Francis or some of his cronies, tell them what he had on them. Needed my help to achieve it ... our help. Who knows what he had in store for you to do.'

'The big league? Holy shit!' I get to my feet and peel out of my constricting coat. 'So he went on his own and they killed him to keep him quiet? God, Cam, this is serious.' I shake the coat and send bark chips flying in every direction. Something flutters to the ground.

Cam picks it up. 'What's this? An empty jelly snakes packet?'

'I found it in a rose bush back at Bryden's old house. It's the same as the ones in your mum's car. Evidence, so I thought, that you'd lied to me about being there.'

He puts his hands on my shoulders and bites his lip. 'I have to tell you something.'

Fear spikes. I wrench from his grasp. 'Let me guess. You

snitched to Francis that Bryden was on the warpath, therefore orchestrating his death?'

'What? No.' He inhales deeply. 'The snakes in Mum's car aren't mine.'

71

CAMPBELL

I steer Ash over to a swing and sit her down. 'The packets in the car are for your dad.'

Her face contorts as if I've just rattled off some techno mumbo jumbo. 'My dad? I don't understand?'

Sitting on a swing beside her, I rock back and forth. 'I guess you don't know, then.'

'Don't know what?' She sounds indignant.

'Your dad and my mum have been ... how shall I put it ... seeing each other.'

'Seeing each other?' She laughs. 'What ... you mean like, dating?'

I nod and wrap my arms around the plastic-coated swing chains. 'Yep, dating.'

'Bullshit. I'd know if they had. Dad tells me everything.'

'Obviously, he doesn't. They've been meeting off and on for coffee, or to catch a movie or whatever for months now ... as friends. But it took a turn a few weeks ago when they went to Surfers Paradise for the weekend.'

Ash leaps up and stands right in front of my swing, her hands gripping the chains. 'No, Dad went to Surfers with some old army mates. A reunion of sorts. I helped him pack.' Her eyes search mine, but I give her nothing. 'You're telling me my father lied? Why would he do that? I'm his daughter.'

'How do you think you would have reacted?'

She shrugs and slams a fist into my shoulder, almost knocking me off my perch. 'You're an arsehole for keeping this a secret from me.'

'Well, Ashley. I wasn't aware you were in the dark about it until tonight. Anyway, we haven't spoken for years, so I didn't really give a flying fuck whether or not you knew.'

She clasps her face. 'Oh God ... they're not ...'

'Having sex?' I scowl. 'That's not a conversation I will ever have with my mother.'

'So your mum keeps a stash of lollies in the glove box of her car for my father. He has type 2 diabetes. He shouldn't be loading up on sugar.'

'Yeah, well, I think it's okay in moderation.'

'Dad doesn't know the meaning of moderation.' Her jaw drops. 'Holy crap! What does the lolly packet in the bushes mean, then?'

'Can you be certain your father didn't read Bryden's note?'

'It was amongst the junk mail, unopened. He never reads junk mail. I've suggested he get one of those letterbox stickers to ward them off.'

I ponder a moment. 'He could have read the note, sealed it back up, and intended to put it in the rubbish before you saw it.'

'Are you suggesting my dad sneakily read the note and met with Bryden on my behalf?'

'It's a possibility. You know how protective he was of you girls when you were young. I remember him stepping in a few times in your defence. Maybe he felt it necessary to do it again.'

'But he knows nothing about what happened between Bryden and me ... or anything else ... unless ... your mum!'

I grip the chains tighter. 'My mum? What's she got to do with it?'

'She knew about the baby ... the miscarriage ... she was there. She must have told Dad.'

'She was where?'

Ash plonks down on her swing seat. 'Cam, when I miscarried, I was at home, alone, scared out of my brain. I phoned you at work, but you were away at some bloody seminar or something, so I phoned your mum. She came and supported me through it.'

'Mum supported you?'

'Yeah, she was brilliant. I wouldn't have coped without her.'

I twirl my swing around to face her. 'Look who's keeping big fuckin' secrets now!'

'Dad may have twigged that Bryden was involved in the Guest House fiasco. I was a mess after that happened ... not quite myself for a long time. There's a chance I let something slip. Did you notice the blood on the carpet?'

'Blood? Carpet?'

'At Bryden's old house.'

I shake my head.

'What if Dad went to the house and argued with Bryden? What if Bryden pulled that gun on him and they struggled, it went off and ...'

'And your seventy-whatever-year-old father tied Bryden up, dragged him into his car, drove to Lake Mitchum, and threw him into the water. Nope, can't see it. Anyway, those nosey neighbours in Percival Street would have called in any loud shenanigans.'

Ash kicks at the rubber matting, letting out a scream of frustration. 'I'm so confused!'

'C'mon, let's go back to the car,' I pull her up. 'We can get another drink somewhere.' I place my hand on her hip to edge her forward, but she swivels away.

Car lights. A vehicle approaching.

We freeze as a black SUV pulls up behind the Corolla, its passenger door still open from Ash's hurried escape.

I push Ash towards a fibreglass fort and shove her inside ahead of me. We kneel, peering through the small windows, as two large figures exit the SUV and walk around Mum's car, shining a torch inside.

'Who are they?' Ash whispers.

'Well, they're not the police, and sure as hell aren't from Roadside Assist.'

'What are they looking for?'

'Whaddya reckon? Me, of course.'

'But why? How did they ... the cops!'

'Christ, they must have done a search on me, unearthed my firebug past, linked me to Bryden.'

Ash jabs me in the ribs. 'Cam, what if they suspect you had something to do with his death? Or worse.'

'Worse?'

'What if Bryden was right? What if they're all in it together? The cops, the judiciary, every corrupt bastard. They murdered Bryden because he confronted them about what he discovered and now, believing you two were in cahoots, they're after you.'

I grimace. Had what Bryden done or said got them all spooked, including Francis? If that's the case, then I have no chance of protection this time. I know where the old man's loyalties lie.

'Hey, Ash, they could also be looking for you, for the same reason.'

'But they don't know my connection. That cop didn't even ask me my name. I could have just been your Tinder date.'

'Tinder? I don't need bloody Tinder to get a date.'

A bright light beams into the park.

I drag Ash down with me and we lay crushed together in the confined space as the light waves over the fort. I feel her warm breath on my face, her heart pounding into my hand squashed against her chest—its tempo matching mine. Her perfume fills my nostrils. Another time, this might be a dream come true. But right now, hiding in fear of our lives is the last place I want to be.

72

ASHLEY

A shout. Car doors slam. Tyres screech.

We wait a little longer and then disentangle our bodies. A quick peek through the fort window shows the SUV and its flunkies have vanished, so we dash back to the Corolla.

'My bag's gone!' I cry, scanning the interior of the car. 'Holy crap! Now they have my details.' I fumble inside my coat pocket. 'Thank God, I still have my phone.'

Cam quickly turns the key in the ignition, and we leave Thornleigh.

It's not safe to go back to Cam's place. Not safe to go back to mine. So we take the motorway heading north out of Brisbane. The traffic on the six-lane highway is steady in both directions.

'What's the plan?' I ask Cam, trusting he's got one.

He shrugs. 'Dunno ... just get away. Find a bolthole in which to lie low and think. Somewhere secluded. The hinterland would be good, possibly Maleny or Montville where we can book a sheltered cabin in the rainforest.'

'Wouldn't it better to hide amongst the masses?' I say. 'On the coast, in a busy resort area teeming with southerners who've migrated north for the winter. Mooloolaba or Noosa.'

'Hmm ... you could be right. We'd have to buy Hawaiian shirts and white sneakers to blend in, though.' Cam grins.

A service station with take-away food options appears up ahead and I'm suddenly hungry. 'Have we enough petrol?'

'Yep, we should be okay. I filled up on the way to the tavern.'

In desperation for something to eat, I open the glove box and remove the unsealed packet of jelly snakes. Offering it to Cam, he takes a snake and bites the head off before sucking in the tail, while I down four snakes in one go.

As Cam drives deep in thought, I check my phone for news updates about Bryden. My chest tightens. 'Bloody hell!'

'What?' Cam glances my way.

'A news report states that a lead weight was found lodged in Bryden's throat. There's mention of a similarity to the Anton Wilkes killing.' A crease forms between Cam's eyebrows. 'Were you aware Francis was questioned about Anton's murder?'

He nods. 'And he was cleared of all suspicion ... or, as Bryden put it, the investigation into Francis was dropped like a hot potato.'

'So, what you suspected was right. Bryden must have told Francis he had incriminating information on him and his associates, and they put a stop to it.'

'Killing Bryden in the same manner as Anton Wilkes. A justice killing. Francis wasn't indicted then, so there's a good chance he won't be indicted now.'

'Bryden knew who he was dealing with. Must have known there was a high probability his plan would backfire. So, why did he go through with it?'

'You heard him. He was tired, ill. Maybe he didn't give a shit about his safety. It was now or never.'

I close my eyes and rest back. My skull feels like it is being crushed by a vice. If I had my bag, I'd swallow a handful of pills I keep in there for moments when I feel boxed in by oppressive clouds. I breathe in slowly then breathe out. My head bangs against the passenger window as the car jerks to the left. My eyes fly open as it then jerks to the right.

I glare at Cam. 'What the hell are you doing?'

His eyes dart to the rear-view mirror, his side mirror, then back to the rear-view. 'I think we're being followed.'

I swivel around. Lines of traffic and plenty of headlights are all I see out the back window. 'What makes you think that?'

'A black SUV. I noticed it a short time ago. Whenever I change lanes, it does the same, always keeping a car between us.'

Cam again swerves the car left, and I clutch the shoulder strap of my seatbelt for balance. We are now in the middle lane, in front of a white hatchback. Headlights swing in behind the hatchback from the right.

'See?'

I turn to the front. 'What are we going to do?'

Cam plants his foot on the accelerator and the Corolla lurches forward. With the engine whining in protest, we pass a VW Beetle travelling on our left and then a Woolworths delivery truck. I check over my shoulder and cringe. The SUV is now directly behind us.

'Cam, it's right up our bum.'

'I know!' he growls, swiftly veering into the left lane ahead of the delivery truck.

I twist around. The rear of a semi-trailer loaded with new Volvos fills the view out the front window. We are now safely cushioned between two large vehicles.

'Good move,' I say, giving Cam a thumbs-up.

He doesn't notice. He's checking his side mirror and shaking his head. 'Bloody hell!' he says, as the SUV comes alongside on our right and keeps pace, matching our speed. The darker-than-legal window tint makes it impossible to see who is inside.

I look in every direction. Vehicles on three sides, guardrails on the other. Like in a losing game of checkers, we are blocked in with nowhere else to go. I shoot a request for help into the universe.

Another glance past Cam and I catch the SUV's front passenger window sliding down. Leaning across Cam's lap for a better view, I watch as a bald scalp inked with a tribal tattoo is revealed, then a face in profile—eyes hidden behind a pair of wrap-around sunglasses. A half-smoked cigarette is flicked out and the face turns, blows smoke through its lips, and smiles at me.

'Oh ... sh-i-i-t!' I squeal, pulling back.

A grunt from Cam indicates he's also seen the menacing thug. Cam's head-tilt shows he's seen something else. I see it too. A huge sign informing there's an off ramp coming up. An extra lane appears to our left. Cars merging into it will have to take the exit. I wait for the Corolla to veer over, yet it continues travelling straight.

'Quick, Cam. Change lanes so we can turn off.'

He says nothing. Does nothing. The man in the SUV still watches us.

Up ahead, a cement barricade splits the merging lane from the motorway. It's coming closer. My heart kicks against my ribs. 'Change lanes now before it's too late!'

Cam is staring at the back of the semi-trailer, his teeth bared, his hands gripping the steering wheel like talons. I feel like slapping him.

'Change now, you dickhead!' I scream.

With only seconds to spare, he swerves the Corolla into the exit lane, narrowly missing the barricade on our right and almost sideswiping a BMW taking the same route on our left. The driver blasts his car horn and shows us his middle finger as he surges past.

As we follow the off-ramp arcing away from the motorway and

merge onto a double lane road, I look back. The SUV is nowhere in sight.

'They'll have to drive several kilometres before they can exit again,' Cam says, a smile playing on his lips. 'See, I'm not such a dickhead.'

At a roundabout, Cam takes the second exit and we travel on until we reach a large shopping centre with a cinema complex. Pulling into the carpark scattered with vehicles, he chooses a space between a Toyota Land Cruiser and a plumber's ute and lets the engine idle.

'I'm confused,' I say. 'What are we doing here?'

'Well, we could buy a box of popcorn and see a late movie … but I suggest we dump the car and leg it. Whaddya reckon?'

'Leg it? Are you serious? Where would we go?'

'The train station's near here. We could take a train north, or out to the bay, or even catch one into the city.'

'Why can't we keep driving? We've lost our pursuers, so we can go wherever we like.'

'Nope. How do you think they knew where we were heading? I didn't see the SUV until we hit the motorway. I reckon they placed a tracking device on the Corolla when they were searching it back at the park.'

'A tracking device? Where?' I run my hands under my seat, along the dashboard—madly tapping, prodding, poking.

'Ash!' Cam grabs my wrists. 'Stop it!'

I wrench free. 'We have to find the bloody thing.'

'No we don't. Let's just get out of here.'

He's about to turn the engine off when a whistling fills the car; the melody is familiar—Bryden's catch cry. Unease surrounds us like drifting smoke as we both eye the cassette player that I must have bumped in my frantic search.

'*I loved you guys; did you know that?*' Bryden's voice says through the speakers.

Cam's shocked expression at realising there is more on the tape mirrors mine.

Bryden clears his throat and continues. '*You were everything to me. Your friendship was a lifebuoy. But now ... I'm tired of toein' the line,*' he warbles, adding a few more lines of the song.

My heart twinges at a memory of a boy standing on a school desk, dancing, singing, showing off.

'*Actually, I'm tired of everything. Life sucks. It's time. Me and my little friend have plans to make. My grand finale.*' He laughs, and a rasping wheeze follows. '*Try to remember the good times, okay? We had a few.*' More coughing. '*When it's done, there won't be a suicide note confessing my sins ... that's not my style. You'll see. Maybe my ingenuity will be lauded, and I'll be the hero I always wanted to be.*' He sighs loudly, then wheezes. '*I'm just sorry I didn't get to say my goodbyes in person. Maybe you'll miss me ... maybe you won't. Well ... adios amigos.*'

A few seconds of whirring are followed by a click as the cassette pops half out of the slot.

I stare at Cam. Neither of us is breathing.

73

CAMPBELL

We leave the Corolla in the carpark and race along side streets, following the direction given by the blare of a train horn.

'How did he do it?' Ash asks, slowing down to match my eased pace. 'How did he make a suicide look like murder?'

'Damned if I know,' I remove my jacket and sling it over my shoulder. 'He was mental, but he was also as clever as shit.'

'Surely forensics will work it out.'

'Probably ... eventually. But, look at all the attention he's getting in the meantime. He would have loved that.'

Ash shakes her head. 'When I saw him last week, I should have pulled over ... gone to him. We could have talked. I could have listened. Changed his mind.'

I halt. 'Christ, will you give it a break! This is what you do. You hate him—justifiably so—and then when he gets all sooky, you forgive him.'

'I've never forgiven him!' she snaps, glaring back at me. 'He just had a way of shining a different light on things.'

'It's called manipulation, Ash. He was a game player, always has been. Have you forgotten all the situations he put us in? Right from when we were kids. When he was doing bad shit to us, he was orchestrating our lives, playing on our emotions, forcing our hand. Take Slade's killing as a big fucking example. It was all planned, I'm certain of it.'

She steps close enough for me to see the dilation of her pupils. 'Planned? How?'

'Why did he include Slade in my birthday celebrations? He wasn't my friend. And why was he sent out to the alley to look for me?'

'As a joke. Bryden told us he knew Slade would try it on with you.'

'But there was more to it. Bryden also sent you out through the same exit to get fresh air, and in doing so, you discovered Slade and me. It didn't happen by chance. He let slip, a couple of years back, that he found out about the rave party and Slade handing out ecstasy a week before my twenty-first. He could have murdered Slade out of revenge for his mother's death anywhere, anytime. But he chose that night. Why?'

'To involve us?'

'Shit, yeah. I believe he took me to the Smooth Cat because he knew Slade would be there. He had it all planned. Then you showed up, making it the perfect opportunity.'

'So the alley was his stage, and we were his audience.'

'No, Ash, not the audience. We were each given a part to play. A part that would tie us to Bryden forever.'

She strides away, turns, comes back. 'Then how could he say he loved us when he made our life hell?'

'I used to think he had such magnetism, and I was powerless against being drawn to him. But over time, I realised that wasn't right. It was he who couldn't keep his distance. That's why he hung around us as kids. We had something he longed for. Normal lives, normal families. Later, when we drifted out of his life, it scared the crap out of him, and he had to reel us back in. Involving us in his drama, causing us pain, and fucking us up somehow fed his need of us.'

'And that's how he showed us he cared? That's some weird fuckery.'

'Damn right, so don't blame yourself. He's the one who determined the events. He's the one at fault.'

I start walking, stopping again when I notice Ash isn't following. 'What are you doing? We have to hurry.'

She was frozen to the spot, so I go to collect her. Grasping her hand, I tug her forward.

She yanks her hand from mine. 'But in the end, we let him down, Cam. When he needed us the most, we weren't there for him.'

Hiding my frustration, I speak slowly so she can take it in. 'We did what we had to do to survive. As horrible as it is, Ash, it's all over now. Bryden's gone. He can't touch us anymore. We are finally free to move on with our lives.'

I feel an urge to wipe away the tracks of moisture glistening on her cheeks.

Her shoulders sag. 'But aren't we on the run? That's not freedom.'

I pat the back pocket of my jeans. 'I have the cassette tape. We'll show it to the police. Tell them it proves Bryden died by suicide, and that we had nothing to do with his death.'

'But can we trust the cops?'

'Not all of them. Remember Barnesy from school? He's now Senior Sergeant Nathan Barnes, stationed at Redcliffe. I reckon we can trust him. We could catch a train there and try to see him in the morning.'

'What about those goons?' She points back the way we've

come. 'They're still after us, aren't they? What if they think we know as much about their goings on as Bryden did? If they find us ...' Her voice fades.

I share her fear. 'We'll ask for protection. Come clean about our knowledge of Bryden's suspicions, say we thought he was loony tunes, which is true. It'll be okay. We have to believe that.'

Ash bends over, hands on her knees. She's panting, hyperventilating. I wonder how I can help when my concern is diverted by the sound of my phone ringing inside my jacket. I recognise the ringtone.

'It's my mum,' I say, puzzled. While I frantically grope through the many jacket pockets, Ash shoves her phone in front of my face.

'Dad's just messaged.'

Her shaky voice alarms me, and I let my mother's call go unanswered as I read her father's text.

'Ashley, where are you? The police are looking for you. They want to know how well you knew Slade Delaney. What's this about? What did you do?'

My stomach churns.

I reach for Ash's hand and this time she doesn't pull away.

74

———————

THE MOTH

WEDNESDAY LAST

A hideous creature glares at me from the bathroom mirror. There's a split lip, a puffy bloodshot eye, a large purple bruise on the left cheek. Further down, a gash on the upper right arm is seeping, and an impression made by a kick to the ribs is turning deep blue. Looks as if I've been in a pub brawl or, better yet, a street fight. I smile. It'll work to my advantage.

Was it only yesterday that I arrived at my old Percival Street home? The house was an eyesore. Broken down, worn out, derelict —just like me. I'd been hopeful, excited even, certain that at least one of my long-time friends would turn up after so long apart. I thought they'd be concerned ... or a little curious. Hadn't I conveyed my desperation in the notes I'd dropped off?

Getting in was easy. No locks to pick, no doorknob, in fact. I'd breathed in the dust-heavy air, catching a whiff of something odd— odd for an abandoned house, anyway. *Aftershave.* Movement from the shadows. The next thing I was splayed out on the floor clutching my face.

'Take that, shithead,' growled the elderly man standing over me, his eyes bulging.

He ranted. We scuffled. He got a few more good hits in, yet I was lenient—he was a senior citizen after all, a devoted father defending his child. Had to admire him for that. Still, I shouldn't have laughed, shouldn't have goaded. Him pulling a knife and giving me a decent slash was a surprise, but not as big a surprise as me pulling the Browning on him. Felt like a game of Rock, Paper, Scissors. Of course, I won. A semi-automatic handgun always trumps a kitchen knife, no matter how sharp the blade. I promised the old war horse I wouldn't bother her ever again if he did one thing for me, tell her I was sorry ... for everything. I meant it. He agreed and left me bleeding on the carpet.

I waited until midnight. I needed to share my plans, let them try to talk me out of it. But no one else showed up. Like Jesus in the Garden of Gethsemane, my disciples were sleeping while I was sweating drops of blood. What pricks! That meant I had to return to the house today to drop off a recording of what I wanted to tell them. If anyone is clever enough to discover the cassette tape, they'll learn the truth.

My head swims. Can't recall when I last ate, but I'm not hungry. I study the haunted face in the mirror: dark eyes leering, twisted mouth sneering.

'You're chickenshit,' it says, scowling.

The face shatters into a hundred sparkling fragments.

I gaze at my bloodied fist; I don't feel any pain. Turning on the basin tap, I wave my hand under the flow and watch swirls of crimson slither down the drain. A memory comes of another's blood snaking from the corners of his mouth, mixing with rainwater.

In my bedroom, I pull on a shirt and reach behind the chest of drawers to withdraw a heavy folder I've stowed there. I find a pen, write my grandfather's name on the front, and scribble beneath it: *lawyer, paedophile, murderer.* Suck on that, you smug bastard. It should generate some interest, and if the evidence doesn't convict you, it'll certainly make you and your cronies squirm a shitload.

I extract several pages from the back and slip them within a large envelope, already stamped and addressed to The Courier Mail newspaper. Placing the folder on the coffee table in the lounge, I unzip the backpack lying on the sofa and feed the envelope inside, making sure everything else I need is there.

The heavy backpack is hoisted over my shoulder as I give the room a cursory glance. A niggle. I've forgotten something. Something important. *What the fuck is it?* I slap the side of my head until the fog in my brain clears. A quick search of the bookcase and I locate the worn comic book, flick through the dog-eared pages of 'The Shadow', and find the photo hidden there for a rainy day.

They look so happy—pissed, but happy. He's wearing that stupid twenty-first badge; her gold sequin top glimmers, reflecting the light from the Smooth Cat neon sign above. As fate would have it, a wall clock to the side indicates the time—a quarter to eleven. Wedged between them, the fat arsehole is grinning and giving a two-thumbs-up, unaware that in thirty minutes he'll be lying dead in the alley in the pouring rain. Funny that no one seemed to remember I had my pocket camera with me that night. They will soon.

Making sure the date is written on the back of the photo, I stand it on the top shelf of the bookcase next to a framed picture of my mother. Blowing a goodbye kiss to Ash and Cam, I tell them that facing their fears is the only way they'll find peace. Tell them to be patient, it will all work out for good. Then I turn away before they catch me tearing up.

I take the stairs down to the apartment block entrance and

walk out into a night that enfolds me like a thick cloak. My car beckons from the roadside.

The drive to Lake Mitchum—via a local post box—is filled with ghosts. My life doesn't flash before my eyes, it stops and starts, lingering on the horrors, mistakes, and regrets. Instead of batting these scenes away, I allow them to empower me to do what I must.

Eventually, the old forest trail comes into view on my right, and I veer off the bitumen, following the dirt road deeper into the bush. The car skids to a stop in a clearing surrounded by tall pines standing in rows like warriors ready for battle. I step out with the backpack, slip on a pair of leather gloves, and open the car boot. I remove a full can of petrol, unscrew the lid, and douse the car, inside and out. Several lit matches and the vehicle is ablaze.

I throw the can, the box of matches, and the gloves into the fire. Flames shoot skyward. It's a beautiful sight. I want to stay and watch it burn, but a coughing fit from the smoke sends me scurrying back down the trail to the main road leading to the lake.

The picnic area is as quiet as a graveyard, the path through the bush as dark as a tomb. When I near the dam wall, I take out what I need from the backpack and shove the items into the pockets of my jacket, checking my wallet with driver licence is secured within a zippered one. Hurling the backpack out past the reedy shallows, I hear a splash as it hits water. The bricks in the outer pocket should sink it quickly.

Evenly spaced lighting newly illuminates the fenced walkway on top of the wall. I reach the halfway point and stop, close my eyes, and listen. So silent. So tranquil. A cool breeze circles me, and I imagine it carrying me to a mystical land, or a distant planet, where I have the ability to morph into a new being. I shake my head free of distractions. I have a purpose. My end will not be in vain.

Placing the small lead weight on my tongue, I seal my mouth

shut with wide strips of duct tape. Then climbing the railing facing the lake, I scale the wire mesh. I drop onto the outer ledge and cling one-handed as I bind the remainder of the duct tape around the lower part of my legs, fastening my ankles together.

I straighten and rest against the railing for balance while I remove a pair of handcuffs and lock them around my wrists—it pays to have friends in low places. Now for the tricky part. I claw inside my jacket pocket, and I lift out the pistol, now wrapped in the monogrammed handkerchief that once belonged to Francis, his black embroidered initials still boldly standing out against the white. With a degree of difficulty, I raise it over my right shoulder and angle the muzzle into the back of my skull. All that is left to do, is shoot. The gun and I will separate in the fall, or on impact as my body either strikes the wall or ploughs directly into the water far below.

I know my plan isn't foolproof, but my death, when discovered, should bring fear to some and retribution to others. Hopefully, certain people will find release and move forward in life's journey.

I inhale through my nose to slow my heart's pounding. Still, my fingers shake, and my knees weaken. A groan rattles in my throat and I drop my arms.

'Coward!' screams the devil in my head.

I grit my teeth and urge my arms to rise.

A sound. My name being called.

I snap my head around. Someone is standing on the other side of the wire.

'Need some help?' asks a soft, familiar voice.

My heart twists and warmth floods over me. Our eyes meet through the open mesh.

'You can do it, Bry,' she says, with a comforting smile. 'I'll stay with you. Just turn around.'

I mumble, 'Thank you,' and face the water.

'Lift the gun like before,' she prompts. 'That's right, tilt the muzzle. You're doing real good. It won't be long now.'

I feel the jab of cold steel against my skull, and want to say how much I love her, miss her. I want to apologise for failing to protect her, to tell her I wish I could have stopped her from dying so young and alone on that train track. Instead, I gaze up at the clear night sky and catch the distant past winking at me in pinpricks of light.

A large orange moth appears out of the darkness and hovers in front of my face ... daring me. I watch as it flitters away, following the path of moonlight shimmering on the lake.

Giving a nod to the man in the moon, I pull the trigger.

ACKNOWLEDGMENTS

Firstly, I want to thank Gary Horwood for being brave enough to collaborate with me in writing a story 'loosely' inspired by adventures and characters from our shared childhood and the world beyond the schoolyard. Who would have thought twirling dance partners from primary school would grow up to spin a story together?

Next, my gratitude goes to Graham Toseland from A Fading Street for his clever editing and wise advice; Writers Rendezvous for their ongoing encouragement and examples of success; and Jane Ireland for frequently picking me up and pushing me forward.

Most importantly, I would like to share my deep appreciation for my family and their support. In particular Ryan for his creative input, and David for his love, tolerance, and frequent coaxing. I couldn't do this crazy life without you all!

ABOUT THE AUTHOR

Vicki Stevens lives with her husband on the rural fringe of Brisbane, Australia. Her keen interest in genealogy and love of clever mysteries inspire her to write her Abby Eaton Mystery series. Reuniting several years ago with **Gary Horwood**, a former school classmate and memoir writer who shares her passion for telling brave and engaging stories, led to a collaboration to write a coming-of-age thriller. *Flames to a Moth* is the result.

You can keep up to date with Vicki's latest news and make contact via her website www.vickistevens.com.au or on social media.

ALSO BY VICKI STEVENS

Shaking Trees

9 780648 383130